# NO PRISONERS!

Through the dirty window on the second floor, Ben Raines could see the troops of Sister Voleta moving down the center of the street. "I love dealing with amateurs," he said with a smile. "Corrie, give the orders to open fire, please."

"With utmost pleasure, sir," Corrie said.

Voleta lost nearly half her troops in the first thirty seconds as the Rebels gave her a taste of Rebel justice. Rockets turned the vehicles into fireballs, 90mm and 105 howitzers, firing at nearly point-blank range, literally blew the enemy trucks off their tires and sent the trucks and those inside into thundering hell, the bodies mangled and burned beyond recognition. Ben's Rebels had been battling Sister Voleta and the Ninth Order for years. He would let his troops vent their anger with hot lead until it passed.

Then he saw her, standing in a doorway, looking at him. "You son of a bitch!" she screamed, her words just audible over the roar of gunfire.

She lifted a pistol and pulled the trigger.

The glass window exploded where Ben had stood an instant before. . . .

WILLIAM W. JOHNSTONE

# SURVIVAL IN THE ASHES

**ZEBRA BOOKS**
**KENSINGTON PUBLISHING CORP.**

ZEBRA BOOKS

are published by

Kensington Publishing Corp.
475 Park Avenue South
New York, NY 10016

Second printing: March, 1992

Printed in the United States of America

"Over the mountains
Of the moon,
Down the Valley of the Shadow,
Ride, boldly ride,"
the shade replied,
"If you seek for Eldorado."

— *Edgar Allan Poe*

# Book One

## Chapter 1

Ben Raines and his army of Rebels had fought many battles over the decade since the world exploded in germ and nuclear war, bringing an end to civilization as people had come to know it. But as Ben and his Rebels drove toward St. Louis, after waging war in the Northwest against the racist forces of Malone, Ben was thinking that this upcoming battle could well be the greatest and most decisive battle of his decade-long career against anarchy and for the restoration of civilization.

On the east side of I-55, massing in great numbers, were the mercenary forces of Kenny Parr, the terrorist forces of Khamsin—the Hot Wind—and the mercenary armies of Lan Villar. Very conservative estimates placed their numbers at ten thousand strong.

Behind Ben Raines and his Rebels, coming up from the west, were the forces of Sister Voleta, Ashley, and a ragtag assortment of human crud, all of whom had but one thought in mind: to destroy Ben Raines and turn the world into an outlaw haven.

The clanking of the engine pulled Ben out of his musings. "What the hell's wrong with this thing?" he asked his driver, Cooper, as the four-wheel-drive vehicle bucked to a halt, smoke wafting from under the hood. Those inside quickly evacuated the vehicle, grabbing equipment as they exited.

"Blew an engine," Cooper said. "Damn, this thing was supposed to have been rebuilt." He lifted his mic.

7

"This is Cooper. Bring the other vehicle up. The Eagle's been grounded."

Rebels quickly extinguished the fire under the hood and the equipment was off-loaded just as a nine-passenger, four-wheel-drive wagon pulled up. It looked enormous sitting next to the disabled Blazer.

"When and where did you find this boat?" Ben asked, inspecting the big wagon.

"Two weeks ago," Dan Gray said, walking up. "I've had people working on it at every stop since then. You need more room. It's armorplated and the glass is bulletproof. The engine is the largest we could find. Four fifty something or another. You'll have a lot more room in this, General."

Ben looked at his watch. "Hell, we're close enough. Let's break for lunch, Dan. Dismount the people and tell them to find shelter. This is where we make our stand."

They were a few miles south of St. Louis proper. Cecil was in command of the battalions in St. Louis . . . or what was left of the city. General Striganov and his people were digging in between the city and Ben and West's position. Ike was north of the city, digging in.

Ben walked to the communication's van and stuck his head inside. "What's the latest word?"

"Hostile forces still pulling in and setting up on the east side of the river, General," she told him. "They're facing us along a thirty-mile stretch. Latest estimates are about eight thousand . . . with more expected. They have artillery, but no tanks as yet."

"Lan Villar is confirmed?"

"That's ten-four, sir. Our scouts report that Khamsin and Kenny Parr have been spotted as well."

Ben nodded and thanked her. He walked away, chewing on a sandwich and washing it down with water from his canteen.

"Traffic coming up from the south, sir," a Rebel pointed out.

Ben turned, squinted his eyes, and smiled. The unmistakable rattle of many VW engines reached his ears. To the rear of the VW column, a shiny black hearse was rolling stately along.

Ben walked out onto Highway 61/67 and waited until the strange convoy drew abreast of him. A familiar face looked out at him from the lead VW van.

"For a peace-loving hippie, Thermopolis," Ben said, "you certainly pop up in the most violent of places."

"We were listening to your radio transmissions, Ben," the aging hippie said. "Actually it was Emil who convinced us that we should lend a hand in this fight. It concerns us all."

"What command do you want to fight under, Therm?"

"Doesn't make me the slightest bit of difference."

"Well, I've got the short battalion, so you can stay here with us." He smiled. "You feel like putting up with Emil?"

"I've been putting up with him for five hundred miles, Ben."

"We've had some additions since I saw you last. Some outlaw bikers have joined up. They're called the Wolfpack; headed by a man called Leadfoot. Another group of female bikers is with them. Wanda and her Sisters of Lesbos."

Themopolis stared at him and finally shook his head. "Ben Raines, you attract the strangest goddamn bunch of people I have ever seen in all my life. And I was a hippie in New Orleans for ten years!"

Ben laughed and looked inside the VW van. "Hello, Rosebud."

Therm's wife returned the smile. "Hello, General Raines."

"What'd you do with the children?" Ben asked.

"Took them to Base Camp One and left them. We felt they'd be safe there." Thermopolis smiled. "Even though by the time we return, their heads will be pumped full of patriotism and duty and all that crap. We may never be able to deprogram them."

"You're a fraud, Therm," Ben told him. "You're just as much a hardass as I am. The only difference between us is that you need a haircut."

Thermopolis laughed and put the VW in gear. "In your opinion," he said, and drove off toward the staging area.

As the van passed by him, Ben caught a glimpse of blond hair in the back seat. He gritted his teeth. Jerre. He nodded his head at her. She returned the curt nod.

As the caravan of hippies passed, Ben nodded and spoke to Zipper and Fly, Santo and Swallow, Whistler and Wren, Wenceslaus and Zelotes, Adder and Ima, Udder and Ura, Willow and the others who made up the large commune.

The platoon of Rebels who had been assigned to the commune passed by and they waved and yelled at the general. Ben tossed them a left-handed mock salute and waited for Emil Hite to pass by. At least Ben hoped he would pass by and not stop.

The black hearse stopped and Emil jumped out. The little con artist who professed to be the earthbound voice of the Great God Blomm drew himself up and saluted.

"Lafayette, we are here!" he shouted.

Ben sighed and eyeballed the little man. Emil had discarded his flowing robes and changed into tiger-stripe BDUs, black beret, and high-heeled cowboy boots. He was a bit unsteady on his feet.

Buddy and Tina, Ben's kids, walked up, both of them smiling. Colonel Dan Gray, CO of the Scouts, stood by them, his little dog, Chester, by his boots. Dan struggled to hide his smile.

With some assistance, Emil climbed up on the hood of the hearse.

"Oh, no!" Ben muttered.

Emil started to slide off the hood and waved his arms frantically, finally regaining his balance. "We have traveled many a hard and dangerous mile to reach you, General Raines. Through fog and rain and gloom of

10

night . . ."

Ben tuned him out as best he could, hoping that the speech would be a short one. For all his theatrics, Emil and his followers had proved to be some tough fighters; they would stand against terrible odds.

Emil finally wound down and managed to get off the hood of the hearse without busting his butt.

"Good to have you with us, Emil," Ben said. And Ben was telling the truth. Ben liked the little con artist, for Emil could always be counted on to provide some comic relief when the situation got grim. "Follow Thermopolis and his people and dig in."

"At your orders, sir!" Emil shouted, saluting. "My people will fight to the death . . ."

"Emil!"

". . . We shall fight on the beaches and the hedgerows . . ."

Ben groaned.

". . . We shall fight in the streets and from the bunkers . . ."

Even the little dog, Chester, was looking at Emil very strangely.

"Right, Emil," Ben said. "I appreciate your coming up here . . ."

"And when ammunition is no more, we shall fight with entrenching tools and clubs . . ."

"Thank you, Emil. Your loyalty is very nearly overwhelming."

"We shall never surrender and ever with liberty and justice . . ." Emil looked confused for a moment. "I said that wrong."

Ben patted the man on the shoulder. "It's all right, Emil. I understand."

With Emil gone, Ben turned to Dan Gray. "Have there been any shots exchanged, Dan?"

"Negative, General. Both sides appear to be too busy digging in."

"So it's shaping up to be an artillery battle."

"At first, yes. But that will change very quickly as

11

those on the east side of the river learn we have them outgunned."

"We're going to have to keep a sharp eye on our rear and our flanks. Voleta and Ashley will be coming up hard and fast."

"I've set up posts stretching from Hannibal in the north to Salem in the south. They're dug in and well concealed alongside every road capable of sustaining heavy traffic."

"Good. All right, Dan. Let's go see how our people are doing."

Dan took the lead and assigned Scouts to the rear of the short column, with Ben and his personal team in the center, Cooper at the wheel of the big wagon.

Everyone who could use a shovel was busy filling sandbags, digging bunkers, and finding heavy timbers to add support. Tanks and artillery were being positioned and fortified. Along the river, working unseen, Rebels were quietly occupying empty warehouses and other buildings and setting up heavy machine gun positions, fortifying their positions with sandbags and railroad ties.

Ben and his teams moved into General Striganov's sector. The Russian had dug his people in deep and quickly. Striganov handed Ben powerful binoculars and moved them toward a window of his CP, located close to the river. "Take a look, General."

The activity across the river jumped into the lenses. "Jesus!" Ben said. "It looks like the staging area in England before D-Day."

"My thoughts exactly," the Russian agreed with a smile. "I, too, have seen old newsclips of the storming of the beaches."

Ben turned to Corrie. "Tell Ike to send his demolition people north and south, Corrie. Blow the bridges that are still standing from Quincy to Cape Girardeau. We'll make the bastards come across the river if they want us. After you've done that, bump Base Camp One and have all PUFFs readied and flown up here.

12

Land them at that strip we cleared at Saint Clair."

"Yes, sir."

Ben and his teams drove into the ruins of St. Louis, using Interstate 55, picking their way along.

Cecil and the mercenary, West, had deployed their troops south to north within the city, from Weber Road in the south to Hall Street in the north.

St. Louis was a study in desolation and ruin. Time and fire and assorted vandals and crud and punks and Night People had turned the city into a wasteland. The suburbs of the city, where Ben had his people to the south, and Ike to the north, were bad enough, but inside the city itself, it was ruin . . . most of it by human hand.

Cecil Jefferys and Ike McGowan met Ben at Carondelet Park and the men shook hands.

"They're dug in tight across the river," Cecil said.

"I've seen. All right, so we've lost the element of surprise. I'm passing the word up and down the line, personally. Let's get all our artillery and heavy mortars in place and the enemy's positions spotted and coordinated. When can you have that done?"

"By 1800 hours."

"Same here," Ike said.

"Approximately the same time Georgi and West gave me." Ben handrolled a cigarette and was thoughtful for a moment. "Cec, you and West were the first ones to arrive. When do the troops across the river roll out for breakfast?"

"Between 0530 and 0600 hours, Ben. It's been that way ever since we got here."

Ben nodded. "All right. At 0600 hours, tomorrow morning, I want all of us to open up with everything we've got in artillery. Willie Peter, HE, Napalm — in that order." He looked at Dan. "Do you know where their supply depots are located?"

"Yes. I have them pinpointed. But they're too far back for anything except our heaviest artillery to effectively strike."

"Drop the other boot, Dan."

"Our one fifty-five's and eight-inchers are not in place; they're not even here yet. And won't be for another thirty-six hours."

"Roads getting that bad?"

"Yes, sir."

"That may be a blessing in disguise," Ben said, grinding out the butt of his cigarette under his boot heel. "They may think the shorter range artillery is all we have and not move their depots." He lifted a map and studied it. "Corrie, bump the convoy and tell them to take one-forty-one at Arnold and then cut east on Interstate Two-seventy, take that on into the city. Dan, have your Scouts meet them there and escort them to here." He punched the map. "Just west of Interstate fifty-five. Have them spread out north to south and get in place doubletime."

"Yes, sir."

"All right, Ike. Let's go see what you've got cooking in your sector."

Ike rode with Ben in the big wagon. "What'd you do with Thermopolis and Emil?"

"Kept them with me. Therm will look after Emil. How far up did you have to stretch your people?"

"I've got a few all the way up to where the Missouri makes its final turn before turning south and flowing into the Muddy."

"That's stretching it pretty thin. How's Lambert Field?"

"Shitty. I've got a crew out there now trying to clear two runways. They say it'll be several days at best."

"Then I'll let the order stand putting the PUFFs down at that strip in Saint Clair."

"At least for a time. Ben?"

Ben met his eyes.

"St. Louis is full of creepies."

# Chapter 2

"It doesn't surprise me," Ben said. "This whole operation started out as a cluster-fuck."

Lan Villar and Kenny Parr were supposed to have been several hundred miles from St. Louis. Instead, Cecil found them digging in on the east side of the river when he pulled in from Base Camp One. Original estimates placed the enemy's strength at about five to six thousand. As it turned out, they were over ten thousand strong.

"Have they tried any crap with your people?" Ben asked.

"No. They've pulled back into the city proper and left us alone."

"Corrie, make a note to keep our people out of the downtown area unless they go in force."

"Yes, sir."

They reached Ike's sector and got out. "I want all the bridges blown simultaneously, Ike. No surprises for us."

"That's ten-four, Ben. My teams have already moved out."

"How about survivors?"

"None," Ike said it flatly. "It looks like they split a long time ago."

"When we leave here, we'll destroy the city."

Defeat never entered Ben's mind, and all the Rebels knew it and adopted the same attitude. That was just one of the reasons they were practically indefeatable. That, and the fact that they knew they were right and just kept on coming.

"That's ten-four, Ben." He stuck a piece of home-manufactured gum in his mouth. "You seen Jerre?"

"Briefly. How did you know she was here?"

"A little birdie told me."

"My kids have big mouths."

"Actually it was Cecil. She brought the twins down to Base Camp One for safekeeping. He said they have their mother's good looks and your eyes." He chewed and grinned at Ben.

Ben met his longtime friend's eyes and returned the smile. "Corrie, make a note to have Jerre assigned to Ike's command."

Ben did not assign Jerre to Ike—he had no intention of doing so—but he did have his friend sputtering for a few moments. Ben had made up his mind to try and make friends with Jerre, if at all possible, and to not be so mean to her as before—as Corrie, Jersey, and Beth had said he had been. Personally, Ben thought he had been cool and aloof rather than mean, but perhaps women looked at it differently.

He went looking for her, and found her helping to set up an aide station on Telegraph Road, just south of I-255. Ben stood in the door, watching her, until she felt eyes on her and turned slowly.

Ben felt a tug at his heart. She was one of those women who would be beautiful as long as she lived. He had all sorts of things he had to say to her; things like, "Let's be friends," for starters.

It all died in his throat.

She stared at him for a moment. "Something, General Raines?"

Ben shook his head. "It's nothing, Jerre. I just wanted to tell you to be careful, kid." He backed out of the building and walked away.

The other people in the room discreetly averted their eyes and tried very hard not to listen.

Jerre walked to the door and stood watching as Ben walked away. There were a lot of things she would have liked to say to him, such as, "Ben, why can't we be

16

friends?" But the words hung in her throat. She sighed and shook her head, walking back into the room and helping the others unfold cots, to be used when the wounded began arriving.

Ben walked up Telegraph Road, past the Interstate, and turned toward the river, making his way through the National Cemetery, located between the old VA hospital and Jefferson Barracks Park. A dozen Rebels trailed along behind and beside him. At the bluff overlooking the river, Ben cut his eyes south, to the Jefferson Barracks Bridge. Ike had anticipated Ben's move and had his divers wire the bridge early that morning, in the predawn hours.

Ben did not like to destroy bridges, for he knew with each bridge he destroyed, another vital link spanning rivers would be forever gone . . . forever at least in his lifetime, and more than likely never to be rebuilt.

Leadfoot, the commander of the outlaw biker Rebels, walked down to join Ben by the river. The outlaw bikers were the newest additions to Ben's Rebel Army, joining up only a few weeks past.

"You know this Lan Villar, General?" Beerbelly asked.

"I know him. He's pure scum. But very, very intelligent and very, very dangerous. So is Kenny Parr. You know about the Hot Wind, Khamsin. We're looking at possibly ten thousand troops just across that river."

"And a couple more thousand comin' at us from the rear."

"That is correct."

"And when we kick these asses, they'll be more comin' out of the woodwork at us."

"That's right. It's been that way for over a decade. No reason to think it won't continue."

"When I was outlawin', I kept thinkin': why don't Ben Raines just carve out a pretty good section of country, secure it, and forget about the rest? But that wouldn't work, would it, General?"

"No. It'd be just as bad, or worse, as it is now. We'd

17

be in a constant state of readiness and swamped with refugees pouring in. Eventually we'd be overwhelmed from the outside."

"How come Base Camp One is never attacked, General?"

Ben smiled. "Because that is the one place where I have allowed nuclear weapons to be set up. Our one fifty-five's and eight-inchers have nuclear capabilities and we have the warheads. I will always have a secure zone, Beerbelly."

The secure zone, known as Base Camp One, now encompassed a half-dozen parishes in North Louisiana, with a standing army of more than two thousand men and women, not counting the doctors, scientists, technicians, and others who kept the factories and hospitals and labs going twenty-four hours a day. Not even Khamsin, Ashley, Voleta, or Lan Villar entertained any illusions about attacking Base Camp One. All enemies of the Rebels knew it would be suicide to attempt that.

True, those who hated Ben Raines and the Rebels's way of life wanted the Rebels destroyed, but they also wanted their advancements and technology and factories intact. That would not happen if by some dark miracle they managed to overrun the standing troops at the base camp. Ben had given orders to destroy it all before allowing it to fall into enemy hands.

Base Camp One was probably the most secure place on the face of the earth.

Since Ben had expanded the perimeters of the secure zone, Base Camp One now extended from the Arkansas line down to approximately forty miles south of Monore, then east to the Mississippi River. There were, in addition to the factories and labs, wildlife refuges, petting zoos, both collective and individual farms, open markets, schools and universities, votechs, hospitals, and all the other vestiges of a normal society.

But on closer inspection, there were some not-so-subtle differences that would have caused many liberals to immediately pull out their hankies and start stomping on them.

There were no free rides in any of the Rebel communities. If a person was able to work, they worked, or they were kicked out. No exceptions. In the schools, children were not only taught the three R's—and taught it well, in addition to fine arts—they were also taught values, respect for other people and their property, and for God's lesser creatures. Many Rebels were strictly vegetarian in their diets, but that was by no means a mandatory requirement. But there were humane ways to raise livestock, and those who chose the Rebel way of life understood that and behaved accordingly.

Trapping and hunting for sport was forbidden in any zone the Rebels controlled. The laying out of any type of ground poison was not allowed. Deer herds were controlled by the careful reintroduction of the animals' natural predators. It was not uncommon now to see wolves and panthers once more roaming free in the designated wilderness areas, as God had intended. If the wolves and panthers ventured outside the designated areas and became a hazard to humans or to livestock, which occasionally did happen, game wardens went after them—taking the offending predator alive if possible—and moving them out of the controlled zone.

If one tree was cut down, another was planted. Land could not be cleared without providing windbreaks of timber to prevent topsoil from blowing away.

It was not a society that everyone could live in. Those who kept statistics on such matters agreed that perhaps one in five could live in a Rebel-controlled zone.

There was absolutely no crime. It was not tolerated. Walk onto someone else's property with less than friendly intent, and there would, in most cases, be a funeral the next day. The selling of drugs called for the death penalty. Killing someone while driving drunk meant a long prison sentence, at very hard labor, without exception. No plea-bargaining, no deals, no lesser sentencing based on social standing. The laws were black and white in Rebel country, without benefit of a gray area. There were no bars or honky-tonks in any Rebel-controlled zone. But if a person wanted to get riproaring drunk in their home, that was their business. Just don't get behind the wheel of a vehicle after doing so.

Abuse a child in a Rebel zone, and the offending party or parties faced the very real possibility of that child being taken from them and placed with couples who would care for it.

There were very few lawyers in any Rebel-controlled zone; or it should be said there were very few practicing attorneys. Many who were lawyers back when civilization was the norm—more or less—before the Great War, were now farmers and soldiers and mechanics and so forth. And those who did maintain some sort of legal practice—just to keep their hand in it, for there certainly wasn't much call for them—soon learned that in Rebel-controlled zones there were very few legal niceties.

The first rule to surviving was: Don't cross Ben Raines.


Standing by the river, Ben looked at Beerbelly. "You and Wanda and the other bikers could have left us at any time over the past few weeks. To tell you the truth, I'm pleasantly surprised you didn't."

Beerbelly smiled. "To tell you the truth, General, it sorta surprises me too. How pleasant it is is up for grabs. But look at it this way: sooner or later, the Rebels are gonna win. It's just a matter of time. It might be months, it might be years; but you're going to win. You and your bunch is gonna have bodies swingin' in the wind from California to New York. There used to be a western sayin' about seein' the gunfighters' graveyards." He met Ben's eyes. "I've seen some of yours, Ben Raines. And the sight scared the shit outta me!"

"Do you find it so difficult to obey the law, Beer-belly?"

"No. I didn't find it difficult before the Great War. But I had me a family back then. Wife and two kids. I worked construction during the week and me and my old lady rode Harley's on the weekend." He smiled. "Had a sidecar for the kids. Both of us used to read your adventure books in my spare time. You were a good writer. I had a good life back then; me and my wife and kids. Then it all fell apart. Oh, don't get me wrong. I'm not makin' excuses for what I done after . . . Alice and the kids died. It was bad and if some-body had killed me for it, well, I would have gone out thinkin' that I sure deserved it. And that's the truth. Those of us who joined up with you . . . we'd been thinkin' of a way out, lookin' for one for a long time. Oh, none of us is altar boys, and we ain't likely to be-come none anytime soon. But what we're doin' now makes me feel a hell of a lot better."

The biker, an Uzi slung over a shoulder, walked back to his group's position, between Telegraph Road and Buckley Road.

Ben walked back south, along 231, inspecting the fortifications his people had built. They all knew it was going to be one hell of a battle, and they were going to take some casualties, so the bunkers were being dug extra deep and fortified heavily.

It wasn't the Rebel way to stop working whenever a ranking officer appeared on the scene, jumping around and saluting and all that crap; not even if that officer was Ben Raines. The Rebels kept right on working and Ben walked on.

He inspected the positions where the 81mm mortar carriers were set up, and nodded his head in approval. With a range of over two miles, the 81s would deal some misery to those across the river.

Then it was back to his CP to look with disgust upon a stack of papers piled on his desk. "What is all this crap?" he asked Jersey.

Ben's diminutive warriorness/bodyguard met his eyes. "Things that need your signature, General. A courier just brought them in from the airstrip at St. Clair."

Muttering, Ben sat down behind the desk and began wading through the stack of reports, proposals, requisitions and recommendations. He slopped his name on some and shit-canned most of the paperwork . . . but he speed-read it all. He had just finished when a familiar voice spoke to him from the open door of his office.

"I often wondered if you ever actually read anything I sent you," Doctor Lamar Chase said.

Smiling, Ben rose from his chair and gripped the man's hand. "I read all of your ramblings, Lamar. When'd you get in?"

"About an hour ago. I want to make an inspection of the aid stations, Ben. At least as many as possible before the balloon goes up. Care to go with me?"

"Lamar, I would accompany you to the gates of Hell to get away from paperwork."

"All in due time, Ben," the chief doctor said with a chuckle. "All in due time."

# Chapter 3

They had inspected a dozen aid stations and Chase found them all well-stocked and meeting with his approval — which was no mean feat to accomplish.

At the next stop, Ben said, "I'll wait out here and grab a smoke."

Lamar gave him an odd look and nodded his head. He walked into the aid station and bumped into Emil Hite. The little man's mouth was swollen and bruised. He could see where several stitches had been taken. "What happened to you, Emil?"

"I was giving a pep talk to my people and fell off the hood of my hearse."

Chase shook his head, thinking: If future historians ever write about this army, it's going to be the goddamnest story ever told . . . with the exception of the Bible.

"I'm very sorry to hear that, Emil. My people took good care of you?"

"Oh, yes, sir."

"Good, good." He patted the little man on the shoulder and walked on. He pulled up short and smiled when he saw the reason Ben had not wanted to come in.

Damnest bunch of warriors I ever did see, he mused. Hardass Colonel Dan Gray has fallen butt over elbows for Sarah Bradford and the leader of the greatest army on the face of the earth won't come into an aid station because of a little blue-eyed girl. One thing about it, though, both of them have excellent tastes in ladies.

Then Chase grinned mischievously as he walked up

to Jerre. "I read the reports on you, Jerre," he said. "You went through combat medic school with high marks."

"Thank you, Doctor Chase."

"You got a promotion, too, I understand."

"Yes, sir. Lieutenant."

"That's good. I have a new assignment for you, Lieutenant. One befitting your rank."

"Oh?"

He told her and stepped back as he noticed her eyes narrowing and her jaw stiffening.

He'd been warned that she had a temper that was close to equalling a wolverine . . . and he believed it.

Then she smiled, with about as much humor in it as a shipwreck. "Why, thank you, sir. Does this meet with the general's approval?"

"It doesn't have to, Lieutenant. Medical people can call any shot they so choose."

"He has been informed of this, of course."

"Ah . . . not yet. Why don't you get your gear together and join the general out in that new tugboat he calls a station wagon. I'll just continue on with my inspection."

"Yes, sir. Whatever you say, sir."


Ben turned his head at the tapping on the windshield and looked at Jerre. He rolled down the window and eyeballed her duffle bag on the sidewalk.

"May we drop you off somewhere, Jerre?"

"Wherever you're going, Ben." When they were alone, she dropped all military titles and courtesies. Considering what they had once meant to each other, and all they had been through, both of them felt ridiculous when she did display military courtesy.

"What do you mean by that?"

She told him.

Ben blinked a couple of times then slowly got out of the wagon, to stand looking down at Jerre. "This is

Chase's idea of a joke. He can't be serious."

"He's serious, Ben."

"Well, by God, you can bet I'll have something to say about this!"

"You have nothing to say about it," Chase said, walking out of the aid station. "Because of your propensity for getting into trouble and taking unnecessary risks, all of your battalion commanders have, at one time or another, requested this. I have resisted because you would have made life miserable for anyone I assigned to you. However, I don't think you're going to make life miserable for Lieutenant Hunter. Because if you try, she'll tell you to go right straight to hell, Raines! My inspection tour is over. Cecil has cleaned up the hospital over on 115. That will be my base. Take me over there now. Lieutenant Hunter is permanently assigned to your personal team, General Raines. Period!"

No sooner were the words out of his mouth when the afternoon air was ripped by automatic weapons' fire. The bullets slammed and whined off the concrete of the building housing the aid station, howling off as flattened and dangerous ricochets. Ben jerked Jerre and Chase to the sidewalk behind the wagon as the rest of his team sought cover.

"Guerrilla attack, Ben?" Chase shouted the question over the whine of unfriendly fire.

"I doubt it. Probably creepies. The city's full of the bastards. Jersey, you have them spotted?"

"That's ten-four, General," the woman called. "Top floor of that building right across the street."

"Corrie, call for tanks."

"Yes, sir."

"You two stay down," Ben told the doctor and the medic. "And in this situation, I give the orders and you obey them."

He opened the door to the wagon and pulled out his M-14 just as the lead from across the street really began to fly in their direction. Ben's team returned the fire and a creepie was knocked out of an already shat-

25

tered window. He hit the sidewalk and splattered.

Ben opened up with the old Thunder Lizard, the heavy .308 slugs pocking the outside bricks of the building and raising hell with anybody inside as the lead found open windows. Screams of pain from those on the top floor drifted over the gunfire.

Sticking home a fresh clip, Ben said, "Corrie, have teams from all battalions clear this city from the river back to Chase's hospital. I'm not going to have three fronts to fight."

"Yes, sir." She began bumping the other battalions, giving them Ben's orders.

Two fifty-ton main battle tanks rumbled around the corner and clanked into position. They elevated their 105's and began destroying the top floors of the building with HE rounds.

"No prisoners!" Ben shouted over the roar of the 105's.

Corrie nodded and spoke into her headset mic.

Dan and a contingent of his Scouts, including Ben's kids, Tina and Buddy, slid around the corner in Jeeps and Hummers just in time to see the top of the office building blow apart.

"Tell the tanks to cease firing, Corrie, and have Dan's people mop it up."

"Yes, sir."

Ben squatted down behind the wagon until a team of Scouts moved into the building, mopping up any Night People who might still be alive.

Ben stood up just as Dan walked up, accompanied by Buddy and Tina. "I heard your orders, General," the Englishman said. "I'll take this sector back to I-fifty-five and commence immediately. Tina and Buddy will accompany you."

"All right, Dan. As you go, set up secure zones and establish perimeters."

"Right, sir."

Ben looked at Chase and Jerre. "Come on, people. Let's take a drive over to Chase's hospital."

Cooper stayed on I-55, making the loop around the city, taking I-70 just past the downtown area and cutting northwest. He left the Interstate at Goodfellow Boulevard and hit 115, taking that to the hospital.

"It's about three miles to the airport, Ben," Chase said, as they pulled up by the emergency room entrance. "Ike tells me a couple of runways should be cleared and patched in a couple of days — with any kind of luck. There is a hospital plant closer to the airport, but it's been vandalized beyond repair."

"It's a good choice, Lamar." He lifted his mic and bumped Buddy. "Rat, take your teams and double-check the area south for creepies. Tina, you go north. Ham, take the west side and I'll take the east." He hooked the mic and said, "Let's go, people."

As they worked along 115, the unmistakable odor of Night People drifted out of the first building they came to. Ben motioned a Rebel with a flamethrower up to him. "Burn it."

A stream of pressure-backed-thickened gas whooshed into the building. It was quickly followed by intense screaming as the clothing of the creepies ignited and their cannibalistic flesh was cooked.

"Hell with this," Ben said. "Get me some Dusters up here right now."

The quick little M-42 Dusters soon zipped into the hospital sector. The five-man crew Dusters looked almost small and dainty when parked alongside the huge fifty-ton main battle tanks, but their 40mm cannon and quad-.50 machine guns could spew out an enormous rate of firepower and destruction.

The explosive warheads in the 40mm shells began pounding the buildings around the hospital compound, knocking holes in the brick walls. Creepies ran from the buildings in a panic, to be gunned down by the Rebels lying in wait for them.

"Stack the bodies inside a building and burn them," Ben ordered. "Look for any prisoners the creepies might have stashed around for a snack and take them to Doctor Chase." He checked his watch. Several hours of daylight left. "Corrie, we don't have time to go house to house, building to building, so I want demolition teams up here right now. I want them to clear a two-block area around the hospital . . . all the way around it. I don't want any building left standing."

"Yes, sir."

"Tell Ham and Buddy to stay up here with their teams and assist. Tell Tina to bring her team and come with me."

"Ben Raines, the one-man wrecking crew," Jerre muttered, not unkindly.

Jersey looked at her and grinned. "Was he always this way? I mean, even when you first met him back in Virginia?"

So everybody knows the story, Jerre thought about that for a moment, as they jogged along the littered sidewalk. She wasn't sure if she liked that or not. But then figured she couldn't do anything about it, so what the hell? "Yeah. Yeah, he was, Jersey. He was tough even back then. He showed me how to use weapons and made me learn to be good with them."

Ben had taken the point, naturally, and waved them to a stop and down with arm and hand motions. Tina was by his side, and they were arguing. Ben didn't look like he was buying any of what she had to say.

"Tina will threaten to call her Uncle Ike if the general doesn't give up the point. He'll bitch and fuss about it, but he'll give in," Jersey said.

"You know him well, don't you, Jersey?"

"I been with him a long time, Jerre. We been through a lot of battles."

Jersey looked every bit of twenty-five years old. But Jerre knew that many Rebels joined the main force as just teenagers.

"Let's go!" Tina called, taking the point.

Tina came to a building whose windows had been boarded up—a sure giveaway that the building was, or had been, inhabited. Tina sniffed at the doorway and grimaced. All watching her knew she had smelled the foul odor of Night People. She removed a grenade from her battle harness and pointed to four others, telling them to do the same. She waved them forward.

Jerre spotted movement across the street, on the rooftops and cut loose with her M-16. "On the rooftop!" she yelled.

Half the team spun to cover their rear while Tina and the others dropped in grenades and scrambled for the protection of rusted-out vehicles parked haphazardly along the curb.

Several creepies were firing from the rooftops just as a main battle tank rounded the corner and opened up with HE and WP rounds, in addition to .50-caliber machine gun fire. The coaxial gun, normally a 7.62 machine gun had been replaced with a second .50, beefing up the firepower. The entire second floor erupted in a roar of flame and smoke and brick and mortar just as the grenades blew in the building behind the Rebels.

"Let's go!" Tina yelled, jumping inside the smoke-filled and shattered room.

Ben was right behind her, his M-14 set on full rock and roll. Father and daughter began clearing the littered room of any living things.

When the first floor was clear, Ben took over and waved the team outside. "Corrie, tell that tank to blast this building."

Ben led the team out of range of falling debris and they squatted behind cars and trucks while the main battle tank dealt some misery to any creepies who might still be alive on the floors above the cleared first floor.

Ben looked up the street at movement. The first of the demolition teams had arrived. Ben looked back at the team. "Everybody all right? OK, good. Corrie, tell the tanks to stick around and cover the explosives people. Let's get out of here.

*The next day.* 0600 hours.

Across the river, the commanders of the opposing forces were having breakfast as they met in a building along Kingshighway Road, laying down the ground rules and clearing the air of any personal grievances they might have.

"I must insist upon remaining in command of all forces," the Hot Wind blew.

Lan Villar laughed at him. "Khamsin, must I remind you that you are in no position to insist upon anything?"

The Hot Wind leaned back in his chair and slowly nodded his head. "You are right, Lan," he surprised them all by admitting. "Thanks to General Raines, my forces have been very nearly destroyed."

Lan softened his usually harsh manner of speaking. "I didn't mean to rub salt into an open wound, Khamsin. But I must point out that if we are to set up any type of empire, it must be in the United States. Europe is . . . occupied, so to speak."

"As is South America," Khamsin said.

The youngest of them all, Kenny Parr, had so far sat silent, listening. Young he might be, but he had his late father's natural ability as a soldier with none of the elder Parr's arrogance. And it was that arrogance that got him killed in New Africa in the early part of the government's attempts to rejoin all of the United States after the Great War.

Kenny finally spoke. "What Raines doesn't know is that Sister Voleta's Ninth Order is much stronger than he realizes. I've been dealing with the sister for several years. She is quite mad, of course, but brilliant in her madness; as are so many of the insane. Voleta has about five thousand personnel in reserve, scattering throughout the United States. She has called them together. They will be massing to the west of St. Louis."

Lan Villar looked at the young man, new respect in

his eyes. The elder Kenny Parr, whom Lan had met in Africa, had been a good soldier, but a rash and impatient man. The younger Kenny Parr had, so far, exhibited none of his father's imperfections.

"Go on, Kenny."

"My father warned me about General Ben Raines. He said above all else, don't trust the man. And don't try to outguess him. You think he'll do one thing, and Ben will turn around and do the opposite."

"I can personally attest to that," the Hot Wind blew bitterly.

"And? So?" Lan questioned. "There is a point to all this?"

"I and my men checked every military base and national guard and reserve armory between Florida and Missouri. There is not one tank nor one single piece of artillery to be found. Ben Raines has it all. Thousands of pieces of artillery and hundreds of tanks. But few drivers and crews, I am thinking."

"Where are they, son?" Lan asked, putting a fatherly tone to his voice. He liked this young mercenary. He might even take him under his wing and guide him along.

"At Raines's Base Camp One."

The Hot Wind leaned forward, his eyes bright and cruel. "Then we take the camp."

"No," Kenny nixed that.

"Why not, son?" Lan asked.

"Raines has nuclear capability all around those hundreds of square miles. And he won't hesitate to use it. He doesn't want to use it. But he will if anyone attacks that secure zone."

Lan wanted nothing to do with nuclear weapons. In the hands of a man like Ben Raines, a damn fanatic for reorganization and law and order and farms and governments and all that happy crap, Raines would certainly use them if pushed. So Base Camp One was out.

Then it dawned on Lan what Kenny had previously said. He looked at the young man and arched one eyebrow.

The young man, quite handsome in a cruel sort of way, smiled. "Yes," he said softly. "Despite our superior numbers, we've got our asses in a crack."

# Chapter 4

"What? What?" Khamsin demanded, both hands gripping the arms of his chair. "What are you talking about?"

"We have short-range artillery," Lan said, his voice low, but not at all soft. "Light mortars and nothing else. We can be very effective with enemy positions along the river. But let Raines pull his people back a few blocks, into the inner city, and we can't touch them."

"But they could, can, pound at us with impunity," Kenny added.

Sixty tanks and dozens of 81mm mortars fired from the Missouri side of the river at the same time the bridges were blown. The impacting incoming rounds knocked the men from their chairs, sending them sprawling on the floor, all of them cursing Ben Raines and his Rebels.

The men got to their knees just as three rounds, HE, WP, and napalm struck the building next to them and tore the center out of it, blowing out the wall facing the street and sending bricks flying through the air; lethal weapons that crushed skulls and broke the bones of any soldier they struck.

Lan Villar grabbed for a mic. "Get me the range of all incoming!" he shouted to anyone who might be listening. "All of it seems to be concentrated in this area."

During a lull in the incoming, Khamsin said, "You think Raines may be limited in range?"

"Yes," Lan said. "From the sounds of the barrage, he's using one-o-five's, ninety's and eighty-one mm. No one fifty-five's or eight-inchers. Order all troops to fall back east of Bluff Road. He can't reach us there."

Khamsin, Villar, and Parr took casualties that morning as the barrage caught them by surprise. Probably ten percent of their troops were either blown to bloody bits, crushed by the falling buildings, or wounded so badly as to be put out of action for the duration. The Willie Peter and napalm rounds set East St. Louis blazing from 270 in the north all the way down to the county line in the south, and from the river to Washington Park.

Rainfall had been far below normal that spring and early summer, and the city was as dry as a tinderbox. With tons of litter on the streets and in the buildings and homes, East St. Louis went up like a huge box of matches sitting under a fireworks' display. Flames were leaping hundreds of feet into the air, and with a hot and very dry wind from the west, the fire was pushed rapidly to the east . . . the same direction the retreating troops were taking.

Lan Villar stopped in his retreat to turn and face the west, a grudging smile of respect on his lips. "You son of a bitch!" he cursed Ben Raines. "So you've won the first battle. But the war is a long way from being over." He jumped in his vehicle and hauled his terrorist ass away from the advancing flames.

"Cease fire," Ben gave the orders.

He had driven up to Cecil's sector and now stood on an overpass of the Interstate, looking through binoculars at the recent carnage across the river. A soldiers' smile creased his lips. "That'll give them something to think about, Cec. And just maybe they've fallen for our short-range ruse."

"We can't send spotter planes up," Cecil reminded Ben. "We know they have a few Stinger missiles."

"As long as they keep it nonnuclear," Ben said, "so will we."

"I don't think they have nuclear capabilities, Ben. I think we're the only standing army in the world who still has that capacity."

"Let's hope."

A runner handed Ben a piece of paper. Ben read it and passed it on to Cecil. All the designated bridges were either down or crippled so badly they could not support vehicular traffic.

"More links destroyed," Ben muttered.

"It had to be, Ben," his longtime friend said. "We had no other choice in the matter."

Ben nodded his agreement, the curt nod also silently stating that while Ben knew it had to be, he certainly didn't have to like it. "Did we receive any unfriendly fire?"

"Negative. Nowhere up and down the line did they sustain any returning fire from across the river."

"All right, that tells us that while they have the superior numbers, they don't have much in the way of artillery. Short-range mortars, probably. Maybe some old recoilless rifles. But Cec, they didn't mass across that river for show. They know something that we don't. And Cec, why don't they have more in the way of artillery?"

Cec met his eyes. "Go on, Ben."

Before he could reply, Corrie said, "General Ike is on his way down."

Ben nodded his head. "I want prisoners. As many as we can grab. Get the interrogation teams ready and equipped. Chase doesn't like it, but he'll do it. I want to know where Lan came from, and more importantly, why. I want to know why he doesn't have more in the way of artillery. I want to know what he's running from." He smiled at the startled look on Cecil's face. "Oh, yeah, Cec. He's running from something. He probably had either Africa or Europe to play in. Why did he leave? What's going on over there?"

"Ben . . ." Cecil knew all the signs and he was reading them in his friend's face and voice. "You aren't planning on? . . ."

"Maybe. Why not? We'll change Ike from general to

admiral and put him in charge of the fleet."

"Jesus, Ben!"

"Are we having a prayer meeting?" the stocky ex-Navy SEAL asked, walking up to join the group.

"It's almost over here in America," Ben said. "Once this present threat is beaten back, all we'll have is the mopping up. The creepies are on the run. Malone's people are in hiding in the wilderness areas out west. Our outpost program is going even better than we dreamed it would. More and more people are realizing that we're going to reclaim this nation and are coming out of hiding to join us. We'll soon be able to field seven full battalions. That's something that those crud across the river don't realize. Why not investigate what's happening in other parts of the world?"

Ike almost choked on his bubble gum. When he stopped coughing, he yelled, "How the hell do you propose to get over there, Ben?"

"By ship," Ben said, taking the offer of a cup of coffee from Jersey. "And when this is over, you're going to be in command of the flotilla, convoy, whatever the hell it's called."

Ike started jumping up and down. He looked like a huge basketball with arms. "Have you lost your fuckin' mind?" he shouted.

"We have to know what threats face us from overseas, Ike. And I believe the threats are dangerously awesome. You both know what our intelligence people have put together concerning the Night People. Through intercepted and decoded communiqués, they believe the creepies have just about taken over the world. If that's true, then it's up to us to stop them."

"Ben," Cecil said. "Those three other battalions are still several weeks away from being ready for combat," he reminded him.

Ben took a sip of coffee and shook his head. "We don't have time." He turned to Corrie. "Bump Base Camp One, Corrie. Have them start the new battalions up this way immediately. Spread them out south

36

to north along Highway 63, from Rolla up to Kirksville. Swing the ends around to cover west to east for twenty miles."

"That's spreadin' them awful thin, Ben," Ike said, after checking a map of the state. "That's about a hundred and fifty miles of highway."

"They're not going to be fighting stand or die, Ike. I think that the good Sister Voleta is much stronger than she's let anyone know. I think she's kept her main force under cover and I think they're going to be joining her as she and Ashley push east. All I want the new battalions to do is keep up a steady fight as they pull back toward us. Buy us some time to contain what's across the river."

"Suppose Voleta comes down from the north or up from the south?" Cecil asked.

Ben smiled. "Then we're fucked!"

The destruction of much of the western part of East St. Louis not only knocked some of the fight from Khamsin, Villar, and Parr, it also gave them some insight into the man who was in command of the Rebel army that faced them across the Mississippi River.

The move also gave Ben a few extra days to get his long-range artillery up and in place.

The three new battalions of Rebels, who had been training for months at Base Camp One and at other hidden locations in the south and eastern part of the nation were on the move. The third day after the bombardment, the first of the new battalions were crossing the Missouri line and moving northward, toward Kirksville. Five Battalion would occupy Kirksville and stretch south sixty miles. Six Battalion would take the line from Moberly down to and including Jefferson City, and Seven Battalion would stretch from the old capital down to just south of Rolla.

These were fresh troops, with the finest equipment available and whose officers and NCO's were all battle-tested leaders. And there was another reason for Ben's committing them to combat fresh out of training: When Ben left the shores of America behind him, he planned on taking three battalions with him—his own, Ike's people, and West's mercenaries. Ben had to make sure that the people he left behind could and would fight.

On the morning of the fourth day after the killing and demoralizing artillery barrage, Dan Gray brought prisoners into Ben's CP. His Scouts had crossed the river at night and did a little silent headhunting with knives, bringing back a dozen scared but sullen prisoners.

"Villar's people are a mixed bag, General," Dan informed him. "From East European to English. No blacks."

"Kenny Parr's men?"

"The worst kind of redneck all the way."

Ben faced the prisoners. "We can do this easy or hard," he told him. "That means with or without the use of drugs, which can be unpleasant to say the least."

The men faced him silently, hate in their eyes.

"Very well," Ben said. "Dan, take them to the interrogation teams and see what we can get. When we've sucked them dry, shoot them."

"Very well, sir."

"Now wait just a damn minute!" a man blurted, his voice trembly from fear. "This is war, and prisoners are accorded some rights."

Ben stared at him. "The same kind of rights you have accorded the men and women you've kidnapped and tortured and enslaved, forcing them to work on your farms in Florida?"

The man shuffled his feet and looked awfully uncomfortable.

Another prisoner spoke, his accent giving away his East European ancestry. "If we cooperate, what do we get in return?"

"Freedom. A chance to start over once the armies

across the river are defeated."

"What kind of freedom?" another asked.

"You'll be separated and placed in a Rebel-controlled zone. We call them outposts. You'll be given a job, depending on what you're qualified to do. After successfully completing a probationary period, you'll be free men."

Four of the prisoners chose to cooperate. The others were led away.

"You're really going to shoot them, General?" Ben was asked by one of the four.

"That is correct."

"Kenny don't know what he's up agin. We should have stayed in Florida."

"We would have gone there to destroy you," Ben told him. "Eventually."

The man shook his head. "I believe that. You're a devil, Ben Raines. You're worser than the ACLU, the FBI, the State Po-lice, and the IRS all combined ever thought of bein'."

"That's a very interesting comparison. How many men does Kenny have in his command?"

"Fifteen hundred."

"All white trash?"

The man stirred at that; but despite his situation, he was forced to smile, very thinly. "You're goin' to make the people knuckle under to you, ain't you, Ben Raines?"

"No," Ben surprised him. "Only those who wish to receive medical attention, to give in a safe and secure zone, who want to work and live and play in freedom, who wish their children to be educated, and who want to see this country regain some of what it once was."

"And them that don't want to live under your rules?"

"Can go to hell."

"Their kids? . . ."

"Will be taken from them and placed in foster homes, to live with decent people and who will see that the young are reeducated."

"That's commomism!"

"The word is communism. But you're wrong. There is a touch of socialism in what we're doing. But in the history of communism, no communist nation ever allowed their people, all of the people, to be fully armed, to vote on every rule or proposition, and to elect their leaders. I never agreed with the saying that everyone has a right to an opinion, because like you, many don't know what the hell they're talking about." He cut his eyes to another. "You are, were, a part of Villar's forces?"

"Yes, General." The prisoner sat at attention in the chair.

And with that, Ben knew Villar's forces would be the ones with the most staying power, the one's with perhaps almost as much discipline as his own Rebels. "And you came here from?"

"All over Europe, sir."

"Why?"

"Those you call Night People, General, had a lot to do with it. There are also armies over there that would make all our combined forces, yours and those across the river, tiny in comparison. All of Europe is an armed camp. The people—many of them—have reverted back centuries. Baron/peasant-type of existence in many cases. The landowner has his or her private army to act as enforcers."

"You speak as an educated man, yet you joined Lan Villar's terrorist army."

"I joined for survival, General. No one stands alone in Europe. To do so is to die . . . and not very pleasantly, I might add."

Ben studied the man for a moment, then told the guards to take the other prisoners out and question them. He asked the man from Villar's army to stay.

When they were alone, except for Dan Gray, Ben asked, "Your name?"

"Hans Strobel."

"German?"

40

"Yes, sir. My parents owned a small business in West Germany before the Great War. I was attending the University at Munich when the world blew apart."

"Majoring in what?"

That thin smile appeared on his face. "Philosophy, sir."

"Your position with Villar?"

"Platoon leader, sir."

"Do you enjoy raping and torturing, Hans?"

"I never raped anyone in my life, General. Nor have I ever tortured anyone, except for a few Night People when trying to find where they had taken prisoners . . . to be eaten."

Ben grunted. He could certainly understand that. "Your opinion of Lan Villar, Hans?"

Hans thought for a moment. "A brilliant soldier, but twisted in his thinking. Personally, I believe the man is functionally insane. He's a cruel man. He once said that he wished he could have met Sam Hartline before you killed him, for he admired him very much."

"Sam Hartline was one of the most vicious people I ever encountered," Ben told him.

"Precisely," Hans replied. "But you will find that Sam Hartline was an angel with wings when compared against Lan Villar."

"What would you do, Hans, if I were to offer you a position within my Rebel army?"

"Accept and fight alongside you and your people. I am a survivor, General Raines. Even though I never held a gun in my hands until I was twenty-one years old. When the Great War came, I fought with the resistance in Germany for five years, before the forces of Lan Villar overran us and took control of the state where I lived. After a year in a forced labor camp, I was offered a chance to enlist. I took it. To stay where I was meant certain death. I am a survivor."

Ben nodded his head. "Outfit him, Dan. Keep him with you for a time. Let's see how he works out." He looked at Hans. "Welcome to the Rebels, Hans."

Hans nodded and stood up. "You will not be disappointed, General. I am a good soldier."

"How many more in Villar's command would switch sides, Hans?"

He answered without hesitation. "Perhaps one half of one percent, General. Most are men with little education; brutes for the most part."

"It always comes back to that, doesn't it, Hans?"

"Only if one keeps a gun close by his books, sir."

# Chapter 5

Dan was back in Ben's quarters later that afternoon with a pleased look on his face.

Ben arched one eyebrow in a question.

"Hans," Dan told him. "He's going to do just fine. One of those we were going to shoot begged for his life in return for information. I pulled him out of the line and interrogated him. He said that Hans was always out of place in Villar's army, and that Villar had threatened him many times with a firing squad if he didn't toughen up. I asked what toughening up meant? He said Hans would never take part in the raping and senseless torture that the others did. He said the only reason Villar kept him around was because of his brilliant mind and because Villar liked to debate with him."

"Did you check his information?"

"Oh, yes. He passed a polygraph and a PSE test. I cut him loose."

"Good. Where did you assign Hans?"

"Buddy's Rat Team. He'll get a workout there."

"What's the word from the new battalions?"

"Moving into place. Two more days and the line should be complete. We move against Villar then?"

"Are the young hellions ready?"

Dan grinned. "Now, General, you don't think I'm going to let all those lads and lassies drop in by themselves, do you?"

"It would have surprised me. I might decide to join you."

Dan suddenly got a very worried look on his face.

Ben laughed and waved a hand. "Oh, hell, Dan! I'm just joking. I may have a couple of jumps left in me, but we'll save them for the future. You've told them it's a one-shot deal? They'll be going in at five hundred feet with no reserve?"

"They know, General."

"They've got a hell of a forced march ahead of them, Dan. Has Chase started his medical exams yet?"

"Started at 1200 hours today, General. So far, everyone looks good."

Ben stood up and moved to a wall map, motioning Dan to join him. "You'll take off at 1800 hours from the strip and fly south for fifty miles before cutting east. Pathfinders are in place and have the DZ all marked out, at least in their minds. They'll flag it for you at 1900 hours. By 0230, no later than 0300 I want you people here!" He hit the map. "That's a twenty-mile forced march and you're going to be staggering under the load of equipment. If you have any doubts, Dan, voice them now."

"No doubts, General. Anyone who falls behind, stays behind. My people all know the rules. The name of the game is march or die."

"I'll see you again before you shove off. I want to talk with all the boys and girls."

"Right, sir."

Dan did a turnabout and left the room as he had been trained to do at the Royal Military Academy near Sandhurst, moving along very smartly.

Ben sat back down at his desk and fiddled with some papers, although his mind was not on it. If he could just figure out a way to go with Dan and his people . . .

Jerre stepped into the room and stared at him. Ben met her eyes.

"Forget it, Ben," she told him.

"Forget what?" Ben asked innocently.

"I can practically hear the wheels turning in your

head, Ben." She closed the door behind her, walked to a chair facing his desk and sat down. "You're not a twenty-one-year-old in the height of physical conditioning, Ben. I know. Remember me?"

"How could I forget you?" Ben replied honestly. "And God knows I've tried."

"Would you believe me if I said I'm sorry about that, Ben?"

"Yes. If there is fault to be placed, it lies with me."

She shook her head. "That's debatable, of course. But beside the point right now. If I have to spend twenty-four hours a day with you until those paratroopers leave, Ben, I'll do it just to keep you from going along. And you know I mean that."

Ben leaned back in his chair and stared at her, a slight smile on his lips. "Yes, Jerre, I'd forgotten. You probably know me better than any woman alive. I'd like to go on the drop; I won't deny that. However, I also know that it's out of the question. I realize that I'm needed here. But I will admit this: I was entertaining thoughts of how to get on board when you came in."

She returned his smile. "You think you could keep up with them, Ben?"

He slowly shook his head. "I'm a middle-aged man, Jerre. So the answer is no. I could not. I'm not even sure how much longer Dan will be able to do it. That's why I'm pushing Buddy along so quickly."

She looked toward the ever-present coffeepot. "May I?"

"Of course."

"Would you like a cup?"

"Yes. Black with . . ."

"I know how you take it, Ben," she cut him off with a smile.

Over coffee they sat and talked for more than an hour; something they had not done — with any degree of friendliness—in a long time. They spoke of old friends, many of whom were dead, killed while fighting in the Rebel Army. And of how well the movement was progressing.

"Are you really serious about taking troops to Europe, Ben?"

"I'm certainly thinking about it. If we can kick Villar and Parr's asses, it will just about wrap it up for the States; except for some isolated pockets. I'll be expanding Base Camp One as soon as this fight is over, taking in half a dozen more parishes, west and south. Cecil is a fine administrator. I'll be handing the reins over to him."

She laughed, and it was filled with good humor. "The first black man in the history of the United States to be completely in charge of the country. But I'll make you a bet that Cecil will be hopping mad about not coming along with you."

"No bet, Jerre. He's liable to call me out for a fistfight. He doesn't know that I'll be placing him in charge, so keep it quiet."

She nodded. "How many battalions are you taking?"

"As it stands now, three. That will leave four battalions in country. My battalion will go, as will Ike's, and Colonel West."

"Doctor Chase?"

"I don't think I could keep him from going."

"I've never been to Europe."

"Then I would suggest you start packing."


Those miscreants that made up Sister Voleta's Ninth Order surfaced at her coded radio messages and began their march toward the west. They came out of the hills and the marshes and the swamps and the caves. Those east of the Mississippi swung north and south, to avoid the conflict at St. Louis, coming up under or over the gathering and then cutting

46

west to link up with Voleta and Ashley and their assorted band of outlaws. Those west of the Mississippi and west of the Rebels who were now stretched out south to north in Missouri simply stayed in place and waited for the main force to reach them.

Those between St. Louis and the three battalions kept their heads down and waited for the signal to begin harassing tactics against both the Rebels in St. Louis and the Rebels between Kirksville and Rolla.

In the ruins of East St. Louis, Villar was pacing the floor of his CP. "What's the bastard waiting on?" he flung the question out, not really expecting an answer. "What's he got up his sleeve?"

Villar had expected the campaign to be short, violent, and of course, victorious for his forces. Food for his people was going to be a problem very quickly. When he hit the shores of America, he had plans to overrun Ben's Base Camp One. Then that was very quickly nixed when he learned that Ben had nuclear weapons there, and that everything in Base Camp One was wired to explode in the event the zone was ever overrun by enemy forces. So that much needed source of food was out of reach.

Twelve thousand people ate up a lot of food every day. And he had no idea where he was to get more. Kenny Parr had huge farms in Florida, but getting food up was a dangerous operation, for Raines had Rebel patrols working everywhere around the nation. One convoy had already been ambushed and the food taken. The bastards and bitches were across the river dining on their food right now. He hoped they all choked on their greens and blackeyed peas and lima beans. The mere thought of defeat was a bitter pill for Lan to swallow. And when he did get it down, it lay like a lump in his belly.

Villar had known that Raines was well-organized; but he had not known just how well. Until it was too late . . . now there was no turning back.

He had thought of and then discarded the idea of

scouring the countryside and taking civilian hostages; perhaps to coerce Raines into letting the food trucks through. But he knew that Raines did not negotiate with terrorists—ever. Another plan out the window.

For the very first time, Lan Villar began to realize just what kind of a man he was facing. In his own way, Ben Raines was perhaps more ruthless than Villar. While the Rebels did not rape and pillage and plunder, Raines and his Rebels did not have one ounce of pity or compassion in their souls for anyone who fought against their dream of rebuilding the shattered nation that was once called America.

"Goddamn you to hell, Ben Raines!" Lan Villar cursed him.

Across the river, Ben looked at his plate of fresh vegetables and smiled. Corn on the cob, navy beans, and hot cornbread.

"Compliments of Kenny Parr," Jersey told him. "Maybe we should send him a thank-you note."

"Corrie," Ben said around a mouthful of food. "Send Villar a message. Tell him many thanks for the fresh vegetables, and advise him that a university here once did a study. They concluded that rats were full of protein and when cooked correctly were quite tasty. Tell him I suggest he try dining on rodents."

When his runner handed him the message, Villar became livid with rage. He screamed out his anger and then ripped the paper to shreds and flung the remnants around the room. "I hate that son of a bitch!" he shouted, his fists clenched.

"Join the club," Khamsin said, looking down at the goop on his plate the officers' personal cooks had prepared for them.

"You know what he's doing," Kenny said softly. "He's waiting us out. He's guessed that by now we're on short rations, so he's pushing us to attack him out of desperation. And we're not far from doing that. If we don't attack, and do so successfully, we're going to have to fall back."

"Fall back to *where?*" Villar demanded, but with no rancor in his voice. "Anyway, we agreed to stay here until this Sister Voleta nut got her forces together and attacked from the west. I never, never expected Raines to blow the bridges. I never did that in Europe. Once they are gone, they are gone forever . . . at least in our lifetimes. We're facing a madman!" He shuddered and regained control. "No," his voice was softer. "No. Raines is not a madman. He is brilliantly ruthless. And he is a man who would see this nation restored no matter what the cost. If I thought he would even remotely entertain the idea, I would . . ." He trailed that off.

But Khamsin had already guessed what he was about to say. "Forget it," the Libyan said. "Ben Raines makes no deals with terrorists. Or at least none that I know of. And you are forgetting your archenemy across the river, Colonel Daniel Gray."

"Yes," Villar said softly. "Dan Gray swore on his sister's grave he would kill me."

"Why does he hate you so?" Kenny asked.

"I had agreed to do some contract work for a offshoot of the IRA back in, oh, eighty-five or eighty-six. I made the mistake, and it was a mistake, of kidnapping some schoolchildren in London. One of the girls was the sister of Dan Gray. All we had been told was that they were relatives of SAS men. She was raped." He shrugged his indifference to that. "Many times. She did not die well. I had learned that she was Gray's sister and tape-recorded the rapes. I sent the tape to him. I was younger then and much more arrogant. I made a mistake. That mistake almost cost me my life. Gray stalked me halfway around the world and shot me with his own damnable brand of hand-loaded ammo. The bastard had sealed cobra venom into the tip. I was near death and paralyzed on one side for months. Don't ever sell Dan Gray short. As a matter of fact, don't

49

sell any Rebel commander short. Ike McGowan is a former Navy SEAL. Murderous bastards! West is ex-FFL. Cecil Jefferys is ex-Green Beret. He isn't as ruthless as Ben Raines, but he is a far better administrator. Word that I've received is that Raines is going to turn the whole operation over to him in the very near future. Can you imagine that? A nigger running the country?"

Ben called for a final meeting of his commanders just hours before the teams of paratroopers took off from the airstrip at St. Clair.

"Dan will be taking off in two hours, people. At 0600 hours in the morning, we shall begin shelling the other side of the river with our long-range artillery. Jersey will give you all the coordinates. Do not overshoot. To do that will endanger Dan and his troopers. Ike dropped sappers in two days ago to mine overpasses and bridges on Interstates Sixty-four and 55/70, east of Villar's positions. As soon as the shelling starts, they'll blow their targets and get the hell out of there, moving north and south respectively. It is my hope that with the bombardment, the sappers' work will not be noticed. That leaves Highway Fifty open to Villar and the others. If he takes it, our plan will work and we'll be rid of a lot of terrorists. If he smells a rat—and he just might—we'll be sitting on this side of the river with our thumbs up our asses while Dan and his people are facing the real possibility of getting mauled."

Ben took a drink of water and then moved to a wall map. "Villar and his people are not going to move far. I'm betting they'll move just out of range of our big pieces and reorganize. Their storage depots are going to be blown to hell and gone. He split them up and located them between Belleville and Highway Fifty, and the second one between Highway Fifty and Collinsville. Those are two more reasons I'm betting he'll head out on Highway Fifty.

"The next logical stop for him is here." He pointed to a town on the map. "Just about ten miles outside the city. It was a town of about twelve or fifteen thousand before the war. If any of you are the praying types, pray that he does choose this particular town."

Ike was smiling. "Dan and his people are all going to be carrying about fifty pounds of cannisters, right, Ben? You've decided to do it?"

"That's right. In addition, fifty others in this drop will be carrying rocket launchers and our own lab peoples' version of the old Dragon antitank weapon. The new ones are lighter and pack more of a wallop. They are also able to launch other types of warheads. Our weather people say the winds will be blowing from west to east that morning."

West chuckled, Ike laughed outloud, and Cecil smiled grimly. Cecil looked at Dan and said, "You people have your shot-kits, Dan?"

"Oh, yes," the Englishman replied.

Doctor Chase pointed a finger at him. "Dan, a few minutes before you fire the gas cannisters, you people inject yourselves. Any trooper who loses his or her kit, or it gets damaged in the drop, get them out of that area immediately, north or south."

"Yes, Doctor Chase."

"The gas will become useless in six to eight minutes," Chase continued, "causing only a mild sickness that will soon pass. But for six to eight minutes, it will kill any living thing it comes in contact with. Only the injection prevents it from doing its work."

Ben pointed to the map. "This large lake is approximately forty-five miles from the target site. The winds will be nearly calm; no more than two to four miles per hour. We anticipate no damage to the lake and its inhabitants, or to any other existing water supply outside of the town.

"There is an old Air Force base southeast of the

town. Part of Dan's drop will include a team to clear a runway there. Now then, another team will go in by plane as soon as Dan gives the signal — whether that signal is mission accomplished or send help." Ben smiled. "I shall be personally leading that other team."

# Chapter 6

The commanders of battalion, company, and platoon all came to their boots at that statement.

"No way, Ben!" Ike shouted over the hubbub of voices. "I'll take that other team in."

The mercenary, West, with a cast on one ankle, was in no position to lead, but he did shout, "My XO will take the team in."

"I'm second in command here!" Cecil roared. "If anybody fronts that other team, I will."

In the back of the room, Jerre stood with Jersey, both of them with smiles on their faces. They knew that Ben was going to lead the other team in, and that was that.

Ben sat back down behind his desk and rolled a cigarette, waiting for all the uproar to calm.

Dan leaned against a wall, sipping at the cup of fresh-brewed tea his batman had brought him.

Chief Doctor Lamar Chase was sputtering like a four-cylinder engine hitting on two, and waving his arms around. Nobody was paying any attention to anybody else.

Another thirty seconds and the uproar had quieted to a low mutter of agitated voices.

"Now that everyone has vented their spleen," Ben said, "let's settle down and return to business. One: are the boats ready, Ike?"

"Yeah, yeah!" Ike said disgustedly. "We've got them hidden behind Mosenthein Island. We can have the third team across the river and in Illinois in a matter of minutes. But it's going to take another eighteen to twenty hours to rig up ferries for the heavier stuff."

"That's all right, Ike. Light mortars and .50's will do. As soon as you receive my signal, start the Dusters west. Main battle tanks, self-propelled, and vehicle-towed artillery will leave as soon as your third team determines the enemy forces in Illinois have had it. West, you will start your westward pullout an hour behind the main battle tanks and artillery. Cecil's battalion will remain in the city and begin laying explosives. Ike will stay with me east of the river until we've cleaned it out."

Ben looked at the crowd of men and women. "If we can pull this off, we can break the backs of Villar, Khamsin, and Parr in a matter of minutes. If they don't take the bait, we're in deep shit. Keep up normal radio traffic so as not to alarm those across the river. That's it, people. Good luck."

Ben and his team drove to the airstrip at St. Clair, Doctor Chase in a vehicle behind Ben's wagon. The young paratroopers were in high spirits, laughing and cracking jokes as they struggled into their harnesses. Ben walked up and down the line, talking for a few seconds to each member of Dan's assault team. Doctor Chase was right behind him, making certain each trooper had his or her inoculation kit against the deadly gas, and then giving each one a smile and a pat on the arm.

Dan walked up, or waddled up would be more like it, equipment hanging all over him. "We're ready to load, General."

"The gas cannisters are packed securely?" Ben asked, for the tenth time.

Dan smiled. "The queen's china would come through this drop without a chip, sir. Even should there be a chute malfunction, the cannisters will not break open. We've tested them repeatedly."

"I'll see you across the river, Dan. Good luck."

Ben turned and walked back to the armor-plated

and bulletproofed glassed wagon, Jerre walking with him.

"All this talk about securing hospitals and aid stations and digging in deep was a ruse, wasn't it, Ben?" She asked. "You knew all along this was what you were going to do." The last was not a question.

"That's correct, Jerre. But only four of us knew it. Lamar didn't even know what was going down until yesterday. Villar has spotters across the river, watching our every move. It was all done for his benefit."

"When we go to Europe, Ben,"—and Ben picked up on the *we*,—"are you taking poisonous gas?"

"Yes. I resisted it for years, Jerre. And perhaps I was wrong in doing so. The cost of Rebel lives in combatting this vermin was what convinced me to change my mind. We just can't afford to unnecessarily lose good, decent people fighting crud. However, it's taken our lab people years to perfect this gas; reducing its killing time down to a matter of only a few minutes and protecting the environment. I've also got them working on gas that will kill humans but not animals. They say they're close. I hope so. The animals have had a tough enough time without us adding to their misery."

Jerre did not have to add that Ben was a strange and complex man. She knew that Ben's philosophy was that it was wrong to blame an animal for being an animal. They could not help what God had made them. But humans could. Animals had no choice; humans did. Humans had the capacity to think and reason, but if they chose not to exercise that ability, to hell with them.

Ben saw no point in keeping them around.

Ben Raines was hard and tough and in many ways, totally ruthless. The one thing that he absolutely could not and would not abide was ignorance when enlightenment was right in front of the person, readily accessible, and the party would not take advantage of it.

Ben had more than his share of compassion for the very young and the very old, and for God's lesser creatures of the animal kingdom. He was totally void of compassion for human trash of any color.

He had told his doctors and scientists that if he ever learned of them using animals for experimentation, he would personally kill that person — on the spot.

Being learned men and women, and knowing that Ben never made idle threats, they knew to take his warning to heart and keep it close.

The second team to land in Illinois would, like Dan's troopers, be carrying a heavy load of equipment. But if the operation proved successful, they would not have to carry it back, for the vehicles of Villar and Khamsin and Parr would be their's for the taking. If the operation was unsuccessful, none of Ben's team would have to worry about it. For the chances were very good that most of them would be dead.

Ben met with Cecil alone in his CP. The planes carrying Dan and his troopers were airborne, the jumpers would be exiting the door in minutes.

"If the operation is not successful, Cecil, pull your people out immediately and head south for Base Camp One. The commanders of the three battalions west of us have the same orders. Do not — repeat: *do not* — attempt to mount any rescue across the river. The Rebel army will stand without me. But it has to have a leader. That's you. If we blow the operation, appoint West your second in command and start over." He smiled at his old friend. "Hell, Cec, we might as well keep it in the family, since I keep getting signals that West is going to marry my daughter."

Cecil did not argue the orders. The two men shared a quiet laugh and a drink of whiskey.

"The chaplains are holding a quiet ceremony this evening, Ben. Praying for the success of this operation. Every Rebel knows the seriousness of what's going down."

After Cecil had left to return to his own sector, Ben poured another drink, added a dash of water — the few months he'd spent back at Base Camp One had spoiled him: he'd gotten used to ice cubes and now missed them — and leaned back in his chair, thinking.

Dan and his troopers had been on the ground for over an hour. They had landed undetected. If there had been any type of fire-fight, Ben would have been notified immediately by radio. So phase one had gone without a hitch. Dan and his troopers were now marching toward their destination, and knowing Dan, he was driving himself just as hard, or harder, than any of his people.

Ben turned his swivel chair so he faced the east. "Come on, Dan. Get in position and say a prayer that Villar and his bunch take the right highway."

*The next morning.* 0500 hours.

"All right, lads and lassies!" Dan rousted his people from a deep, almost exhausted sleep. "Get your Tommy Cookers out and light your tabs." He grinned at a grimy-faced young Rebel and affected a Cockney accent. "Get ye char abilin'."

"Do we heat up our MRE's, Colonel?" another asked, knowing very well what the answer would be.

"Not a chance, me boy. Heat up your coffee and douse the tab. Cold rations for us all."

"I got meatballs," a Rebel said. "Anybody want to trade?"

"I got tuna and noodles," another said.

"Anything is better than meatballs for breakfast. Here, catch, and toss me yours."

While the Heximine tabs were heating the water, Dan walked up and down the line, inspecting each trooper's inoculation kit. Then he settled down to drink his morning tea (a carefully hoarded supply of Earl Gray Breakfast tea he had found in a warehouse; he would have enjoyed some cream but one can't have everything in the field) and eat his cold MRE's. Chicken stew. For breakfast.

After eating, he carefully buried the wrappings from the MRE's—no Rebel littered unless it was necessary—and chewed his gum. These weren't really the MRE's American GI used in 'Nam, but a newer creation from the Rebel's lab people down at Base Camp One . . . they might have been newer and contain more vitamins and so forth, but they weren't any better.

Light was touching the eastern sky when Dan said, "Let's get into position, gang."


0555 hours. *The landing strip at St. Clair.*


The planes' engines were silent; they would not start their warm-up until the artillery began their barrage. Ben and his people stood on the runway, all of them loaded with equipment.

Buddy was standing beside his father and his sister, and the young man was pissed.

"I really wish you would reconsider, Father. I would like to accompany you across the river."

"No, boy, and that is final. If something gets fouled up and your sister and I don't return, you and Cecil have to piece together the remains and get this army moving. Now get off my ass about it." He looked at his son and softened his statement with a grin. "But

58

you are going to Europe. Now does that make you feel any better?"

"Somewhat," the young man replied, smiling. "I can take some consolation that I will be with Ike in the boats later on."

"There you go."

Thirty miles away the graying sky was suddenly lit up as the thunderous barrage began. The very first shell of HE from the eight-inch guns struck true, landing smack in the middle of a supply depot. Ammo, gasoline, mortar rounds, and rockets lit up the sky across the river.

The Rebels on the airstrip cheered.

"Tell the pilots to check their engines," Ben told Corrie.


The salvo knocked Lan Villar out of his bunk and tumbling to the floor, grabbing for his boots and clothing. The door to his quarters burst open.

"They've got us zeroed in, Lan!" his XO shouted to be heard over the whine and roar of incoming.

A round landed very close and blew out what windows remained on the ground floor.

Lan pulled on his boots and looked out to the north, then ran across the room, the glass crunching under his feet and looked to the south. Huge fires lit up the early morning skies.

Lan cursed for a moment. "That's it, Karl. We've had it. Without those supplies we're screwed. Why in the hell wasn't I informed that Raines had guns capable of reaching this distance?"

"We didn't know, Lan. We thought the heaviest he had were one-o-five's."

"The son of a bitch is dropping rounds in from twenty miles away. How is the evac route to the north?"

"No good. The explosion at the depot took out part

of the Interstate."

"South?" Lan knew the answer to that even before he turned and looked south. A wall of flames greeted him. Defeat clutched at him in a cold sweaty grasp and the copper taste was unpalatable on his tongue. "It seems we have only one other option, Karl. And might I add that we had better exercise it."

"After you, sir."


"It worked!" Dan said, after receiving a curt and coded radio message. "They're heading this way." He lifted his walkie-talkie, set on a scrambled high band frequency. "Use your injection kits now. Now!"

He laid the walkie-talkie aside, opened his kit, and took out the syringe, the small needle capped. He removed the cap and jammed the needle into his leg, emptying the vial. He experienced a moment of nausea, fought it back, and then the sensation left him.

He lifted the walkie-talkie and spoke into the cup. "Lay out cannisters but do not activate or load—repeat: *do not*—activate or load. Activate and load only on my orders."

The Rebels were spread out from one city limits sign to the other, running west to east in the deserted old town. Others were on rooftops, flat on their bellies, waiting.

"The town up ahead." Lan pointed to his radio operator. "That seems to be out of range of the guns. Tell the others to center around me there."

The message was sent down the line of fast-moving vehicles, the cars and trucks taking up both lanes of the highway in their haste to escape the deadly fire from the Rebels.

The dead calm air began moving as a very slight breeze from out of the west picked up.

"Activate and load," Dan gave the orders.

Lan Villar told his driver to pull off on the shoulder and waved down the command vehicles of Khamsin and Parr. He got out and walked back to the other commanders. "Have your people use this next town as a staging area. We're out of range of the guns."

"The barrage has almost stopped," Khamsin said, pointing out the obvious.

"I noticed," Villar said coldly. "And why not? Ben Raines has us running like scared rabbits." He looked at Kenny Parr. "Have your radio operator order one battalion from each command to lay back just behind our position to act as rear guard, Kenny."

Kenny gave the orders that saved a few lives.

"I hate Ben Raines with all the passion in my heart," the Hot Wind verbally farted.

The town limits, which extended for nearly six miles, began filling up with troops from the terrorist and outlaw armies.

At St. Clair, the planes filled with Ben's team began lifting off the runway.

With a smile on his lips, Dan Gray lifted the walkie-talkie and said, "All teams fire! Fire!"

# Chapter 7

Rockets exploded vehicles on the clogged roads leading into and out of the town, completely blocking many of the littered streets. The burning vehicles caught other cars and trucks on fire and the exploding gas tanks, ammunition, mortar rounds and grenades hooked onto battle harnesses only added to the confusion.

The deadly gas cannisters were fired from rocket launchers and exploded out of mortar tubes. Since the gas was invisible, many of the members of the terrorist armies trapped in the burning streets did not know what was taking place until their lungs and throats began burning and waves of nausea struck them, driving them to their knees with unseen hammer blows.

Even from their positions several thousand yards from the town, Lan Villar, Kenny Parr, and Khamsin could hear the screaming from several thousand tongues. But it was not until they saw dozens of men stagger out of the smoke, clutching their chests and their throats that Villar put it together.

"Gas!" he screamed. "The bastard's using poisonous gas."

Many miles to the south, the planes carrying Ben and his contingent were just making their northern turn.

The young Kenny Parr was the first to react sensibly. He quickly consulted an old map and said, "Everybody backtrack to one fifty-nine and cut north," he said, his voice firm. "We can't stop for anything. Raines will surely have another larger force coming in as soon as the gas clears. Let's go!"

The three terrorists and what was left of their armies ran for vehicles, running in a near-blind panic as the screaming began to fade from the death town. "Take the lead, Kenny," Villar shouted. "We'll follow."

Atop a roof, Dan watched the frightened exodus through binoculars, a grim smile of satisfaction on his face as death clogged the streets below him. He turned to his radio operator. "Let them go. They'll be out of range for us in less than a minute anyway."

As the frightened remnants of the terrorist army escaped, many of those still on foot were run over and crushed under the tires of the vehicles used in the rush of retreat. In many cases their dying took much longer than their comrades trapped in the town. A few managed to pull their crushed bodies off the roadway and into the ditches, where they died amid the litter and twinkle of years'-old soft drink and beer cans. The cans would still be twinkling years after their bones had turned to dust.

As the planes flew over Belleville, they turned toward the east, the pilots reporting the hurried retreat of the terrorists to Ben.

"Let them go," Ben radioed to the cockpit. "It's twenty miles from the river to their present location. No way Ike could possibly catch them. Transportation on this side of the river is uncertain, at best. We'll catch up with them another day." He changed frequencies and said, "Eagle One to Scout Leader."

"Go Eagle One," Dan's calm voice sprang into Ben's headset.

"Situation report."

"Wall-to-wall bodies, Eagle. There is no sign of life on the streets. The team at the airstrip where

63

you will land says to stay clear for another five minutes."

"That's ten-fifty, Dan. We've already injected ourselves. We're safe. We'll be landing in three minutes. Send trucks on the way."

"That's ten-four, Eagle." He changed frequencies and ordered, "Drivers commandeer enemy trucks and meet the Eagle at the strip. Go!"

Rebels literally climbed over the bodies of dead terrorists and outlaws to get to the enemy vehicles. They cranked up—many of the engines were still running—and headed for the old Air Force base south of town.

A quiet fell over the town as the Rebels left their positions to stand and look in awe at the sight before their eyes. More than six thousand men lay in the streets and on the sidewalks; some hung out of the windows of cars and trucks and Jeeps. Their faces were forever frozen in that last agonizing moment of death as the deadly gas took their lives.

Dan walked down the steps from the rooftop to the street below. He stood for a moment, looking at the stiffening carnage. "You may begin stripping the bodies of weapons and ammo," he ordered. "Take all radio equipment and anything else you see that we might be able to use. Start moving the usable vehicles clear of town. After General Raines makes his visual, we'll burn the town to eliminate any health hazard."

Ben pulled in moments later. The Rebels had all seen death many times, but none of them—including Ben—had ever seen death like this; not on this wholesale level.

The faces of the dead men were turning black; the death grimaces an awful sight to witness. Hands had turned into claws as the respiratory systems shut down and fingers tore into the flesh of throat in a futile attempt to suck in air. Nervous systems had refused to function, leaving limbs twisted in near-impossible positions. Some lay on their backs, arms, and hands stiffly outstretched heavenward, as if seeking some godly relief to help them cope with this awful moment of death.

If God heard the silent pleas, He did nothing that Ben could see to aid the terrorists and outlaws.

"Some of the enemy trucks have scraper blades on them. 'Doze the bodies onto the main street," Ben ordered. "Douse them with gasoline and burn them. When that's done, have artillery lay back and destroy the town with napalm and Willie Peter."

"Right, sir."

"How long do you anticipate recovering the captured supplies?"

"We should be finished by noon, sir."

Ben nodded. "You've dispatched trucks to pick up Ike and his people?"

"Yes, sir."

Again, Ben nodded. "West has some of his people rigging barges to use as ferries across the river. Start the convoys moving westward as quickly as possible."

"Right, sir."

"Corrie, radio Cecil and have him start his demolition teams planting explosives around the city and other teams clearing a way for us through the city. I want the first units moving toward our battle lines in Central Missouri by dawn tomorrow." He turned to his daughter. "Tina, move out ahead of them and set up my CP in Jefferson City . . . or what's left of it."

"Right, Dad."

"Double your usual team size and move with Dusters, mortar carriers, and main battle tanks. Voleta will have people between the river and our lines. Destroy them. No prisoners. Move out now, Tina."

Ben had not expected Thermopolis and his people to accompany Ike's people, but they did. Thermopolis stood at the end of the street and stared at the sight.

"My God!" he whispered. "There is death wherever one looks."

Rosebud took it much more stoically and pragmatically. "They had a choice," she said. Then she leaned down, plucked a wildflower that was growing out of a crack in the street, and stuck it behind one ear. "They just didn't make the right choice."

Her husband fixed her with a jaundiced look. Every fiber in his being wanted to debate that remark, but he wisely decided against it. He couldn't remember ever winning an argument with her anyway.

Twisting curls of black smoke arched into the sky moments after the bodies of the dead were set blazing. The dead had been bulldozed onto the main street, doused with gasoline, and torched. As soon as the flames began to wane, Ben ordered the artillery barrage to begin and the afternoon was filled with long-range booming, the napalm and WP shells setting the town blazing.

Rebels had taken up positions around the town, digging firebreaks to prevent the flames from spreading, and in some case lighting backfires to arrest the forward motion of the leaping flames.

Ben motioned Dan to his side. "You want the job of pursuing the terrorists, Dan?"

The Englishman smiled coldly. "I would be offended if you gave it to anyone else. Naturally, since you are moving against Voleta, you would like me to take Buddy and his Rat Team with me." It was not a question.

"Yes. Pick your people and equipment."

66

"I shall be in pursuit by dawn tomorrow."

Ben watched the former SAS officer walk away, yelling for Buddy and his Rat Team to form up around him. If there was a man alive who could track down and kill Villar and what was left of his army of terrorists, Dan Gray was that man. And with the addition of Hans Strobel, the German might be able to give some insight as to what Villar could possibly do next.

One thing was for certain at this time: Lan Villar was no longer much of a threat to the Rebel movement.

With rear guard personnel radioing that there was no pursuit from the Rebels, Lan called a halt to the frantic retreat.

They were just north of Litchfield when the battalions regrouped on the shores of a lake and began counting heads.

It was discouraging to all.

Out of an initial force of nearly twelve thousand men, twelve hundred had been killed or wounded in the first bombardment by Raines's Rebels. Another thousand had been killed or wounded by the surprise assault early that morning, and more than six thousand had been killed by the gas. Another thousand or so had scattered like paper in the wind when the first gas cannisters popped. Whether they had survived or not was anybody's guess.

Personally, Lan figured at the most, maybe half of them made it. He knew he would probably never see one tenth of those survivors again.

"Twenty-three hundred men able to fight, sir," Lan's XO reported to him later that afternoon. "And most of them belong to us."

"Khamsin?"

"Four hundred troops."

"Kenny?"

"Two hundred and fifty troops."

Villar snorted bitterly. "And we are left with less than three full battalions."

"Your orders, sir?"

Villar sighed. Earlier he had watched the clouds of black smoke darkening the sky south of their position, and knew what it was: bodies burning with the town. "Karl, I just don't know."


Ben went back across the river on the ferry's first return trip. It had been a most fruitful morning. The Rebels had captured more than five hundred vehicles; more than two hundred of them Volvo and Mercedes trucks. Ben ordered them carefully gone over and stored. These would be the vehicles they would take to Europe; it would be easier to find parts for them over there than for American-made trucks.

With Khamsin's army crushed, that meant they would more than likely leave from some port in South Carolina. As soon as Ben could spare the people, he would have the trucks driven out to South Carolina, fully loaded with supplies for the voyage.

He cleared his head of those thoughts. That was in the future. For now, he had an army to destroy.

And his son's mother to kill.

# Chapter 8

Ben stepped outside into a still dark but already busy morning around his CP just south of the city.

He could tell by the way his people moved that they were in high spirits. They had come out of what at first appeared to be a brutal fight without losing one single troop—Chase had already closed the hospital, packing everything for the move west—and the Rebels had handed the enemy a devastating defeat.

They had reason to be in high spirits.

And the scuttlebutt was that General Raines was taking three battalions and heading for Europe, just as soon as Sister Voleta and her nuts of the Ninth Order were defeated. All in all, they concluded, it shaped up to be a very interesting summer.

Ben sat down on the curb, a cup of coffee in his hand, and watched the loading of equipment preparatory to their pulling out of the city.

Jerre came out and joined him on the curb. She studied his face for a moment and then said, "You don't seem as happy as the troops, Ben."

"Voleta is not going to be as easy to defeat as Villar, Jerre. For one thing, she isn't as arrogant as he appears to be. Another reason is that she's been fighting me for a long time. She knows better than to mass her people as Villar did. We'll be fighting nasty little pitched battles. Ambushes. And we'll be fighting along a one-hundred-and-fifty mile front. Probably two fronts, for that bitch will have people behind us as well. It isn't going to be a piece of

69

cake, Jerre. Anything but. It's going to be long and bloody and nerve-racking."

"By long, you mean? . . ."

"End of summer before we're through. Then a four-thousand-mile boat ride to Ireland."

"Why Ireland?"

Ben smiled. "Because we're going to hit it before we do England."

"Smartass!" She grinned at him. Her smile faded. "What do you expect to find, Ben?"

"Trouble."

Dan had crossed over into Illinois by ferry, taking with him four hundred and fifty handpicked infantry personnel. He took a section of Dusters, half a dozen main battle tanks, three mortar carriers, and heavy trucks carrying spare parts for all equipment, food, treads for the tanks, tires, and ammo for all weapons.

"You get your butt in a bind, Dan," Ben told him, "you get on that horn and radio in. I can have birds in the air within the hour."

"Will do, General. Ta-ta, now." He saluted smartly and wheeled about, yelling at the top of his lungs for his people to mount up.

"Let's split, people!" Ben yelled.

"Split?" Rosebud said, looking at Thermopolis. "General Raines actually said let's split?"

"I think he's really a hippie in disguise."

"Damn good disguise if he is. He sure fooled me. Are we in this for the duration?"

"What do you think?"

"Have you asked the others?"

"Yes."

"And they said? . . ."

"They always wanted to see Europe."

That topic was put to rest by the arrival of Emil Hite and his band of followers. Emil rolled up in his hearse—there was a bed in the back so he could take a nap when he felt like it—and got out, his people grouping around him. Emil faced Thermopolis.

"Are we ready to go do battle with the wicked witch of the west, Therm?"

"We're gung ho and ready to go, Emil," Thermopolis told him.

"That's the spirit, Therm. We've been assigned to the center of the column. We're off, Therm."

"Right, Emil." In more ways than one, he silently added, then felt a small pang of guilt for thinking it. Emil wasn't that bad a person. He was just a con artist and always would have one scam or the other going for him; always harmless scams that never really hurt anybody. But the little man would stand and fight when he had to . . . one could not take that away from him.

Emil waved his group to their vehicles and they drove off, to take their positions in the miles-long column.

Leadfoot, Beerbelly, Wanda, and their bikers pulled in behind Emil, with Emil twisting in the seat to keep a close eye on them. He wasn't too sure about the bikers.

Thermopolis and his crew got in their VW Bugs and vans and pulled in behind the bikers. Thermopolis rather liked the bikers, seeing through their façade and knowing that despite their toughness—and they were a tough bunch—most of them were just full of horseshit and quite likable when you got to know them. And the bikers liked Thermopolis and the hippies. They knew a kindred spirit when they found one; although the kindred spirits of the over-the-hill hippies were of a gentler nature than

71

the bikers.

Downtown St. Louis began to explode and burn as the Rebels moved out. Rebel sharpshooters with .50-caliber sniper rifles were stationed all along strategic points surrounding the city. They took a fearful toll on the Night People as the creepies ran to escape the explosions and flames.

Ben and his personal team were the last to leave the burning city. He halted his short column on an overpass on Interstate 40 and got out, to face the east and the smoke and flames. The killing gunfire of the Rebel snipers could be clearly heard over the roaring of the wind-fed and unchecked flames.

"The wind is out of the west," Ben said. "So the river will stop the flames from spreading any further."

"You seem especially sad to see this city go, General," Jersey observed.

"I used to spend a lot of time in St. Louis as a teenager, Jersey. But they all have to go, I'm afraid. Like it or not. Every city in America has to be brought down. The creepies have to be flushed out of their holes and killed. We've learned that they cannot be rehabilitated—no matter how hard we try—so that doesn't leave us much choice. Corrie, is Tina in place in Jeff City?"

"Yes, sir. She encountered no resistance along the way. She has your command post set up and waiting."

"Cooper, we'll take the old river road, Highway Ninety-four. Corrie, order Scouts out along that route and advise them to be on the lookout for survivors. People have a habit of settling along waterways. I want more outposts set up as we move along."

"Right, sir."

"Let's go."

Cooper cut off the Interstate just after crossing the Missouri River and linked up with Highway 94. As Ben had expected, they saw no signs of human life until they were a good thirty miles west of the burning city. The creepies had been working this area hard, in their search for human flesh.

"Bastards," Jerre muttered from the third seat in the wagon.

"We'll defeat them," Ben said. "We've got them running scared and scared people make mistakes. In the past year we've killed thousands of them, and we'll kill thousands more before the land is reasonably safe once more. Every city has to go. Once Voleta is dealt with, we'll probably take a month for another search and destroy before we go sailing on the bounding main."

Cooper looked at him. "Before we do what, sir?"

"Your education is sadly lacking, Coop," Ben told him. "I think I'll ask one of Therm's bunch to be your tutor for a time. You need to be better versed in literature."

Cooper grinned. "That redhead will do me just fine, General."

"Santo was, I believe, a teacher before the war. I'll ask him."

Cooper groaned and the others laughed.

"Scouts are stopped just up ahead, General," Corrie said. "Little town called Marthasville. The people aren't hostile, just curious."

"Tell them we'll be along presently. How do the people look?"

"Tough and capable, Ham said."

"Very good." Ben looked at his map. "That would be an excellent spot for an outpost. We'll see if the people are amenable to that."

"Do what?" Cooper asked.

Ben sighed. "Cooper, you are definitely going

73

back to school."

"Will it help my driving?" he asked.

It was too good to pass up. "Nothing would help your driving, Cooper," Jersey said. "It's a miracle we're all still alive."

After the laughter, Ben said, "Just remember this, Coop: in Ireland and England, you are to drive on the left side."

"We're all dead," Jersey said mournfully.

They'll do, Ben thought, his eyes touching the neat gardens and well-kept homes of the people who lived close to the small town. He had already mentally noted and approved their defense system.

The man Ben assumed to be the leader of the small group of people came forward, his hand outstretched. "You passed by us several years back, General. When you and the Russian were slugging it out. I'm glad you made it this time."

Ben shook the hand and came right to the point. "You've heard about our outpost system?"

"Yes, indeed. And we're ready to join you. We know the rules."

"And do all the people here agree?"

"Ninety-five percent of them."

"What's the trouble with that five percent?"

"They say they'll educate their kids the way they see fit and nothing you or anybody else says is going to change their minds."

"Take any child younger than twelve and tell the adults to hit the trail."

The spokesman smiled. "That might not be as easy as you think, General."

Ben returned the smile. "I assure you, Mister Leathers, it will be very easily done."

Ben accurately pegged the people inside as soon

as he saw the falling-down homes they lived in, with animal skins tacked to the sides, drying out. They had big four-wheel-drive vehicles parked alongside what were once called luxury cars in the driveway.

"Their degree of learning, whether they finished high school or not, is near a sixth-grade level — if that much," Ben said. "They don't like anybody not of their skin color and religious beliefs. They're cruel to animals and beat their kids at the slightest provocation. If they read at all, it's some old hunting or fishing magazine or book. They are inherently lazy and fond of saying something like: 'Hit's God's will,' if anything goes wrong. And they place the blame for all their many misfortunes on everybody except themselves."

Leathers looked startled. "How in the hell did you know all that!"

"I've been studying them for years, Mister Leathers. They're commonly called trash. What's this man's name?"

"Bannon. Ed Bannon."

"Ham, get on a bullhorn and tell Bannon to get it out here."

Bannon had been watching from a dirty window of his shack. But solider boys had never impressed him much before and this long drink of water with a funny-looking hat on his head, standing beside Leathers didn't impress him either. He stepped out onto the rotting porch and Ben noted that the man was massive.

"I'll take 'at thar horn and jam it up your ass, boy!" Bannon yelled at Ham.

Ben's voice stopped Ham as he started toward the man. "I'll handle this, Ham. Back off." Ben walked into the front yard, littered with wornout tires, rims, various engine parts, and several very weary-looking and malnourished hound dogs.

Thermopolis had seen it all before. While he agreed with Ben in theory, he felt there were better ways to accomplish it, other than Ben's blunt and oftentime brutal methods.

Thermopolis also knew that while he could discuss it all he wanted with Ben, in private, one did not question commanding generals in front of their troops. Therm also could recall several times when members of his group had questioned his decisions in a rather sarcastic and demeaning manner . . . in front of the others. He also recalled that he had knocked them on their ass.

"I'll lay it out for you, Bannon," Ben told the brute of a man. "This town is about to become a Rebel outpost. A clean zone, so to speak. In more ways than one . . ."

"Shet up!" Bannon told him. "And git off my property."

"I have been informed that this isn't your property," Ben replied. "And kindly do not tell me to shut up. When I am finished then you may have your say. Now then, how many children do you have under the age of twelve?"

"Why . . . hale's-fire, I don't know. A whole damn passel of 'em."

"Damnit, man, they are your offspring! Don't you know how many you have living under your roof?"

Bannon tensed up and glared at Ben.

"Get them out here!" Ben told him.

"I'll be damned if'n I will!"

Ben lifted the muzzle of his M-14, pointing it at Bannon's chest. "You will most certainly be dead if you don't," he said coldly.

Bannon sucked in as much of his gut as he could. He hunted with a .308. He knew what kind of damage that big slug could do. He turned his head and hollered, "Thelma! Git all them younguns

76

of ourn out here!"

The porch literally filled with people, most of them kids. Ben guessed their ages from about three to twenty-one, and he pegged the older kids as impossible to rehabilitate. He smiled at a little boy of about eight and the boy shyly returned the smile. Ben noticed the lad's face was swollen and there was a large bruise on the boy's face.

"How'd you get that bruise, son?"

The boy pointed to his father.

Bannon slipped down another notch in Ben's estimation. "You like to read, son?"

"Cain't," the boy admitted.

Ben turned to Leathers. "You told me you had schools, Mister Leathers."

"Of course, we do!" the man replied indignantly. "Nothing on the order of what we were used to before the war, but we certainly have schools! But the only way we could have taken these children into schools would have been to kill Ed Bannon."

"Then why didn't you?" Ben asked the question with about as much emotion in his voice as if he were requesting a cup of coffee.

Leathers knew then that everything he had heard about Ben Raines was true. Both the good and what many, both before and after the Great War, would consider the bad. Leathers shrugged his shoulders.

Ben looked back at the young boy. "What's your name, son?"

"Adam."

Ben pointed to a huge battle tank parked by the curb. "You ever seen one of those, Adam?"

"In pitcher books."

"Would you like to go for a ride in one?"

The boy's face brightened. "I shore would!"

"Then go on. Your father doesn't mind. Do you,

77

Bannon?"

Bannon's eyes were bright with hatred. He knew exactly what Ben was doing; and it was being done as smooth as owl shit was slick.

"As a matter of fact," Ben said, "all you kids can leave the porch and go riding in the tanks and APCs. That's all right with you, isn't it, Bannon?"

"Can I go too?" a weary voice came from behind the screen door.

"You shet your mouth, Thelma!" Bannon yelled over his shoulder. "An' git your ass back in the kitchen and to cleanin' and cookin' them fish for us."

"Of course you can go for a ride, Mrs. Bannon," Ben said. "Come on. Your husband won't bother you."

The woman stepped out onto the porch, grabbed the hand of a tiny girl, and hurriedly walked toward the line of Rebels by the road, all the rest of the younger kids following her.

"I'll take a strap to your ass, woman!" Bannon squalled. "You'll pay for this, I promise you."

"Shut your goddamned ignorant mouth," Ben told him.

Bannon glared hate at Ben. "I ain't never gonna see them kids agin, is I?"

"No. They'll be taken to Base Camp One and placed with people who will care for them and see to their education. You stupid son of a bitch!" Ben lost his temper, as all gathered around knew he probably would, for Raines hated ignorance above all else. "Can't you understand that education is the key to rebuilding this nation? Unless we educate our young, we're doomed! Can't you see that?"

"I got a high school education," Bannon said. "Hit never done me no good. All them smartass college boys always a-tellin' me what to do on the job.

78

After I whupped four or five of 'um they wouldn't nobody hire me."

"No, Bannon. You didn't get a high school education. You got socially passed from one grade to the next. But that's as much your fault as the teachers. You didn't want to learn. But I bet you were a star football player, weren't you?"

"Damn right."

"That figures. And an ex-coach was the superintendent of schools, right?"

"Damn shore was."

Ben looked at Leathers. "It took a world war to break that cycle of stupidity in America. And I'll be goddamned if I'll see it repeated." He turned to Bannon. "Bannon, this is now a Rebel-controlled zone. There is no place for you or your kind here . . . not living the type of life you have been. I was informed on the way over here that you are a bully; probably been one all your life. That you've killed several men in fights and seriously injured others, and that most of them were people who had done you no harm. Is that right?"

" 'At's rat," Bannon said with a grin. "I lak to fight. I laks to whup up on them that thinks they's better than me. And if you'd lower that there gun, I'll come off this porch and stomp the guts plumb outta you, General soldier boy bigshot."

Ben measured the man carefully with his eyes. He guessed Bannon was a good ten years younger, and probably outweighed him by a good fifty or sixty pounds, but forty pounds of that was in the gut.

The tanks and APCs had rumbled off, taking the kids and the battered wife with them.

Ben lowered the muzzle of the M-14 and handed it to Jerre.

"Oh, shit, Ben!" she muttered. "What don't you

let Ham do it."

" 'Cause then it wouldn't be any fun," he returned the whisper.

Ben stepped back, slipping on leather work gloves and then holding his hands wide apart. He looked up at the wad of bully. "Well, come on, you jelly-belly son of a bitch. What are you waiting on?"

# Chapter 9

Bannon came off the porch roaring like a maddened bull, his big feet pounding the earth. He took a wild swing at Ben. Ben ducked the punch and gave him a right to the wind, his fist sinking into the softness of belly.

Thermopolis shook his head in disgust at the very idea of the commanding general of the largest standing army in the country fistfighting with a redneck bully . . . but he understood why Ben was doing it. He looked at Rosebud. She was jumping around shadowboxing the air.

"The campaign is certainly bringing out the baser instincts in you," he remarked.

"Punch his lights out, Ben!" Rosebud yelled.

Ben caught a looping left to the side of his head that stung and backed him up. He knew he could not hope to win by standing and slugging it out with the man. Bannon was too powerful. But Ben knew he could win by keeping the man moving, using up his air, and by concentrating his blows to the man's body.

Ben danced away and drove a fist above the man's kidney, then moved to the other side and popped the man a good, solid right directly on the man's ear, bringing a howl of pain from Bannon.

Bannon tried to hook a toe behind Ben's boot and trip him. Ben grabbed onto the man's shirt with his left hand, maintaining his balance, and drove the stiffened fingers of his right hand into

Bannon's throat. The 'neck gagged and choked and Ben busted his nose with a short, savage right fist.

With blood streaming down his face, Bannon coughed and backed up, the light in his eyes telling Ben that Bannon was desperately trying to figure out how best to fight him.

Ben didn't give him much time to ponder the situation. He faked a left and Bannon followed it, dropping his guard. Ben drove a combination through the opening, the left catching the man on the side of the jaw and the right hitting him flush on the mouth, splitting the man's lips and loosening rotting teeth.

With Bannon's face registering his shock at being punched so easily, Ben pressed the attack with a left to the gut and a right to the jaw.

Bannon closed, fighting to regain his wind, and grabbed Ben in a bear hug, trying to break his back. Ben stomped on the man's instep with his jump boot and Bannon screamed in pain, his grip lessening. Ben slipped free and hammered at the man's kidneys with left's and right's.

Bannon turned and flung one big arm out, the forearm catching Ben in the mouth and knocking him off balance and to the ground. Bannon lumbered forward, trying to kick Ben. Ben rolled and came up on his boots, his mouth bloody.

Ben stopped the 'neck in his tracks with a hard right to the mouth, then followed that with a left to the man's belly. Bannon backed up, trying to clear his head.

Ben gave him no time. He stepped forward and hit him twice in the face: another right to the man's mouth and a left to the jaw. Ben stepped back and kicked the man on the kneecap. Screaming his pain, Bannon staggered and Ben gave him the toe of a jump boot to the balls.

Bannon dropped to his knees, both hands holding his throbbing crotch. Ben kicked the man in the face, the toe of his boot shattering Bannon's front teeth and knocking the man backward.

Bannon struggled to get to his feet. But Ben had no intention of allowing that. He kicked the man in his big fat ass and knocked him sprawling on the ground, on his face.

Walking to the man, Ben kicked him as hard as he could in the belly, doubling the man up into a wad of painful and largely self-imposed ignorance.

The fight was over.

Ben pulled off his gloves and stowed them in a back pocket of his BDUs.

"You kilt our daddy!" one of the cretinous-looking young men on the porch squalled.

Ben ignored him and walked over to Leathers. The civic leader involuntarily backed up at the advance.

"What about these older boys?" Ben asked.

"Just like their father. Thieves and bullies."

Ben turned to Ham. "Let them get what clothing they want out of the house. No guns. Then burn this shack to the ground." He swung his glance back to Leathers. "They'll be back, Leathers. And they'll cause you trouble until you finally make up your mind to shoot them. Or hang them. That will be your decision to make. But I assure you, unless Bannon changes, you will have it to do."

"You ain't got the right to do this," Bannon moaned from the ground. "This ain't no decent thing to do to a hooman bein'."

"I wouldn't do it to a decent human being, Bannon," Ben told him, after taking a sip of water from his canteen. "But the only resemblance between you and a decent human being is your ability to walk upright." He took his M-14 from Jerre.

"Don't ever let our paths cross again; not if you insist upon living the way you have been. Because I'll kill you without hesitation."

Ben watched the light in the man's eyes change from cruel defiance to defeat. Social workers and shrinks would argue the point until exhaustion felled them, but Ben knew, and knew without doubt, that there are people in the world who can respond only to brute force and violence. They cannot relate to compassion because they do not possess even a modicum of that emotion. They have to be hammered into the ground, picked up, and hammered again. Once they realize that unless they change, to fit into the established mores of whatever society, they will know only pain. Then they will understand that society has but two choices: allow them that change, or dispose of them.

"I ain't got no place else to go," Bannon pushed the words past battered lips. "I was borned around here."

Ben looked at Leathers. "It's up to you. You're the leader of this zone. You make the decision. I can't make all of them for you."

"We'll have a town meeting on the subject."

"Good. That's the way it should be."

"You'll delay burning down this house?"

"No. We don't allow shacks in any controlled zone."

Leathers sighed. "I agree with that. To allow filth would be unfair to others who try to maintain a clean living area."

"We're pulling out now. Have your town meeting and make your decision about Bannon."

"Whichever way we vote, you won't interfere?"

"No. Not unless I learn that the man has returned to his old ways and you people refuse to do

84

anything to correct the problem."

"And then you will? . . ."

"Dispose of the problem."

Leathers stared at him. "Bannon's wife and kids."

"They're on their way to Base Camp One now. He will not see them again."

"You're a hard man, General Raines."

"Hard times, partner."


Ben and his column pulled out, heading westward, following the river road.

"You think Bannon will change, Ben?" Jerre asked, as they rolled along through the afternoon.

"Others have. So there is a chance. But my guess would be that he won't. He's lived too many years as a bully and a slob and a petty thief and a thug . . . and society let him get away with it."

Cooper said, "The people back in the town said there is a town about thirty miles up the road that's filled with a gang of punks and crud, General."

"I know. Leathers informed me. They've been having trouble out of them for months. Shooting trouble. It's a pretty well-organized gang of thugs. Ham should be radioing in any time."

"Wonder why Thermopolis and his bunch decided to break off from the main column and follow us?" Jersey asked.

Jerre answered that. "He likes to study Ben. Says the general is a walking contradiction."

"So is he," Beth said.

"That's very true. We're more alike than you think," Ben spoke. "Cut off his hair and the only difference would be our tastes in music. Thermopolis claims to hate big government, but he knows that the only way to survive in these times is with a form of centralized government. Cut through all his rhetoric and you'll find that's one of the main reasons he joined us. He and his bunch will always live apart from us, but not too far away. And I can appreciate that."

"Ham calling in," Corrie said.

Ben picked up his mic. "Go, Ham."

"Fifty to sixty men in the town. Maybe that many women. They have kids, General."

"How are they armed?"

"Pretty well. Mostly small arms. I haven't seen anything in the way of heavy stuff."

"Stand clear of the town. We'll be there in a few minutes."

As soon as the thugs and outlaws in the town saw it really was Ben Raines coming at them dead on, they left their women and kids and hit the trail in cars, fender-flapping pickup trucks, and smoking motorcycles.

"Nice brave bunch of people," Jersey said. "Really care a lot for their families, don't they?"

"Most animals will die protecting their offspring," Jerre said. "So much for the theory that humankind is superior to animals in all ways."

Ben didn't argue that. He felt the same way about it. Looking at the thugs and punks in wild retreat, he knew that the battle for America might be very nearly over. Six months back, the outlaws would have stayed and fought the Rebels—now most of the slimebags they encountered just ran away in fear.

Ben knew there would always be some that would stand up to his people, but those were becoming fewer and fewer, with wider intervals between battles.

"What do we do with the women?" Ham asked, walking up to the wagon.

"Any suggestions, Cooper?" Jersey needled him.

Cooper shook his head. "Don't look at me. I wouldn't touch one of them with a sterilized poker."

Yes, one very long battle was maybe, just maybe, drawing to a conclusion in the United States. But the Rebels had discovered that a large percentage of outlaws and their women who were taken alive and given medical tests were walking germ factories. Sexually transmitted diseases, such as gonorrhea, syphilis, and AIDS were running rampant. Another battle was waiting in the wings. TB had reared up again. But for some reason cancer, per capita, had taken a dramatic nosedive and the doctors and researchers at Base Camp One could not explain that.

But Doctor Chase had a theory. Chase had a theory about everything. "The factories have stopped belching millions of tons of crap into the air each year," he theorized. "Farmers no longer poison the earth and the air with chemicals . . . all in the name of progress, of course. And," he would add, eyeballing Ben's cigarette, "those things are harder to come by."

Ben shook his head and said, "Line the women and kids up, Ham. Tell the medics to break out the equipment and let's check them over. Corrie, bump Jeff City and tell Tina we'll be there when we get there. Tell her what we're doing."

He got out and walked up to the line of women, and a sorry-looking lot they were. He stared at them for a moment. "Good afternoon, ladies. It appears that your menfolk have deserted you. You have any plans for the future?"

They all returned his stare, sullenly and silently.

Ben decided to try another tact. "How long has it been since you and your children have seen a doctor?"

That struck a responsive cord. One woman, holding an infant in her arms, said, "We haven't ever seen a doctor. There's doctors around, a few of them, but they refuse to see us."

"Perhaps they don't like the company you keep," Ben suggested.

She shrugged. "What's that got to do with treating babies?"

"Good point." Ben smiled at her. "The sins of the father are often passed onto the child. I'm not saying it's right; but that's the way it is many times."

"My baby's sick," the mother said.

"We have doctors." Ben tossed the decision back to her.

"With strings attached," she countered.

"Not for the first go-around."

"I don't know what that means, but my kid's sick. And it isn't right to let a baby suffer."

"I agree. The medics are setting up in that building right over there." He pointed.

"How are we supposed to pay?" another asked. "We ain't got nothin' to barter that y'all'd want." Before Ben could tell her there would be no charge, her eyes shifted, to touch Thermopolis. "You a funny-lookin' soldier, man. You look like one of them hippies I seen in a book."

"I share the philosophy of the sixties," Thermopolis told her. "Even though I was barely walking at the time and hardly able to grasp the social significance of the movement."

She blinked and shrugged. "Whatever that means." Her gaze shifted back to Ben. "How do we pay?"

"It's free," Ben told her.

"There ain't nothin' free, mister whatever-your-name-is. We'll have to pay for it, one way or the other."

"Why don't we just treat your children first. Then we'll talk."

"Are you really Ben Raines?" another asked.

"Yes."

"Them ol' boys we took up with, and who just took off like their asses was on fire, is scared to death of you, Mister Raines."

"They probably have good reason to be. We've left their kind lying dead all over this nation."

"You gonna kill our men if you catch them?"

"If we decide to go after them and if they choose to fight."

"They ain't much good, for a fact," she admitted. "But when your whole world has been tore down and it don't look like it's ever gonna be put back together again, a body does what you can to survive."

"As long as what you do does not involve killing and stealing from others who are working to rebuild a better society."

She nodded her head. "You ain't givin' people much of a choice, Ben Raines."

"It's all spelled out quite clearly in the Bible, Miss."

"Don't hand me that crap! There ain't no God, Mister Raines. God wouldn't have allowed the whole damn world to be destroyed. Little babies sufferin' and dyin' all over the damn place. I can't believe a smart man like you would even think there ever was a God."

"Oh, there is a God, Miss. But He is a very vindictive God. He said he would never again destroy the earth by flood. Maybe the Great War was His way of telling us we'd better shape up."

"So now you're God's right-hand man, huh?" It was not said sarcastically, but it was spoken with a very slight smile.

Ben laughed. "Oh, no. I'm a mortal being. With all the mortal faults and frailties built in. I'm just a man who is trying to restore the nation to some semblance of what it once was, that's all."

"But on your terms." It was not put as a question.

"That is correct."

"You know that there are them who think you are a god, Ben Raines."

"I know. They are wrong. I am a mortal man, and nothing more."

She shook her head. "No. I don't believe that. I don't think you're a god. But there's something about you that makes people want to gather around and listen to what you have to say, and then act on it. Follow you. What am I trying to say?"

"Charisma," Thermopolis said.

"Yeah," the woman replied. "Maybe that's it. I don't know."

"Your baby looks feverish," Ben said.

"She is. And a lot of the others kids as well. We run out of medicine a long time ago. Been takin' the babies to see an old woman back in the hills; she's been treatin' them with herbs and plants and the like."

"Does it work?"

"Sometimes."

"We're ready, General," Jerre called from the hastily set up aid station.

"You make my baby well," the woman asked, "you gonna take her away from me?"

"That depends entirely on you."

"Like I said, there ain't nothing free in this world."

"That's right," Ben told her. "That was the problem before the Great War. Too goddamn many

90

people wanting something for nothing."

He turned and walked away, before he lost his temper.

# Chapter 10

Villar, Khamsin, and Kenny Parr traveled hard, knowing that Ben Raines would have Rebels hot after them.

"Is there anything left of Chicago?" Kenny asked. "If there is, we could go there. Although food would certainly be a problem."

"Stay out of the cities," Khamsin said. "Ben Raines and his Rebels are experts at combat in the streets. Believe me, I know firsthand."

Even Villar had been awed when Khamsin told them about the Rebels taking on impossible odds in New York City — and winning. Villar was beginning to see why Ben Raines was unstoppable. And he did not like the taste it left on his tongue.

Still, he believed it was better than what he had left behind in Europe and Khamsin had left behind in South America.

Death was preferable to being eaten alive or put on a forced-labor farm or being forced to fight to the death in an arena against some trained gladiator . . . all for the pleasure of those who had proclaimed themselves kings and queens of this or that section of whatever country.

Many parts of Europe had reverted back to the Dark Ages . . . and done so very quickly.

And, Villar was reluctantly forced to admit, at least to himself, he had certainly had a hand in bringing about that change.

The battered armies of the terrorists and the outlaw had taken refuge in an old state park just south of Peoria, and just east of the Illinois River. They would stay only for a day and a night, and then move on. The three of them had decided that the woods of Wisconsin or Minnesota would probably be the safest spot for them to hole up and try to rebuild their shattered armies.

But Villar knew only too well that unless they could beef up their forces, and do it quickly, eventually the Rebel Army of Ben Raines would find them and wipe them out. He also wondered who Raines would send after him; he thought he had a pretty good idea.

A runner confirmed his suspicions.

"We just intercepted a communication, sir," he panted the words that Villar quickly and accurately guessed that he did not wish to hear. "It was an open transmission from a small group of survivors living somewhere not too far south of here. Colonel Dan Gray and a battalion of Rebels just left their zone, moving north."

"No idea where it came from?"

"It was a very strong signal on low band. So it probably was not more than fifty miles away."

"Damn!" Villar cursed his luck. Dan Gray. He knew the Englishman would track him to the ends of the earth and beyond for an opportunity to kill him. Lan Villar got to his boots and gave the orders to his tired men. "Get up and get moving. We've got to leave and leave now! We'll cross the river just up ahead and cut straight north. Get moving, people. If you want to live."

"If we are to believe the transmission, there is only one battalion of Rebels," Kenny pointed out. "And many Rebel battalions are short compared to normal size. We have approximately twenty-five hundred men."

Villar did not lose his temper with the young

man. For he, too, had once been young and reckless. "But they have tanks and long-range artillery, Kenny. And for more than a decade, one Rebel in battle has been proven to be the equal of five other soldiers. So if you take that into consideration, *they* have *us* outnumbered!"

Less than forty miles to the south of where Villar and the others were pulling out, Dan brought his column to a halt and called Buddy and his Rat Team members back in from the point.

"We have about two hours of good daylight left," Dan told his people. "We'll make camp here for the night. Too risky rolling after dark. Believe me when I say that Villar is an expert in ambush."

They had made less than a hundred miles that day, due to the constant sending out of patrols in all directions in search of the terrorist army. Dan knew they were not far behind, due to the signs his people had been picking up: a fresh oil slick, a bloody bandage, a piece of uniform carelessly discarded or blown out of the back of a truck by the wind.

Dan prepared his four o'clock tea and leaned up against a tree trunk, sipping the fragrant brew. Dan also felt the general was a bit optimistic with his predictions of ending the battle for North America by fall. But Dan seldom argued with superior officers . . . unless his opinion was asked for, and this case, it had not been.

A runner from communications broke into his thoughts with a message.

"Sir, we've received another of those messages from Malone up in the Northwest."*

*Death in the Ashes—Zebra Books

"Still calling for men and women to join him in his fight to, in his inimitable prose, purge the earth of all nonwhites?"

"Ah . . . Yes, sir."

"The swine! I wish we could have finished him when we had the chance. If Villar hears the message, he'll perk up like a vulture sensing death."

The runner waited.

"Thank you," Dan said with a nod and a smile, dismissing the young Rebel.

Dan leaned back against the tree and sipped his tea, thinking. He knew from looking at all the gear captured outside East St. Louis that Villar had very fine electronic equipment; capable of scanning all bands, high and low. So the odds were good that he had caught the message.

All right—assume that he has. So? What to do?

Dan took a map from his case, intending to study it carefully. He knew Villar was close. Probably no more than fifty or sixty miles away. And Villar, if he was to survive, had to beef up his forces. And Villar, Dan knew, would make a pact with the devil if he had to.

Dan waved Hans Strobel to him.

"Yes, sir?" The German stood at very loose attention. Experienced soldier that he was, he knew not to salute or to show any obvious signs that he was facing an officer. Snipers looked for that.

"Go to the communication van and have the operator send a coded and scrambled message to General Raines. Advise him that I am breaking off pursuit and will begin a hard drive westward. This is in response to Malone's messages. He'll know what I'm talking about. We cannot let Villar and his people link up with that nut."

"Yes, sir. Right away, sir."

"Hans?" Dan called to his back.

The German stopped and turned. "Yes, sir?"

Dan smiled at him. "Loosen up, my friend. We're a pretty informal bunch most of the time. Relax — you've made the team or you wouldn't be here."

"Thank you, Colonel. That's the best news I've had in years."


"What do you know about this Malone person, Khamsin?" Villar asked.

"He's a nut," the Libyan said flatly. "But he's still got a lot of men."

"And with groups monitoring those messages he's sending out," Kenny added, "I'll make a bet he'll add considerably more to his force."

"How large a force currently under his command?" Villar directed the question at Khamsin.

"I would say between fifteen hundred and two thousand," the Libyan said. He opened a map of the West. "All of them holed up in this wilderness area."

"Food supplies?"

"Voleta told me they have many gardens planted all over this area. It's a short growing season, but they do quite well with it and have canning facilities to prepare and store food for the winters, which are extremely harsh, I was told."

"This Voleta woman seems to be more of a nut case than I care to align myself with," Villar spoke. "At least for any period of time. However, we might be able to use her to our advantage." He sat back, hard in thought. "We have to get to Malone. That's our second objective. This Malone might not agree with us philosophically, but he needs our strength as much as we need his. If Voleta can keep Raines occupied in Missouri, we just might have a chance of linking up with Malone."

Kenny looked at the terrorist. "You said that was our second objective. What's the first?"

"Avoiding Dan Gray in order to stay alive long enough to accomplish the second objective!"


The women and kids had been checked over and medicine dispensed where needed. Ben was in his tent, listening to Jerre's report.

"The children are all anemic, and of course none of them have been inoculated against the normal childhood diseases. They've been very fortunate in that no epidemic has struck them . . . yet. Blood-test results show that about half of the women are either alcoholics or addicted to some drug."

"Drugs!" Ben straightened up. "What kind of drugs?"

"Amphetamines, mostly—what we used to call speed. PCP, the old angel dust, which can be man-ufactured anywhere is also widely used. Several of the women told me that was their boy friends' chief line of business. They trade drugs for food and medicine."

"Good God! I thought all that nonsense was years behind us."

"Obviously not."

"Are they worth our time and effort attempting to salvage, Jerre?" Ben had already made up his mind about that; but he wanted some input from Jerre.

The younger woman sighed. She had suspected Ben would throw that question at her, and she had dreaded the moment. "They're all human beings, Ben."

"They walk upright," Ben tossed that back to her. "I looked around this town while you people were checking them out. Nothing to resemble a school.

The older kids can't read or write. No gardens planted. The houses they squat in are filth-filled. They have no plumbing facilities. They've made no effort to improve themselves or the town in which they live. In several of the homes, human excrement was two feet deep in the bathrooms. They lie, they steal, and they are accomplices to murder, torture, and rape. They're losers. We'll take the children and tell the women to hit the road." He turned to Corrie. "Make arrangements to have the kids flown to a secure zone."

"What if the women decide to make a fight of it, Ben?" Jerre asked. "We didn't disarm them . . . at your orders."

"It will be a very brief fight."


Few of the outlaw women kicked up any fuss at having their kids taken from them. Most of them seemed relieved and glad to be rid of the children.

Ben had spoken to Leathers by radio, advising him of their actions and warning that the outlaws were still in his area.

Only two of the women were allowed to keep their children and be flown to another zone; one of them was the woman who had the brief debate with Ben. There was a spirit in both of them that Ben liked, and he made up his mind after seeing where they lived. The small houses were clean and some effort had been made toward plumbing and their own personal hygiene. Whether or not the women could make it in a controlled zone was up for grabs. Time would tell. The older kids were allowed to leave with their mothers. Many bitter and heart-tugging past experiences had effectively shown the Rebels that once a child passed into their teens, and became hardened to brutality and crime, rehabilitation was nearly impossible to achieve. The Rebels had the inclination and desire to try, but neither the time nor the facilities to expel trying. It was a hard decision, but one that had to be made. The Rebels would not jeopardize four younger children in order to save one older teen. It was a situation that none of the Rebels — including Ben — enjoyed seeing; but it was a decision that was made almost daily somewhere in the shattered nation, by some Rebel commander.

The Rebels pulled out just after dawn, following the river road toward Jefferson City. Ham and his team of Scouts took the point. They were followed by two Dusters, five hundred meters behind the point.

The Rebels saw no other living being on the way to Jefferson City. They passed through towns that were rapidly falling apart, having been looted dozens of times over the decade since the Great War. Many of the buildings had burned . . . most of them deliberately set on fire by crapheads who enjoyed seeing things burn, and knowing they could get away with it now with only a degree or two more impunity as they had when the nation was whole.

Ben said as much as they rolled and rumbled through the charred remnants of a small town.

"What do you mean, General?" Corrie asked. "They were punished back before the Great War, weren't they?"

Jerre laughed, knowing more than the others what was coming.

Ben smiled. "They were slapped on the wrist by judges, told they were naughty, naughty boys, and usually turned loose to do it again."

"That doesn't make any sense," Beth said.

"Neither did our judicial system. And as long as

I'm alive it will never return to that ridiculous degree of incompetence."

Ben looked out the window of the big wagon. "We're going to be an island standing in the middle of anarchy, people. Surrounded by human sharks with nothing in their pea brains but blood lust. Once this continent is secure, we're going to have to shift our base of operations — or somebody is — and secure the rest of the world, country by country. And that is going to take a lifetime. Maybe several lifetimes. We cannot permit our ideals and goals to die. That is why I put so much emphasis on education.

"When this nation was intact, our public schools — mostly due to court decisions — failed the nation for several decades. Our school systems became staffed with personnel obsessed with excellence in athletics and rot of the mind. We allowed games to reach the stature of a religion. It was downhill from that point.

"Our society became the most materialistic society on earth. Many of our elderly died alone and afraid, hungry and cold; the young could not receive proper medical care; victims of crime were ignored while we sobbed and moaned over the poor criminal, and endangered species of animals were slaughtered into extinction, while a good fifty percent of Americans spent literally billions of dollars pleasuring themselves on the most idiotic and meaningless of games or events . . . stepping over the homeless and mentally ill and young and old and sick and dying on their way to those dubious proceedings.

"As long as God allows me to live and pick up a gun, and as long as one person will follow me — or if I have to do it alone — I will never see this nation return to those shameful days."

Those in the wagon were silent for a mile or so

until Jersey wiped her eyes and broke the silence. "That was beautiful, General. If I wasn't a soldier, I think I'd just bust right out and bawl. I might anyway."

Ben started laughing at the expression on her face and the laughter became infectious. They were still laughing and wiping their eyes when they rolled into the ruins of Jefferson City, with Rebels they passed looking at them and wondering what in the hell was going on?

# Chapter 11

Ben drove through the looted and trashed city. He was not surprised to see several trucks with the bodies of dead creepies in the beds.

"Have a little trouble, Tina?"

"A little. Six and Seven Battalions stayed out of the city. As soon as we rolled in the creepies attacked. It didn't take them long to realize they'd made a bad mistake. By that time it was too late. Jefferson City isn't that big a place so there weren't that many creepies here. I think we got most of them. Only a few of them escaped. Dad, have you heard from Dan and Buddy?"

"Both of them are all right. They haven't made contact with Villar yet."

He explained Dan's change in plans and his daughter nodded her head in approval.

"If they link up with Malone and his squirrels we'll be right back in the fire again. And you can bet that Villar will never again allow his men to be trapped like they were in Illinois."

Ben certainly agreed with that. The Rebel's victorious battle with Villar was the only campaign that Ben could remember where the Rebels had no dead or wounded. Odds of that ever happening again were astronomically high against it.

"Dad? We don't really know the size of Malone's army, do we?"

"No. Conservative guesses place his strength as few as seven hundred and fifty, as many as three thousand. I'd guess fifteen hundred fighters. Add the strength of Villar and Khamsin and Parr, and it kicks it up considerably. To about four thousand. So we can't allow that to happen. Tina, I'm going to send Georgi and his men to beef up Dan and chase Villar. In addition I'll send Five and Six Battalion with them. We cannot allow Villar to link up with Malone."

Ben lifted his mic and gave the orders. He turned to Tina. "Ike will move into the northernmost sector of the state. You join them. Stretch out up to the Iowa line."

"We're going to be thin."

"I know. It has to be. Georgi will stretch his people, and Five and Six Battalions up into Minnesota. I'm placing all units north of the line under Georgi's command. Cecil's people will beef up Seven Battalion south of us. I'll take this sector. Ike will replace Five Battalion north of us up to the line."

He drove back to his CP and Tina gathered up her gear and her team. "See you, Pop," she called.

"Take care, kid."

He called for a meeting of his commanders.

"Risky, Ben," Ike pointed out. "But I see the need for it."

"Voleta could mass her people and punch through the lines, Ben," the Russian said. "Specifically your lines. It's you she wants."

"I know," Ben acknowledged.

"If she punches through, Ben," Cecil said, "She could cut off Jeff City and really have you in a box."

"I am aware of that."

They all knew then that Ben had some plan working in his head, but was not yet ready to tell them the details of it. Perhaps he hadn't finalized it as yet. They all knew that he would tell them when he was good and ready, and not a moment before.

"When do you want us to pull out, Ben?" Georgi

asked.

"Now."

"General Raines is splitting up his people," Sister Voleta was informed. "Our people behind his lines report a massive pull-out from Jefferson City."

"Which direction?" Ashley asked.

"Mostly to the north."

Ashley smiled. "He's trying to stop Villar and the others from reaching Malone. It's a good move on his part. Albeit a very risky one."

"We take him now!" Voleta said, smiling like a shark in anticipation of blood. "We can punch through his lines and surround him."

"No!" Ashley nixed that. "Don't be so impetuous, my dear. Bear in mind that Raines used poisonous gas to stop Villar and the others. It might be that he wants us to enter the city so he can do the same thing. He has a plan for us; bet on that."

"So we do what?" Voleta asked, her eyes shining with dark hatred for Ben Raines.

"We've got to wait and watch the Rebels very carefully . . . and as closely as is possible."

Voleta paced the room and cursed Ben Raines and her traitorous son, Buddy. The years had taken their toll upon the woman. Where she had once been beautiful, the years of intense hatred had poisoned her, turning her beauty into ugliness. Her face seemed to be frozen in a perpetual mask of hideous scowling. Her dark eyes burned with a strange light.

Ashley, on the other hand, seemed never to change. He had been a pretty boy rich kid when Ben Raines had whipped his ass back in Louisiana, long before the Great War, and he was still a pretty man . . . and just as vain. He hated Ben Raines, but not to the point of it being all-consuming.

Lance Ashley Lanier had long forgotten just why he hated Ben so, but that was no matter. He was content to just hate. It made him feel good.

Oh, yeah! Now he remembered. Ben Raines had insulted his sister, Fran—he couldn't recall just what the insult was—and Ashley had called the man out. Big mistake on his part. Raines didn't fight fair. Ben had stomped the shit out of him and to make matters worse, had done it in front of witnesses. It had all been so humiliating. Ashley had been a super-duper football hero in school. Super-duper football players were not used to getting the snot kicked out of them by trashy people like Ben Raines.

Ashley sighed. Well, he thought, it was all moot, now. The great mansion he had been raised in down in Louisiana was in ruin. The last time he saw it a bunch of Mexicans had moved in and had goats grazing on the front lawn.

His sister, Fran, had taken up with Hilton Logan, the president, and had later been shot to death while screwing the secretary of state. Ashley never could make up his mind whether Ben Raines's Death Squads had been responsible for that or if the President, Hilton Logan, had ordered it.

No matter. Hilton had been killed by Raines's Death Squads after the Tri-States had been destroyed by government troops.

That was back in? . . . Hell, he couldn't even remember. But some points he could remember was that a lot of people, fronting a lot of armies, had tried to defeat Ben Raines over the years.

No one had ever succeeded.

He brought himself back to the present and looked with some disdain upon Sister Voleta, pacing the room and ranting and raving and cursing Ben Raines until she was so breathless she had to stop and sit down. No doubt about it, the woman was a basket case, all right. But a nut with thousands of followers. His own army paled in comparison with the troops of Sister Voleta.

And he knew what would be the first words out of her mouth when she caught her breath.

She had never disappointed him before and she didn't disappoint him this time.

"I hate Ben Raines!" she screamed.


Two days had passed since Ben had ordered his troops to spread out, and not one move had been made against them from Sister Voleta or Ashley. Ben chose to inspect the pitifully thin line of Rebels that were stretched along the almost seventy-mile sector that was his to defend.

About fifteen Rebels to the mile, he mused, enjoying a little game of mental arithmetic. Or one Rebel every three hundred and fifty-two feet, if he had chosen to spread them out in that manner, which he had not.

What he had done was blow bridges and overpasses on secondary roads from Highway 24 in the northernmost part of his sector, all the way down to just below Highway 50 to the south of him.

He knew Voleta had people watching him from a distance, so he loaded up West's people in trucks and sent them north, all the way up to Ike's sector. The trucks then promptly turned around, with West's mercenaries lying down out of sight in the canvas-covered beds, and dropped them off in the center of Columbia—or what was left of the city.

Ben pulled most of his people into Jefferson City and waited.


"Don't you see what he's done?" Ashley wanted to scream the words at Voleta; he struggled to keep his voice calm. "It's the most obvious trap I have ever seen. He's left us two options, and only two options. We can only go in two ways, Interstate Seventy or Highway Fifty. He's crippled the bridges and overpasses on every other road."

"There is a flaw in that logic, Ashley," Voleta pointed out.

"What?"

"Ben Raines is sitting down there in Jefferson City with less than a thousand Rebels—far less than a thousand, for we know he's put outposts all up and down Highway Sixty-three. Correct?"

"Yes, that is correct. I would think that Raines probably has less than seven hundred Rebels in Jefferson City."

"The nigger general has his people down south of Jefferson City with the fresh battalion from Base Camp One, right?"

"That is correct, Voleta."

"The Russian and the Englishman and the two new battalions of Rebels are off chasing Villar and Khamsin and Parr, right?"

"That is correct."

"Our own people saw, with their own eyes, the mercenary, West, and his men move into Ike's sector, right?"

Ashley sighed. Something about that move had caused a warning bell to ring in his head. He knew that Ben Raines liked to take chances, liked to tempt the Gods of Fate . . . or make people think he was doing that. But he couldn't deny the obvious. West had moved into Ike's sector.

"Yes, Voleta, that is fact."

"So even you will have to admit that Ben Raines is alone with less than a thousand personnel."

"It looks that way, Voleta."

"We leave token forces north and south, Ashley, and we throw everything we have against Raines in the city. There is nothing to stop us from being victorious."

Nothing except the trick that Ben Raines has up his sleeve, Ashley thought. But for the life of him—and his life was what he was betting—he could not think of what it might be.

He pointed out the one thing it might be. "Gas, Voleta."

"I thought of that. And rejected it."

"On what basis?"

"I spoke to the Gods last night."

"Oh, shit, Voleta! You're no more of a witch than I am a warlock! Give me something real on which to base commiting my people in this."

"Ashley," she spoke the words contemptuously, "I hardly think that piddling little battalion of yours would make the slightest bit of difference in the outcome of this campaign."

Ashley stiffened at the slur upon his men and himself. "If that is the way you feel, Voleta, I can certainly take my . . . piddling little battalion and move on."

"As you wish, Ashley." Her words were as cold as her heart was evil.

"Then I must wish you good luck, and good day, Sister Voleta."

"Good-bye, Ashley. I and my people will get along just fine, so don't worry."

Ashley was sorely tempted to say, "Frankly, my dear, I don't give a damn what happens to you." But he knew that would have been pushing his luck with Voleta.

Voleta watched the man leave her headquarters, located some fifty miles west of Jefferson City. She felt nothing at seeing him leave. Ashley Lanier was a pompous coward, and those were his good points.

"Screw you, Voleta," Ashley muttered, safety outside her HQ. "Crazy bitch. I hope I never have to look upon your face again."

He drove to his headquarters and gathered his commanders around him. "We're getting out of here," he told them. "Voleta has gone totally around the bend and is going to get herself and everybody connected with her killed."

The leader of the outlaw motorcycle group that had remained with Ashley after seeing his people slaughtered by Ben and his Rebels in Wyoming and Montana only a few months before, walked in, hearing the last part of Ashley's statement.

"As usual, Ashley, I don't agree with you . . . at least not all of what you said," Satan told him. "Me and my bunch is stayin' with the broad."

"That's fine with me, Satan. It's your damn funeral. She's crazy."

Satan shrugged. "Hell, I know that. You just remember this: I'm gonna kill you someday, pretty boy, and don't you forget it."

"How can I? You keep reminding me of it, you . . . lout!"

Satan laughed and walked away.

In his CP in Jefferson City, Ben leaned back and sipped at a mug of coffee. "Come on, Voleta, take the bait. Our son is not here now, so Buddy doesn't have to see me kill you. Come on, you crazy witch. Come on!"

# Chapter 12

Buddy Raines grunted as a sharp pain grew behind his eyes. Then the pain faded.

"What's wrong, son?" Dan asked, looking at him.

Buddy looked at the man. "You know I am marked, Colonel?"

"I know. I'm not sure what it means, but I've heard you mention it a time or two to your father."

"It means there are times I know what is about to happen. Not often, but at times."

"And what is happening now, boy?"

"I must return to my father, Colonel—now!"

To his surprise, Dan did not argue the request. "All right, Buddy. Take your Rat Team and head on back. I know you well enough to know that if you didn't believe it important, you wouldn't ask. But I don't know how your father is going to take this."

"If I get there in time, my father is going to rant and rave and cuss and wave his arms all about."

"If you get there in time? In time for what, son?"

But Buddy was gone in a run toward his Jeep, yelling for his team to get their shit together and come on!

Dan lifted a map. Buddy had a good four to five hundred miles to go. All the way down through what had once been the state of Iowa.

"Godspeed, boy," Dan said.

"Buddy did what?" Ben roared.

"Don't yell at the messenger, Ben," Jerre told him.

"I am only telling you what Dan Gray radioed in to communications about ten minutes ago."

Ben glared at her. She smiled sweetly at him. All his roaring and glaring didn't have any effect on Jerre; it never had.

"Why in the hell would Buddy do some damn fool thing like that?"

"He didn't say. You can ask Buddy when he gets here."

"I damn sure will!"

"Calm down, Ben. Calm down. How's your blood pressure?"

"My blood pressure is fine . . . at least it is until members of this army start disobeying my orders. Goddamnit, Jerre, I'm trying to pull the boy's mother into a trap so I can kill her. That's why I sent Buddy with Dan. So he wouldn't have to witness this."

"I know, Ben. But don't you remember telling me that Buddy said he felt he would be the one to stop his mother. That he knew these things somehow. Maybe Buddy feels that you are in danger. Real danger."

Ben sat down behind the old, battered desk and drummed his fingertips on the desktop. With an effort, he calmed himself. "Well, hell, I guess I can't fault the boy for trying to protect me, can I?" Without waiting for a reply, he said, "And I'm reasonably sure he asked Dan's permission to leave." Ben shrugged. "It's done. Now I just hope Buddy makes the run in one piece. He'll be traveling through some dangerous country."

"Buddy has a lot of you in him, Ben. He'll make it."

Ben smiled. "I'm just damn glad he's got more of me in him than his mother. Buddy would have made one very dangerous enemy."

111

Dan had set his CP up just south of Minneapolis. Buddy took his Rat Team and pulled out, driving hard down Interstate 35. He did not stop until he reached the Iowa line. There, he was forced to use pumps to bring up gas from old storage tanks, and to wait until the gas was filtered for impurities.

One of his team had climbed on top of a two story building and was inspecting the terrain through binoculars when thin fingers of smoke caught his eyes. "Company," he called. "To the east about five miles."

Buddy squatted on the old littered main street of the town. Colonel Gray had concluded that Villar had broken up his army into smaller teams and was moving the smaller units westward; platoon-sized units would be more difficult to detect and more stood a better chance of making it through in that manner.

Buddy felt that his mother would launch an all-out offensive against his father very soon, and Buddy felt he had to be there. But as a soldier, he was obligated to check out the smoke the lookout had detected.

At the call from the sentry, the other members of his team had stopped their building of fires to cook the evening meals and make coffee.

Buddy pointed at two Rat Team members. "You and you. Check it out and shoot us a line to follow and radio in the heading. Then maintain radio silence until you get a visual. If it's Villar's men, give us three clicks a couple of times and stay put. We'll join you. Paint up and take off."

After his team had put on night camouflage, Buddy hid the vehicles and sat down to eat cold rations and wait for the signal. It soon came: three

112

clicks over the radio, repeated twice.

Darkness had dropped around them as they moved out, shrouded them in gloom. The night was cloudy, the humidity high, the sky threatening rain. The Rat Team was armed with rocket launchers, grenades, and automatic weapons. Buddy carried an old Thompson SMG, identical to the one his father had carried for years. Ben had put it aside, choosing an M14, after so many people were beginning to view the old Chicago Piano as something more than what it really was . . . as many viewed still viewed Ben.

As powerful as he was, Buddy carried the heavy, drum-fed weapon as effortlessly as a sack of marshmallows. The .45-caliber spitter was awesome at close range, the big slugs capable of stopping nearly anything they hit.

Taking the point, Buddy shot his azimuth and followed the course. Anything that might jingle or jangle on the team had either been removed or taped. Buddy's Rat Team was made up of young men and women in the height of physical conditioning, and they could and did move like silent wraiths in the night.

They moved across fields that had not been plowed in years, through timber that grew tall, now that man was no longer destroying it in the name of progress. They were conscious of the eyes of forest animals on them as they moved through the animal's kingdom. The natural inhabitants of the woods had nothing to fear from the Rebels, and they seemed to know that. Rebels would kill a forest critter only in self-defense or if they had run out of food and no chance of getting resupplied.

They came up on the two-person scout team abruptly and went belly down on the cool earth. They talked in sign language whenever possible, using a system the Woods Children had shown the Rebels years back.

The camp was a thousand yards ahead. Guards were few and security was lax. Probably a hundred men in the camp. They were eating their evening meal.

Buddy told his team to swing in a half circle around the camp, then once more he took the point. He came up on a guard just as the man was lighting a hand-rolled cigarette. A breech of security that his father would have had the offender court-martialed for.

Buddy cut the man's throat with a big, razor-sharp knife and softly and silently lowered the bloody, cooling body to the earth. All around the half circle, other members of his team were taking out the guards with silent kills.

Buddy waved a team member with a rocket launcher up to him and patted the weapon. The woman smiled and filled the tube with death.

A nightbird seemed to sing a gentle tune, the melody floating through the darkness. But it was not a nightbird and the tune did not signify anything gentle.

A bird answered the first call. A bird that was earthbound and carried violent death in its hands. One by one, the Rat Team members called out that they were in position.

The men around the fires paid no attention to the bird-calls. Perhaps it was because most of them were not a part of this land; had not been born in this country that was once called America and were not familiar with the nightbirds' sound. Perhaps they were just tired and more than likely frightened.

The outlaws and terrorists would soon know no more fear and they could rest forever.

Buddy tapped the young woman on the shoulder

114

and she fired the rocket. The rocket, an antipersonnel type invented by Ben's weapons' experts down at Base Camp One, turned a dozen men into bloody, mangled, nonhuman looking lumps. A second after the first rocket was fired, the other rocket-wielding Rat Team members fired and the campsite was transformed into a fiery hell on earth for those enemy troops gathered there.

The weapons set on full auto, the Rat Team members made very short work out of any who survived the rocket blasts and had the bad timing to stand up.

The Rat Team ceased their fire and bellied down on the ground and waited, motionless. Only a few moans came from the burning camp. The Rat Team waited.

"No more," a man called out in a heavily accented voice. "No more—please!"

The Rat Team lay still and very quiet. Another man began crying in the firelit night.

"We need a few prisoners to take to the Eagle," Buddy said.

"Vehicles?" a Rat Team member asked.

"No. We don't have the time to check them out for prolonged road use. But we will use them to get back to town. Grab some prisoners and we'll move some miles down the road before making camp. Go!"

They drove twenty-five miles south before stopping to make camp for the night. There, they patched up the prisoners as best they could and tied them securely. Buddy remarked that they were certainly a sorry-looking bunch.

"Go to Europe," one said. "And you'll leave looking a lot sorrier. If you leave at all."

Buddy knelt down beside the man. His wounds had been only superficial. "What is in Europe that

115

frightened you so?"

"Chaos. It's ten times worse than here. Those you call the Night People — Kannibales — are everywhere. They surfaced just after the Great War and began taking over. They have huge farms where they breed humans . . . for food. In other parts of the Continent, there are warlords and land barons and God only knows what else. Each with their own army. There are thousands of people living in the countryside who were burned and disfigured — both mentally and physically by the blasts. Their genes were affected. Their offspring are twice as horrible. There are parts of the countryside where no one dares venture. It is indescribable. One has to see it to fully understand the terror of it all."

"You're German?"

"Yes."

"You know Hans Strobel?"

"Yes. He's a good man. Too good a man to ever have become involved with us. He's alive?"

"Yes. Then why did he join Lan?"

"To get away from the labor camps. To remain there would have meant death for him. It was a simple matter of survival."

That jibed with everything Hans had said. Buddy had initially sized him up as being basically a good person after only a few minutes of conversation with the man. But to have corroboration from several different sources was always good.

"And you?" Buddy asked.

"What?"

"Are you a good man?"

"I am a soldier. I have been a soldier all my life. Since I was fifteen. I have spent twenty-five years soldiering with one army or another."

"Are you going to tell me that with all that experience behind you, you joined Lan Villar to sur-

116

vive?"

"No. I could have survived in Europe. I am a survivor. One does not spend twenty-five years at war without learning to survive. I joined Villar because he was a winner."

Buddy tapped his own massive chest. "You are looking at another one."

The man smiled. "I got that impression."

"Are you a true leopard?"

For a moment, the man looked puzzled, trying to understand what Buddy meant. Then it came to him. "You mean can I change my spots?"

"Yes."

He hesitated. "I honestly don't know. From what I have been able to learn about the Rebel movement, I don't think I could live under Ben Raines's rules."

"That's an honest reply. Tell me this: if you were set free, would you rejoin Villar?"

"I can answer that quickly. No. But not because of any moralistic reason. I would not rejoin him because the man has changed from a winner to a loser. I can see the change in him. Villar has never known defeat. What happened in Illinois marked him."

"Hear me well," Buddy said. "Whether you live or die depends on how cooperative you are when we reach my father's sector. And give some thought to joining the Rebels. Give a lot of thought to it. People who don't conform to what few laws we have are outcasts. They receive no help from us—none at all. No medical help, nothing; only for the very young, which we take from them. It's a harsh rule of my father's, but in these times, a necessary one. He's trying to rebuild a nation from out of the ashes of ruin."

The German nodded. "I owe Villar nothing. I

gave him years of loyalty; now he is near defeat. I know all the signs of that. So I will be as cooperative as I can be with my interrogators. But General Raines probably knows as much about Villar's plans as I do."

Buddy nodded his head in the murk of darkness. "Our way of life is probably not as restrictive as you have been led to believe. Anyone who really tries can adjust very quickly to our philosophy. Think about it."

The man smiled. "With my hands and feet bound, there is not much else I can do, is there?"

"Oh, yes," Buddy returned the smile. "You can die if you try to escape."

# Chapter 13

"Patrols in the western part of Missouri report that a battalion-size group is moving westward out of the central part of Missouri," Corrie told Ben. "They appear to be well-armed and organized."

"That would be Ashley," Ben said. "He's not going to take the bait I offered. Advise our patrols not to make contact."

"Yes, sir."

"Any word from Buddy?"

"He'll be here by noon tomorrow. He and his Rat Team destroyed about a platoon of Villar's men last night. They have prisoners."

"No movement reported out of Voleta's people?"

"Nothing. Generals McGowan and Jefferys report that all is quiet in their sectors."

"Thank you, Corrie. Have Buddy report to me when he arrives."

She left the CP, returning to her communications room down the hall.

Ben's constant shadow, Jersey, sat across the room from him, her M-16 across her knees. Jerre was with Doctor Chase, at the hospital. Cooper stuck his head into the room.

"Thermopolis to see you, General."

"Send him in."

"Getting bored?" Ben asked, after coffee was poured and the men seated.

"Peace has never been boring to me, Ben. But it has been rare over the past few years. Do you think this Sister Voleta is going to take the bait and attack?"

"Oh, yes. She hates me so much she's blind to anything else."

"This will not be as easy as St. Louis, will it?"

"No. This will be house to house and hand to hand in many instances."

"The reasoning behind that?"

"I want her in this city and I want to personally see her dead body. That kook and her followers have been a thorn in my side for years. I want the thorn plucked out and destroyed."

"And then? . . ."

"We move against Malone. I want all the major resistance forces against us crushed by the end of summer. That does not include, of course, the creepies still in the cities."

"And then? . . ."

"Maybe Europe. I don't know. That all depends on whether some new, as yet unknown to us, force appears on the horizon."

"May I make a suggestion?"

"Of course."

"Alaska."

"What about it?"

"Oil. I know that everything was shut down after the government fell . . . for the second time. That area needs to be reopened."

"I agree with you. And I've given it a lot of thought. Are you volunteering to settle up there?"

Thermopolis smiled. "No. Emphatically, no. But I wouldn't mind a short visit."

"Neither would I. All right. Let's do some thinking on it. Tell you what: why don't you pick some people and start prowling the city's libraries during this lull in the fighting. One thing about looters: they seldom steal books. See what you can find concerning Alaska."

"Me and my big mouth. I might have known you'd give me a damn job."

"Your idea."

"We all make mistakes." But it was said with a smile. He drained his coffee cup and stood up. "I'll get right on it." He started for the door.

"Thermopolis?"

The man turned around.

"A lot of buildings have not been one hundred percent checked. You people go in armed and careful. Another reason for that is I don't know when Voleta is going to strike. We've got to be ready at all times."

"I understand."

"Tell Corrie to get you some trucks, and some help rounding up crates." Ben smiled. "I always take books wherever I find them."

"I will admit, Ben Raines, that you do have some redeeming qualities."


"All right, boy," Ben said to Buddy. "Let's have it."

Buddy had been hustled to his father's CP before his feet were firmly on the ground.

"My team destroyed one full platoon of Villar's men about twenty-five or so miles inside Iowa."

"That's not what I mean."

"We saw no other signs of the enemy on our move south."

"That's good to know. But not what I wanted to hear from you."

"General Striganov and Five and Six battalions are in place."

"I *know* that, boy! I am in radio contact with them. Why in the hell did you pull out from Dan's group and come here?"

"To help you fight my mother."

121

"You know I deliberately sent you away from this fight."

"Yes. I know. But my place is here. I sense it. So here I am."

"And you are going to do what?"

"Take over your personal security."

"I appreciate the thought, boy, but I don't need a goddamn nanny! I've been taking care of myself for a good many of my fifty years. Oh, hell!" He waved his hand. "Go get something to eat."

Buddy turned to leave.

"And close the damn door."

"Yes, sir." Smiling, Buddy stepped out of the office and closed the door behind him.

"That wasn't too bad," Beth said.

"Not as bad as I thought it was going to be. He didn't try to spank me."

They all got a laugh at the mental image of Ben with Buddy over his knee, applying a belt to the young man's butt.

Buddy looked at Jerre. She and Cooper and Corrie were playing cards. "There has been no word from my mother?"

"No. We know she's going to strike. We just don't know when. Ashley has left her, though. He and his men were seen in Western Missouri."

"They'll be linking up with Malone, then. And we don't have a large enough force west of here to stop them."

"Your father doesn't seem to be too worried about Ashley," Beth said. "He just wants this business with your mother over and done with."

"She's hard to kill," the heavily muscled young man said. "But she's evil and must be stopped. She is past redemption."

"What do you mean, Buddy?" Jerre asked.

He sighed and rubbed his chin with a big hand.

122

He needed a shave and wanted a shower. He and his Rat Team had been pushing themselves hard on the drive south, stopping only when absolutely necessary.

"I mean, Jerre, that I think if Voleta is to be stopped, I will have to be the one to stop her."

"I hope it doesn't come to that, Buddy."

"It's already come to that, Jerre. I know it." He walked out of the room.


"Still no contact with Grumman and his platoon?" Villar asked.

"No, sir," the radio operator told him. "And I've tried repeatedly."

"They've bought it. We can scratch them off the roster." He lifted a map and studied it closely. His forward recc teams had radioed back distressing news. Raines had shifted his people, stretching them all the way to the Canadian line. The Rebels were thin, very thin, but still a force to be reckoned with. Splitting his people up into small groups had seemed, at first, to be a good idea. Now he was having second thoughts. Villar sighed heavily and shook his head. "We've got to mount an offensive and punch through. That's all we can do."

Again, Villar studied the map. Finally he nodded his head. "We'll start pulling all units in Wisconsin to our position. They'll move only at night, using slit headlamps. That will be slow, but will lessen the danger. We won't cross into Minnesota here. That's the first route in north of the river and that would be too obvious. We'll make our crossing just south of Duluth. We'll punch through and do it fast and hard. Cutting north, we'll hit Highway Two and stay on it. Karl, tell all units south of the Wisconsin line to cut east for a hundred or so miles, then

123

drive south just as fast as they can. Get under the Rebels' position and cut west. We'll make the link in Idaho. Or in hell," he added grimly. "Whichever comes first."

The morning after Buddy's return, he stepped out of his quarters, relaxed and refreshed after a good night's sleep. He could not feel his mother's presence so he concluded the Rebels had bought yet another day of waiting. No one laughed when Buddy talked about his being marked. The Rebels knew that even Ben Raines believed there was some truth in it.

And they all knew why Buddy had returned.

After breakfast, Buddy got in his Jeep and drove to the westernmost section of the city under Rebel control and parked, getting out.

"Yo, Buddy!" a sentry called, looking around his sandbagged position. He was not there to die if Voleta attacked. Just radio in and get the hell back to friendlier lines.

Buddy called him by name and walked over to the position. "Anything going on?"

"Dead, man. Coffee?"

"Yes, that would be nice."

Buddy took powerful binoculars and scanned the sentry's perimeter. The terrain leaped into his view. There was nothing out of the ordinary anywhere he looked. He lowered the binoculars.

"Did my father Claymore the area?"

The Rebel smiled. "General Raines didn't do nothin', man. That area is as clean as a needle. If Voleta attacks, I got orders to call in and bug out."

"He wants her to attack," Buddy muttered. "He wants this to come to a head so he can pinch the boil and expel the corruption."

"That's why he wanted you out of here, Buddy. Aw, he isn't pissed 'cause you came back—and I got that from close to him. He just wanted to spare you the . . . you know."

"I know. The death of my mother. She is meaningless to me now. She is a cancer that must be cut out and destroyed. I knew that even before I left her."

"Did you?" The sentry shook his head. "No. Forget I even said anything."

"Ever think of killing her when I had the chance? Yes. Yes, I did. It was the Old Man, my grandfather, who prevented me from doing that. More than once. And I have never admitted that to anyone."

"It won't go any further, Buddy."

"It's all right if it does. It's time for me to be truthful. God knows I'm going to have to face up to it all very soon. Tonight. Tomorrow night. The next night. But soon." He faced the young sentry. "When they attack, you get out very quickly. Use the radio in the Jeep to call in. Don't waste time staying and playing hero. And above all: don't let any of them take you alive. The Old Man shielded me from most of what those people are capable of doing, but I saw enough to know it would be an insult to a rabid dog to call them that."

"I can just imagine what they would do to a Rebel."

"No, you can't," Buddy told him. "Not in your wildest screaming nightmares. My mother likes fire, and sharp knives. And she can make the act of dying much more preferable to living. She has kept many prisoners alive for days, slowing skinning them. She is pure evil—if that connection is grammatically acceptable. Her brain is pus and her heart belongs to Satan."

The young sentry shivered as chill bumps covered

his flesh, although the day was very warm. "This Old Man you talk of . . . he helped you get away?"

"Yes."

"What happened to him?"

"She tortured him to death, so I later found out."

"What kin was he to her?"

Buddy's eyes turned cold. "He was her father."

# Chapter 14

The scattered men of the terrorist armies made their night runs to the north with much caution, taking back country roads, avoiding any town that might be populated with anyone with a radio who could call into Ben Raines. And that was getting very nearly impossible to avoid.

"The bastard has outposts all over the fucking nation," Villar cursed Ben. "He's stuck up a clean zone everywhere a hog roots."

"And it's just as bad in Canada," Khamsin told him. "The damn Canucks put a gun in a child's hand practically at birth."

"Blame that on Ben Raines," Kenny said. "That's the one thing he and my father agreed on."

Villar consulted a map. They had miles to go and it looked like everybody that was coming in, had arrived. It was obvious that more than half of the terrorists had elected to push south. With a sigh of frustration, he flung the map to the floor and began cursing Ben Raines until he was breathless.

Kenny read the man's anguish accurately. "We don't have the men to punch a hole, do we?"

"I don't think so. Not without losing more than we can afford to lose."

Khamsin spoke softly, and no one in the room doubted him for an instant. "I will never surrender to Ben Raines. I will die fighting him. Allah be praised!"

Villar looked at him, a faint light of amusement in his eyes. "How in the hell do you justify calling on your God when you've spread unnecessary death and destruction all over the damn world, Khamsin?"

"I am a believer, that's why?" The man seemed surprised he would even be asked such a question. "There is a place in heaven for me."

"Horseshit!" Kenny said. "People like you fry my ass. At least me and Lan aren't hypocrites about what we do and what we are. I got a spot in hell reserved for me, and so does Lan. And if the truth be known, so do you, Khamsin. So do you."

The outburst didn't startle or upset Khamsin. He merely shrugged them off as words out of the mouth of an infidel. Like so many people of all faiths, Khamsin was smug about his convictions. He felt in his heart that when he died he would follow the golden path to sit by the side of Allah. What these two nonbelievers thought meant absolutely nothing to him. And he certainly wasn't going to debate his beautiful religion with anyone who boasted that after death they would have a seat next to Satan.

"I will lead the assault against the lines of the Rebels," Khamsin said. "Show me where you wish to break through, and it shall be done."

Villar studied the man for a long moment, then slowly nodded his head. The fool believed he could do it, so maybe he could. Let him lose his men trying or succeeding. Villar pointed to the map. "Right here, Khamsin. Right here."

The Hot Wind looked at the spot. "It shall be done. Praise Allah!"


"When nothing is heard from that bastard, Villar," Dan spoke to Georgi Striganov, "brace yourself. He's certainly up to something."

"I agree," the Russian said. "He's had me worried

128

ever since he dropped out of sight."

"The bridges are covered on the west side and wired to blow. Villar will have guessed that. He won't try the bridges. We have people all along the river and they report no sign of the man. My guess is that he'll try to punch through between these two spots." He pointed them out on a map. "Probably just south of Duluth. That will give him good access to this highway."

"That is by no means our strongest spot," Georgi said.

"Yes." He glanced at his watch. A couple of hours before dark. No way he could get his people up there in that time. The Interstate was in bad shape and getting worse. But Dan knew he had to try. The assault was coming tonight; he could feel it. "I'll take my people and pull out now. We'll be traveling fast, so we won't have artillery to back us."

"I'll start artillery moving north now. Just in case you're wrong about the timing."

"I pray that I am wrong. But I fear that I am correct."

Duluth was filled with creepies so the Rebels stayed well away from the city. They would deal with the cannibalistic creeps at a later date.

Khamsin and his men turned west off a state road in Wisconsin and entered Minnesota on what was left of a country road, crossing over the state line about fifteen miles south of Duluth. Only two squads of Rebels were at that point and Khamsin's men butchered them, knocking a hole in the thin line through which the terrorist armies poured into the state.

Dan was on Interstate 35, south and west of the breakthrough when he got the news.

Dan lost his cool and cut loose with a steady stream of profanity. Not so much that his prey had broken through, but for the men and women lost in the assault.

He jerked up his mic. "Rebet and Danjou join up with me," he ordered. "General Striganov, they have broken through. When Voleta hears of this, she'll attack."

"I'll start my people moving south to beef up the forces in Missouri," the Russian radioed. "Do you want the artillery I sent to continue following you?"

"That is ten-four, General. The logical route for Villar to take is Highway Two-ten, so I'm betting he'll cut north and take Highway Two. I'm taking my people and Rebet and Danjou's forces and taking two-ten. I'll stay under him and try to cut him off somewhere along the way."

"That is affirmative, Colonel Gray. I will have the artillery cut east, following you. Godspeed."


"It was a friggin' piece of cake," Villar said to his driver. "And I let that goddamn Libyan take it. I'll never hear the end of it."

The driver wanted to say: So what? We got across, didn't we?

But he didn't.

They crossed the Interstate, picked up Highway 33, and took that to Highway 2, cutting west.

Villar had no illusions: he knew that Dan Gray would be hot after them. Only one thing would stop Colonel Gray, and that was death. Villar also felt that if there was some sort of existence after death, if Dan Gray didn't get him in this life, he would in the next.

Villar knew something else, too; something that he had not shared at length with the others: there was no way they were going to win this fight, or any other fight against Ben Raines and the Rebels.

130

Raines had thought it all out and had it perfected. The son of a bitch had spent years going all over the nation, collecting every tank, every piece of artillery, and hauling it off to only he and God and a few Rebels knew where. And no one was going to win against Ben Raines without long-range artillery and tanks. And to make matters worse, Raines had done the same thing with cars and trucks too. He was more than a warrior. He was a thinker, a planner, a teacher, a philosopher, and a doer.

"We're going to look this situation over with Malone," Villar said. "We might even stay awhile. But we'll eventually pull out."

"To where?" his driver asked.

"The one place that, to the best of my knowledge, Raines had never shown any interest in."

"And that is?"

"Alaska!"


"Here they come!" sentries all up and down the line shouted into their mics as Voleta's army began advancing toward Columbia and Jefferson City.

"Fall back!" the order from Ben went up and down the line.

The sentries on the east side of the river beat it back across the bridge and watched as Voleta's forces took control of the airport.

"Airport's in their hands, now," they radioed to Ben's CP.

"Let them have it," Ben said, as much to himself as to the others in the room. "They won't do anything with it. They damn sure don't have any planes and if they try to cross that river at night, we'll be waiting for them when they step ashore."

In Columbia, as Ben had done in Jefferson City, West had pulled his battalion into the center of the

131

city. Tanks had been rammed inside buildings and hidden, the muzzles of the 90mm and 105's lowered to the max. The .50-caliber machine gun emplacements were set up and heavily fortified with sandbags. Each Rebel had food enough for several days and boxes of ammo, grenades, rockets and mortar rounds.

In both cities, the Rebels waited.

Voleta halted her troops on the outskirts of the suburbs and called for a meeting of her commanders.

"Not a shot has been fired," she said. "Have we been mislead? Is Ben Raines even in the city?"

"He's there," she was told. "And we have not been mislead."

"Then why is he doing nothing?"

"Perhaps the man has lost his mind," another commander offered that. It got him a dirty look from Voleta but she let him continue. "He's placed himself in a death trap. He can't cross the Missouri River. Our people have taken control of the airport and Highway Fifty-four. . . ."

What the commander failed to realize was that Ben had heavy artillery up and down West Main and Capitol Avenue, and it was slightly less than two miles from there to the airport. Ben could annihilate Voleta's forces across the river at any time he so desired.

". . . As far as I can see, Sister, General Raines has put himself in a box and nailed the lid shut . . ."

Ben was in a box, all right, but it was a box of his own construction. Over the years, the Rebels had become not only the most feared guerrilla fighters anywhere in the nation — and probably around the globe — but they had also become highly expert at urban warfare. Voleta's army was made up

132

of dedicated men and women, but damn few true, disciplined soldiers among the bunch. They outnumbered the Rebels in this battle, but the Rebels were used to being outnumbered. They would have felt they were taking advantage of the enemy if they were on a par.

". . . Before you halted the advance, Sister, our troops in Columbia had penetrated well into the city limits and had met no hostile action. The city appears deserted . . ."

Columbia was anything but deserted. Like Jefferson City, it was a deadly trap waiting to be sprung. West, limping around with a cast on his foot, had laid out his battle plans well. His mercenary troops lay still as death's touch, waiting.

". . . We have intercepted radio messages that tell us the Russian is on his way south, to beef up General McGowan and his troops. Sister, without Ben Raines, the Rebels will fall apart. If we are to succeed, we must strike now, and strike hard!"

There was truth in what the man said, but still Voleta was not convinced. She knew Ben too well; knew him for the fanged poisonous snake that he was; knew how treacherous the man could be. If Ben Raines had put himself into a box, he had a hole from which to escape. She would bet her brassiere on that. If she wore a brassiere. Which she didn't.

And Ben had guessed accurately on another point. He had guessed that after the debacle in the Northwest, where Voleta's troops had taken a battering, she would be low on mortar rounds. And she was. She still had plenty of ammo for light weapons, but practically no rockets or mortars.

"Get those damnable motorcyclists up here," she ordered.

The leader of the bunch, Satan, stepped into the

tent moments later. He didn't like this bitch, and knew she didn't like him. But for Satan's bunch, it was the best game in town, so he'd take orders from her . . . for a while longer, anyway.

"I want a recon team sent into the city, Satan. I want them to penetrate as far as Southwest Boulevard. Here!" she showed him the map. "And report back to me."

"That ain't no sweat, lady," the huge, evil-looking biker said. "I don't even think Ben Raines is in the damn city."

"There is one way to find out," she said, smiling as sweetly as was possible for her. Her smile held all the warmth of a striking cobra. "Go in and look."

Satan stood his ground. "You know what I'm gonna do when all this shit is over, lady?"

"I couldn't possibly imagine," she replied. "Or care," she added.

"Oh, you'll care, all right. You an ugly whore, but I think you got a couple more good fucks in you. When this is over, me and you is gonna get it on."

She spat in his face and flung out a hand just in time to prevent the others in the tent from shooting the biker.

Laughing, Satan left the room. "Yeah, baby," he called over his shoulder. "I might even let you get some lipstick on my dipstick."

"That is the most disgusting creature I have ever encountered, Sister," a commander said. "Why don't you let me shoot him?"

"Because while he is a loathsome being, we do need him," she said sourly. "At least for a little while longer."

"Or some stain on my thing!" Satan hollered from the outside.

"Ashley was a coward," a woman said. "But at least he would show some respect for you."

"Ashley was a fool," Voleta said, as the sounds of motorcycles leaving the camp roared into her ears. "But I have to admit, he was a pleasant fool."

"Leave the light on, baby!" Satan screamed as he roared past. "I might decide to jolly you tonight."

Voleta grimaced and gave the voice the finger.

# Chapter 15

"Don't fire on the bikers," Ben warned his people. "Don't make a sound. Keep your heads down and let's see how far they penetrate."

The Rebels burrowed deeper in the homes and buildings and dark alleyways. Most had changed from lizard and tiger-stripe to dark urban BDUs. With the moonless night, they were almost invisible.

The team of bikers split up, some traveling on Highway 50, others turning onto Stadium Boulevard and then onto Edgewood, with all of them stopping at Southwest Boulevard. Satan waited at the intersection for his bikers to regroup.

"Shit, Satan!" one said. "There ain't nobody left in this town."

Satan looked all around him, doing his best to peer through the darkness. "Shut 'em down," he ordered.

The bikers cut their engines and the following silence was heavy.

"Fan out," Satan said. "Inspect the buildings." Satan left his Hog and walked across the road, to a line of office buildings. Cautiously, he pushed open the door with the muzzle of his Uzi and clicked on a flashlight, the beam strong in the murk.

The narrow beam of light picked up the litter on the floor. It showed him the unmarked dust and undisturbed cobwebs. What it did not show him was how the Rebels had entered the building without disturbing anything.

Ladders. Few Rebels were on the ground floor anywhere in the city. They had climbed up ladders to the second and third floors and set up their machine gun emplacements, then another team removed the ladders and went on to another location.

The outlaw bikers inspected a dozen buildings along the road and found nothing to indicate the Rebels were anywhere close.

Which is exactly what Ben wanted them to think. Soon, if all went according to plan, Ben and his Rebels would not be the only ones in a box. But Ben and Rebels would be in control of that box.

"It was a damn trick all the time!" Satan said, kicking at a beer can that had laid in the street for years, still just as shiny as the day it rolled off the line.

"What you mean?"

"I bet you Ben Raines ain't even in this city. I bet you he left a few soldier boys and girls downtown and he hauled his ass off to the north, chasin' that Villar-what's-his-name."

"I bet you right, Satan."

The outlaw biker lifted his walkie-talkie. "It's clean in here," he radioed. "They might be some Rebs downtown, but they ain't any out here. Come on in."

"Fall back," Voleta ordered. "We'll enter the city at dawn."

"That woman beats all I ever seen," Satan said. "If she don't screw no better than she gives orders, I don't think I want any of it."

"She's ordered the bikers back," Corrie told Ben, after monitoring the transmissions. "They'll enter the city at dawn."

"Stay on the tach frequency and order no fires, no lights of any kind. Maintain noise discipline. Tell them to get some rest. Tomorrow is going to be a busy day."

At dawn, Voleta ordered her troops into the cities of Jefferson City and Columbia.

"Take what few Rebels are in the cities alive," she ordered. "I want to torture them. We can have days of pleasure with them."

Satan shook his head. It wasn't that he minded seeing people tortured — he kind of liked it, especially when it lasted a long time and they screamed a lot — but with Rebels this close around them, wherever they were, it just seemed like a waste of valuable time.

"It's chancy from here on in," Ben said to his staff. "At any time, one of those kooks could look up and see a gun emplacement or the muzzle of a tank; or a Rebel could sneeze. Anything might happen. We can't wait much longer."

"You were very lucky last night," Voleta told Satan. "The Rebels are famous for booby-trapping buildings." She turned to her radio operator. "Tell the people to stay out of the buildings. Inspect them through the windows."

Ben listened to the orders being given and smiled. "That's right, Voleta. Play it cautiously, you witch. And come on in."

Buddy's face was impassive as he stood in the command post, listening to his father. This had been a very chancy move for his father to make, and not one that the other Rebel commanders liked. But so far, it was working.

"The points of the column have moved past Boonville Road, Ellis Avenue, and have reached

Fifty-four near the downtown," Corrie informed them.

"Let them come," Ben said, his voice calm.

"Father," Buddy said. "Taking chances is one thing. But we are going to be *smelling* the stink of them in a moment."

"That's right," Ben said cheerfully.

The sounds of the advancing vehicles could now be clearly heard on the second floor of the CP.

"Goddamnit, Raines!" the voice of Doctor Chase came over the scrambled tach frequency. "The bastards are outside my hospital. Will you please give the orders to open fire?"

"Tell him staying here was his idea," Ben told Corrie. "And to shut up."

Through the dirty window on the second floor, Ben could see the troops of Voleta moving down the center of the street. "I love dealing with amateurs," he said with a smile. "Corrie, give the orders to open fire, please."

"With the utmost of pleasure, sir," she said, with just a touch of nervousness in her voice.

Ben smashed the window with the butt of his old Thunder Lizard and emptied the clip at the followers of the Ninth Order.

Voleta lost nearly half her troops in the first thirty seconds as the Rebels popped up and gave her a taste of Rebel justice. Rockets turned the vehicles into fireballs, 90mm and 105 howitzers, firing at nearly point-blank range, literally blew the enemy trucks off their tires and sent the trucks and those inside thundering into hell, the bodies mangled and burned beyond recognition.

The .223, .308, .50, and .45 caliber slugs tore into flesh. The streets and gutters of the city ran red and slick with blood.

There was no place for the troops of the Ninth

139

Order to escape. Ben had plugged all the holes with his orders to open fire.

Those troops of the Ninth Order laying back outside the city limits did not escape, nor did the followers of Voleta who sat smugly within the perimeters of the airport across the river.

Heavy artillery began shattering the morning, the booming of shells impacting against the ground rattled the city. The gunners had the range and dropped them in with deadly accuracy.

In Columbia, those troops of Voleta met the same fate at the hands of Colonel West's mercenaries. Ben had given the orders that no one was to be left alive. No prisoners taken.

He wanted to end this scourge upon the earth now. He wanted to crush the Ninth Order . . . crush it so badly it could never recover. Wipe it from the face of the earth and have the pleasure—perverse though it might be—of looking down into the dead face of Voleta.

Corrie kept glancing at him, wondering when Ben was going to call for a cease fire.

But Ben was not. His Rebels—and they were his—had been battling Sister Voleta and the Ninth Order for years. He would let his troops vent their anger with hot lead until it had passed.

He walked out of the room, turned, and went down the hall, to the old fire door that faced an alley—an alley now littered with the bodies of those who chose to follow Sister Voleta.

Then he saw her, standing in a doorway, looking up at him.

"You son of a bitch!" she screamed at him, her words just audible over the roar of gunfire.

She lifted a pistol and pulled the trigger.

The glass exploded where Ben had stood an instant before.

On his back on the floor, Ben kicked the old door open and crawled out onto the catwalk, cutting his arms and legs on the broken glass.

He peeked over the edge of the catwalk. Voleta had disappeared.

He looked back over his shoulder. No one in the building had noticed the lone shot and apparently, no one had any idea Ben was anywhere other than safe.

They probably thought he went to the bathroom.

Ben caught a glimpse of a black robe in the shadows of a doorway and began bouncing lead around the small enclosure. He heard a scream and then something lurched out of the doorway, staggered, and fell to the bloody alleyway.

Voleta.

She was down, but far from out and far from staying down for very long.

The woman jumped to her feet and ran across the alley, into a building.

Ben started to use his walkie-talkie, to advise his people that the witch was near. He decided against it. Ben reached up and slipped a grenade from his battle harness, pulling the pin and holding it down. This was his fight, and he wanted to settle it personally.

Ben leaned out of the metal catwalk as far as he could and tossed the grenade into a window just opposite the door he'd seen Voleta enter. When it blew, it set her robe on fire and she came screaming out of the building, running blindly with her hair burning.

She ran into a brick wall and fell backward, just as a main battle tank picked that time to round the corner. Ben could not turn away, even though he really did not want to see the treads crush the life from her.

141

In an effort to get away from the burning woman, the tank swerved and slammed into an old brick building, knocking part of the wall down. Ben stood on the catwalk and looked down at what was left of Voleta: two bare legs, from the knees down, protruding out from under the bricks, in a puddle of blood. From where Ben stood, it looked like her feet were dirty.

Jerre told him that Buddy had gone to the place where his mother was lying under several tons of bricks. He had stood silent for a long time, and then knelt down by her bare legs. Jerre felt uncomfortable watching him and had walked away, leaving him alone. She had not looked back.

The Ninth Order was no more. If the Rebels found any alive, they shot them where they lay. Leadfoot told Ben that Satan and his bunch had got away. They headed west out of the city.

Ben ordered his Rebels out of Jefferson City and Columbia and told his demolition people to bring the cities down to ruin.

He had not seen Buddy all that day.

He waved Jerre over to him. "See if you can find Buddy, will you, Jerre?"

"He's getting his team squared away, Ben. Said you'd probably want him to take the point and he wanted to be ready to go."

"How is he?"

"Seems to be fine. A little quieter than usual, but that's to be expected. He knew his mother was evil, but her death still was a jolt to him."

"Sure it was. I wish I'd had a dozer push those bricks off of her just to make sure she was dead."

"Good God, Ben! A *tank* ran over her!"

"Yeah. At least it ran over her legs. But I'll always wonder."

Jerre shook her head. "If she survived that, Ben, I'll believe she really is a witch. Do we rest now?"

"No. We can't take the time. We're pulling out within the hour. The demolition crews can catch up with us along the way. I've already told Corrie to send Ike and Georgi on their way behind Dan. Cecil is to link up with us anytime now and we'll head west."

Behind them, dull explosions began erupting throughout the city and buildings began coming down in great clouds of dust.

Buddy rode up and got out.

"Son," Ben said. "Your Rat Team about ready to pull out?"

"All ready, sir."

There was something in Buddy's voice that sounded odd to Jerre. "You want me to leave, Buddy? So you can talk to your father alone?"

"Oh, no! No. Please stay. Father," he said with a sigh. "I don't believe my mother is dead."

It took several seconds for that to register with Ben. "What did you say, son?"

He repeated it.

"Son, I shot her. Personally. Then I tossed a grenade in on her and she was a ball of fire when she bounced off that wall. Then a goddamn tank ran over her. Jesus, boy. Nobody could survive that!"

"She did. I don't know for how long, but she survived it."

"After I walked away, Buddy," Jerre said, "leaving you alone with her. What did you do?"

"Reached down and pulled on her feet. The tank obviously severed her limbs at the knees. I felt sort of . . . well, stupid, standing there holding her by the feet. Sort of macabre. I dug into the bricks. She wasn't there, Father. I dug all the way to

143

where the wall was. There was a trail of blood leading into the building. I looked all over the place for her. She was not there, Father. She's beaten us again. She's alive."

# Chapter 16

Dan and the Canadian forces, commanded by Rebet and Danjou were hot after what was left of the terrorist army as they moved west. But despite everything Colonel Gray did, he could not catch up with them. They had too big a head start. With both sides traveling night and day, Villar and his people managed to stay a good half a day in front of the Rebels.

Striganov and his people headed west on 212, taking them through South Dakota. Ike and his battalion took off on Highway 36, heading through Kansas. Cecil linked up with Ben and West and they began their trek westward on Interstate 70. Those units south of Dan would gradually work their way north. Seven Battalion, always short, had been incorporated into Five and Six, beefing them up.

Villar, knowing that with the slaughter of Voleta's troops, every Rebel under Ben's command would be hot after them, never let up. They traveled night and day, pushing the vehicles and themselves. If a vehicle broke down, it was abandoned along the road. They could not risk the time needed to make repairs.

"Break it off," Ben finally gave the orders. "We can't keep up this pace. We're losing ground anyway according to outpost reports."

Ben ordered his people to rest and work on the vehicles. And he was debating whether or not to order Dan to halt. Ben knew the Englishmen would pursue Villar, but would not endanger his men tackling a much greater force should he not catch Villar before he reached the wilderness area and linked up with Malone.

"What's the last report on Dan?" Ben asked Corrie.

"Wyoming, sir. He had to stop for major repairs on some of the vehicles."

Ben made up his mind. "Get him for me, please."

Colonel Gray on the horn, Ben told him, "That's it, Dan. Just hold what you've got. I'm ordering all units to link up with you. So for now, you stay put and get some rest. We know where Villar is heading. We'll deal with them all."

"That's affirmative, General. I'd about made up my mind to stop when the vehicles broke down. I just never could catch up with the bastard."

"You gave it your best shot, Dan. Get some rest. We'll be there in a couple or three days. I'm not going to push it."

Ben and his columns were in Western Kansas, south and almost even with the Rebels who had taken the more northern route. He checked his maps and turned to Corrie. "Tell the others to rendezvous just east of the Continental Divide, on Highway Two-eighty-seven. On the Sweetwater. Tell them there is no hurry. Malone and Villar aren't going anywhere." He smiled at Thermopolis. "One thing about it, Therm: it's going to put us a hell of a lot closer to Alaska."

The hippie fixed him with a jaundiced look. "I do hope, General, that this upcoming battle will be a short one. I have no desire to be caught in Alaska in the dead of winter."

"Well, there is a bright spot should that happen."

"I'm afraid to ask what."

146

"All those books you're toting around from the libraries back in Jeff City."

Thermopolis walked away, muttering about transporting approximately twenty-seven tons of books all over the goddamn United States.

Ben called his son to his side. "You and your Rat Team take off, boy. See what you can find out about Malone and his bunch. How many people answered his call and so forth. Stay out of the Wilderness area. And that's an order."

Buddy tossed his father a very sloppy salute. "On my way, pops."

"Pops!" Ben muttered, watching his son jog away.

Ben walked back to the communications truck and joined Cecil, who was talking with the man he'd left in charge back at Base Camp One. "Trouble, Cec?"

"Oh, no. Just checking in on Patrice and the kids."

"And? . . ."

"She told me to be sure to take my blood pressure medicine," Cecil said sheepishly.

Laughing, Ben walked away, wandering through the camp, stopping to chat with small groups of troops as he strolled among the resting and relaxing men and women, Jersey always a few steps behind him.

"We goin' to Alaska or Ireland, General?" the question was tossed at him.

"I don't know, Pete," Ben replied. "As much blarney as you have, you'd be right at home in Ireland."

"You reckon there's any redheads left over there, General?" another asked.

"You got a redhead, Marty," Ben reminded him. "Back at Base Camp One."

"Yeah," a woman called out. "And the truth be known, he can't even take care of her!"

147

Red-faced, Marty shook his head and grinned.

Ben walked on, liking what he saw as he walked. His people had been resting for two days, and they were ready to go. They were ready to get this fight over with and see some new country.

He turned to Corrie. "Use your walkie-talkie, Jersey. Bump Corrie. Tell her to alert all commanders. We're pulling out at dawn."

Hundreds of miles away, in a farmhouse, a hooded figure asked, "Will she live?"

"Despite what she had been through, her signs are good. She'll live if she has the will to do so. But I don't know that she wants to live."

"Why do you say such a thing?" the man cried.

"Because of the damage done to her. Infection set in. We had to amputate most of what was left of her legs. Her face is horribly scarred from the fire as is most of her body. She will never again have hair."

"She must live! She still has hundreds of followers."

The medical man shrugged.

"Has she said anything since her surgery?"

"Yes. One sentence. Over and over."

"And that is? . . ."

"I hate Ben Raines."

The man smiled. "She'll live, Doctor. She'll live."

Satan and his outlaw pack caught up with Ashley and his men. It was not a joyous encounter for either of them, but with Ben Raines on their butts, they both knew the stronger they were, the better.

Ashley had shaken his head at the news of the crushing of the Ninth Order. "I tried to warn her,

148

Satan. I did try."

"I know. For once, you was right and the rest of us was wrong. Miracles still happen, I reckon."

Ashley ignored that. "So what do you propose to do, Satan?"

"Beats the shit outta me, man. It's done got to the point where there ain't no safe place no more. Ben Raines has got people all over the damn country. I figure we might as well go out in a blaze of glory, maybe."

"Whatever in the world are you babbling about?"

"I ain't babblin' about nothin'. I'm tellin' you that I ain't gonna spend the rest of my life runnin' from that goddamn Ben Raines. I'm gonna find me a spot to defend and make my stand. Just like I seen John Wayne do one time in the movies, fighting a bunch of Mexicans or Indians or Puerto Ricans or somethin' like that."

Ashley sighed. "Satan, why do something like that? We don't have to die just because Ben Raines is on the prowl. That makes no sense. Look, I've been doing some thinking on this matter, and I have discovered that there is one place that Ben Raines apparently has no interest in. Why don't we check out what's happening with Malone, and then head there?"

"Where's there?"

"Alaska."

"Welcome!" Malone shouted, spreading his arms wide and smiling at the tired terrorists.

His men had stopped the convoy miles from the entrance to what had become known as the wilderness area: over twenty thousand square miles of country located in the northwestern section of Montana and the northeastern section of Idaho.

"You would be General Villar? I have been monitoring the events of this summer. Indeed I have."

"I am Lan Villar. You are Malone?"

"Indeed I am."

The men stood inspecting each other, both liking what they saw. They were about the same age and both of them in good physical condition. Both of them wore their hair short and it was peppered with gray. Malone was stocky, well-built. He considered himself to be a very religious man, and could point to passages in the Bible that he construed to mean that everybody who wasn't white was inferior. More specifically, white, Anglo-Saxon, and Protestant.

Malone stepped closer to Villar and whispered, "That dark fellow over there, he's a sand-nigger, ain't he?"

"I beg your pardon? Oh. Khamsin. He's a Libyan."

"That's what I said. An A-rab. Sand-nigger. Is he worth a damn for anything? Can he fight?"

"He can fight."

"Did they bring their own women with them?"

"Some did."

"I don't want none of them fooling around with white women. The Bible forbids mixing of the races. Says so right out. You tell him that."

"I shall certainly advise him."

"You don't have any Jews or Mexicans with you, do you?"

"No," Villar said with a smile. Already he could understand why Ben Raines hated this man so.

"That's good. We'll get along then. I'm a good Christian man, General Villar. I don't drink hard liquor or smoke and won't allow it in my presence. I've been married to the same women for years and have never lusted after another woman. That's a sin. We go to church here every Sunday morning and Wednesday evening. But that's not something you will have to do if you so choose."

The only thing that Villar had done with churches over the past quarter-century was blow them up; preferably with people inside them. But just the thought of attending some religious ceremony filled him with amusement. "Oh, but I enjoy a good sermon, Malone. I'm looking forward to attending your services. Aren't you, Kenny?" he turned and winked at the young terrorist.

"Oh, yeah," Kenny said, with about as much enthusiasm in his voice as a long-distance runner with an ingrown toenail. "My daddy always told me to go to church whenever I could."

"Excellent! Wonderful!" Malone cried. "Enter my territory, gentlemen." He waved toward the vast wilderness area. "The new land of milk and honey and freedom from the inferiors."

Back in their vehicles, Kenny said, "This guy is as loony as a road lizard, Lan. I hope to hell you don't plan on staying here any length of time."

"Let's reserve judgment until we see how many men he has in his army, and what kind of soldiers they are. I'd join hands with the devil if that would insure getting rid of Ben Raines."

"The devil might be an improvement over this screwball," Kenny muttered.

# Chapter 17

Ben pulled his contingent out the next morning, with Buddy and his Rat Team at the point. The long column turned northwestward, heading for the rendezvous point in Wyoming. Ben stopped at several outposts along the way, and was pleased at the progress the settlers had made. The so-called secure zones were clean and neat, and stores were slowly being reopened, many of them using barter as a means of exchange, but with newly printed money now also being accepted. The nation was once more back on the gold standard, with Ben's accountants controlling the gold and the flow of paper money.

At an airstrip not far from the rendezvous point, heavily guarded planes were sitting. Ben had a surprise for his people.

Payday.

"You're kidding?" Jerre said, looking at Ben.

"Nope. Payday."

"Where are we supposed to spend it?" Beth asked.

"There are shops and stores in the outposts that accept paper money. Also a lot of individuals who do work in their homes are accepting it. Crafts people and the like. I'm going to reopen several vacation spots around the nation; secure-zones just like the outposts, and start running airline flights to and from outposts to the vacation zones. For a fee, of course. It's a small start, but it most definitely is a start."

"Well, I'll be damned!" Cooper said.

"Probably," Jersey told him.

Many of the older Rebels just sat and stared at the money in their hands after the long lines had been paid. Things were beginning to come together once more. For the first time in a long time, the men and women of the Rebels began to really sense that all the fighting they'd been doing, for over a decade, was paying off.

Ike was rubbing two brand new bills together and grinning. "I love the sound of money," he said. He frowned and squinted one eye at Ben. "But you know what this means, Ben."

Ben waited and smiled.

"This means I got to send most of this home to the wife."

"That's right," Ben said cheerfully. "We've had the good life for a long time, old friend. No money worries because there was no money. But as the nation grows and builds, pure barter can't stand as the sole means of exchange of goods for service. All the freebies we're used to just picking up as we go along are running out. It's the old law of supply and demand."

Chase looked at the pay in his hand. "Damned if I don't feel like crying," the crusty old doctor said. "I saw this nation destroyed, now I'm seeing it put back together—all in one lifetime. I never thought I'd live to see it, Ben."

"It's a start, Lamar. Just a start. We'll get this nation secure. But we can't stop there. We've got to secure the world or our enemies will eventually cross the waters and destroy us."

General Georgi Striganov nodded his head in agreement. "I would like to see the motherland once more before I die. I want to see if those left are

153

friends or enemies."

"What if we do get there, General?" Dan asked. "Would you want to stay?"

The Russian shook his head. "No. No. My future is here, just above the line in what was once Canada. I have my wife, my family, and my farm. I will come back here."

"Enjoy the feel of your first paycheck, people. It isn't much when compared to what we were making before the great war, but then, there isn't that much to buy."

"Not much?" Georgi said with a smile, holding out the bills in his hand. "Oh, but it is, Ben. You don't know what Russian generals were paid!"


Thermopolis's crew immediately got together and began scrounging up canvas, old leather jackets and boots and snaps and zippers. They began making billfolds and purses and selling them.

Up to this point, the only thing Rebels had to carry were the dogtags around their necks. Now they had money to carry around with them and soon they would have ID's with their pictures on them, encased in plastic. Billfolds were needed, and Thermopolis's bunch saw the need and provided the goods . . . for money.

A few Rebels found decks of cards and poker games sprang up around the camp. This army was no different from any other army that ever marched the earth . . . in many respects. Ben sent the word down the line that anyone caught cheating at cards or dice was in for some bad trouble. But he didn't try to impose laws forbidding gambling among his troops. Cavemen probably tossed stones into a small circle, the hunters gambling among themselves for the best cuts of meat.

Ben and his commanders spent the time going over maps of the wilderness area.

"OK, people, here it is: Buddy's Rat Teams report that Malone and his bunch are spread out from the northern tip of the old Beaverhead National Forest all the way up to British Columbia. That's more area than we first thought. Somewhere between twenty-five and thirty thousand square miles, taking in parts of two states. It isn't going to be a cakewalk by no stretch of the imagination. Ashley and the outlaw bikers have linked up with Malone, as have Villar, Khamsin, and Kenny Parr. We'll be able to use tanks in some areas . . . but not many. This is going to be a rough one. It's going to be march in and slug it out eyeball to eyeball. Dan, you get your riggers busy drying out the 'chutes. There might be a drop during this campaign, and if so, you and your people will be dropping into some rugged country. Cecil, get the birds coming up this way with supplies. Depots at Conrad, Fort Benton, Lewistown, and get with Georgi on a location in B.C."

Georgi leaned forward, over the briefing table. He studied the map for a moment. "Right there," he said, pointing. "Creston. There is a strip large enough for the planes to use. And that's right over the panhandle of Idaho."

"Good enough," Ben said, as Beth took down all the planned depots. "Now then, once we get in this area and our quarry sees we're in this to the finish, there is no telling where they're going to go. I wish we had the people to seal this area off, but that's a pipe dream. It would take several divisions to do that—and they would be stretching it."

"What we could do," Cecil said, after studying the maps, "is take Five and Six battalions and spread them at the bridges along this stretch of Highway

Two-hundred down to Thompson Falls. Then do the same along the Interstate down to the junction with Ninety-three, and then all the way down to the Idaho line south. But that would be spreading them thin."

"Not if we used our tanks to beef them up," West pointed out. "We could get them moving right now, and be in position by the time we are fully resupplied and ready to go in."

"We sure won't be able to use main battle tanks once we get off what few highways are in there," Ike added. "Dusters will be about all we'll be able to use."

"Get the spotter planes up," Ben ordered. He traced the several meandering rivers from British Columbia down to the Idaho line at Lost Trail Pass. "See how many important bridges are still standing along this route." He met the eyes of Colonel Gray. "Any whose connecting roads from the east or west have deteriorated to the point of being unusable . . . blow them."

"Right, sir."

"Cec, bump Base Camp One and our other main depots and get every tank we have drivers and crews for started up here on flatbeds. I want them to roll twenty-four hours a day. Tell the drivers I want them up here day before yesterday. And tell them to come up from the south and work north. Five and Six battalions will not move into place until we have supporting tanks in; we don't want to give away what we're doing."

Ben paused to take a sip of cold coffee. "Yekk!" he said with a grimace, and sat the cup down.

"Did the general let his coffee get cold?" Jerre asked sweetly.

Ben almost popped right back at her, but changed his mind as he realized that's what she wanted him

156

to do. "Yes the general did, Lieutenant," he said just as sweetly. "Why don't you be a sweet girl and make a fresh pot . . . and then pour us all some fresh coffee?"

Sitting in a chair, Jersey looked heavenward and her beret fell down, covering her eyes. She made no attempt to pull it back up. She really wasn't sure she wanted to see the rest of this exchange—hearing it might be volatile enough.

Corrie and Beth moved out of the deadly, eye-locked shooting gallery between Jerre and Ben. Cooper quietly left the room. The others froze in their boots.

"Oh, it would be a pleasure, General," Jerre said, enough ice in her voice to air condition all of Mississippi in August. She moved to the door, turned, and mouthed the silent words Fuck you! She shut the door behind her.

After the dust in the room had settled from the impact of door into frame, Ben muttered, "One for me. I think," he added.

"I wouldn't bet on it," Ike said.

"You do enjoy living dangerously, don't you, friend?" Georgi said with a smile.

"I gotta go to the john," Jersey said, and left the room.

Beth moved and Ben said, "You stay. I need you in here. You're the only one in here that makes legible notes."

"Lucky me," Beth muttered.

Ben gave her a dirty look that had about as much impression on her as it would on a porcupine.

"Oh, hell," Ben said. "Everybody take a break. Damn, can't anybody take a joke anymore?"

Ben sat down at his desk and told Beth to take off with the others. Be back in fifteen minutes.

He was going over maps when Jerre came back in and set the coffeepot down on the grill of the portable burner, only bending it a little.

Rolling a cigarette, Ben said, "You used to be able to take a joke better than that, Jerre. I recall that we used to insult each other a hell of a lot rougher than that. Alone and in a crowd."

She stared at him for a very long minute until finally some good humor came back into her eyes. "Yeah. But you caught me off guard that time, Ben. You want an apology?"

He shook his head. "No. You want a transfer out of here."

She shook her head. "No. That wouldn't accomplish anything. We're becoming friends again, Ben. It's just going to take some time, that's all."

Ben stood up and poured two mugs of coffee, handing one to her. "Have you heard any word on how the twins are doing?"

"Yes. They're fine. I don't think they miss me at all."

"That's bullshit, Jerre, and you know it."

"I'm not the world's greatest mother, Ben. I have too much wanderer in me."

"Well, stay with us, kid. We're damn sure going to do a lot more wandering."

She nodded her head and sipped her coffee. "Yeah, Ben. I plan on doing that."

One by one, the others wandered back into the big room. They were wary at first, until they saw Ben and Jerre joking with each other.

They watched as Ben spread clear plastic over the table map and began making small black X's on the plastic. "What Malone and his people did when they settled in here was very smart. After our fly-by's charted each smoke they saw, I compared the smoke with an old tourist guidebook and a map.

Back before the war, there were over fifty lodges and guest ranches in this area, ranging in size to accommodate anywhere from twenty to five hundred guests. Malone just put his people into those quarters. And it was a good move on his part. For many of these lodges and their outbuildings are way to hell and gone from paved roads and civilization . . . as we once knew it.

"Now then, with the addition of Villar and those with him, the use of PUFFs is out of the questions. They'd just knock them out of the sky with missiles. But," Ben held up a finger and smiled. "We can get our one-o-five's in damn close to these places, and make it awfully uncomfortable for Malone and Villar. So everybody has their jobs to do. Let's get to it." He smiled. "I would like to get to Alaska before winter."

# Chapter 18

Villar was the first to put it together.

A week had passed since Ben laid out the battle plans, and Villar had personally driven over as many roads in the so-called wilderness area—actually much of it was referred to as glacier country—as could be driven over in the time he'd spent in the area.

It was beautiful country. Even a man such as Villar, with all the compassion of a cobra could see that. Whether or not he appreciated the beauty was something he never revealed. What he did reveal were his thoughts on defending the area.

"It's a death trap," he told Malone.

"Whatever in the world do you mean?" Malone looked at him. "There is no way Ben Raines is ever going to flush us out of here."

"Ben Raines can do just about anything he sets his mind to," Villar bluntly told the man. "I've had rec patrols out since one hour after I got here, Malone. It didn't take me long to put together what Raines is doing."

"And what might that be?"

Villar bit back his anger. Malone was more and more reminding him of video tapes he'd seen—years back—of certain TV preachers and those who wanted to set the moral standards of others: smug, arrogant, and self-centered. "He's putting us in a box, Malone."

"Nonsense! Villar, do you have any understanding

of the thousands of square miles we control?"

"Let me tell you something, Malone. All along our west side there are rivers. To cross rivers, one must use bridges. The explosions you asked me about? Ben Raines's troops blowing certain bridges. At all the other bridges? Rebels backed up by battle tanks and heavy artillery. He's effectively sealed off that route. To the north, the same problem: rivers and bridges. To the south lies the Continental Divide, with mountains ranging from six thousand to eleven thousand feet. Raines has blocked every access route out. To the north, going into Canada, he's placed the Russian, Striganov, and his army. Ben Raines and Ike McGowan and their troops are to the east. Do you understand, Malone, that Raines has artillery that can drop rounds in on top of our heads from twenty-five miles away? All he's going to do, to soften us up, is take control of several roads—which he has the people to do—and then tear the guts out of us with long-range artillery."

Malone was sitting quietly. The smugness was gone from his face.

Meg Callahan was seated beside him. Meg had been a part of the Rebels for a time, until Ben had flushed her out of his ranks, after learning that she was a spy. She knew from firsthand experience what the Rebels were capable of doing; and she knew that Villar was telling the truth.

Ashley nodded his head in agreement with Villar and Malone took note of the nod.

"Is there no place on the face of this earth that is safe from that heathen?" Malone practically screamed the words.

"I'm beginning to think not," the terrorist replied. "Besides, what good would that knowledge do us now?"

"What do you mean?" Malone demanded.

"He means," Meg told him, "that we're trapped in here. Ben Raines has sealed us in. Right, Villar?"

"To a degree, yes. We could get out; but it would have to be on foot. We'd have to march out, leaving anything we couldn't carry."

"Ben Raines has no right to do this!" Malone screamed, spittle spraying from his mouth. "He has no right to displace us from our homes."

"Fine," Villar said. "Then do you want to tell General Raines that you will live under the Rebel rules?"

"Certainly not! Don't be ridiculous! I will not allow genetically inferior people into this area. That's why we came out here in the first place, to get away from niggers and Jews and wops and spics and polocks and the like. There used to be a couple of Indian reservations in this area. Those we didn't kill we ran out. Oh, there are some still in this territory. We use them for houseboys and maids and cooks. Menial jobs." He waved that off. "You know all that, Villar. I'm not leaving, Villar. I will order my people to gear up for a sustained battle, and we'll fight to the bitter end."

Villar's smile was void of humor. "With your philosophy, Malone, you don't have a great deal of choice in the matter." But I do, he silently added.


Trucks had rolled into the area from Base Camp One, carrying supplies and instruments of war. They rolled in twenty-four hours a day. Planes were landing around the clock, off-loading their cargoes of ammunition, food, medical supplies, generators, and boots, bras, and fresh BDUs.

Inside the wilderness area, Malone had set up his CP at a once beautiful resort near the Pinkham

Mountains, some thirty-five miles from the Canadian border.

Satan and his odious crew had personally inspected many of the roads leading out of the area, roaring around on their motorcycles, disturbing the animals and fouling the pristine air.

When they tried to cross over into the Bitterroot Range, they came under heavy fire from the Rebels stationed along Highway 200, 135, and Interstate 90.

"Shit," Hogjaw said. "We in a hell of bind in here, man."

"Yeah," Moosemouth agreed. "I ain't likin' this worth a damn."

"I think I'll kill that goddamn Ashley for bringin' us in here," Satan said. "It's all his damn fault."

"No, it ain't," a biker called Axehandle said. "It's our fault. If I git out of this mess, I'm hangin' it up, boys. I'm fixin' to find me a good woman, git me a little farm and settle down."

"What damn woman that's any good would have you?" Satan fixed him with a baleful look.

Axehandle shrugged. "Plenty of 'em, once I git shut of the likes of you?"

Satan wanted to slap him off his Hog. But Axehandle was just about as big and just about as mean as Satan, so the leader of the outlaw bikers held his temper in check. Instead, he said, "I don't want you in my bunch no more, Axe. Carry your funky ass."

"With pleasure," Axehandle said. "But you ride out first. I don't wanna git shot in the back."

Satan grimaced, kicked his Hog into life, and roared off, the others with him.

Axe rode south, down the Ninemile Divide to within shouting distance of the Interstate. "That's it!" he yelled across the expanse of concrete. "I'm quittin.' I done broke with Satan and them others. Y'all hear me?"

"We hear you," Leadfoot hollered from the other side. "Is that you, Axe?"

"In person. That you, Leadfoot?"

"In the flesh. You wanna join us?"

Axehandle thought about that for a moment, then sighed. Anyone with any sense ought to know there wasn't no way Ben Raines was gonna be stopped. Him and his Rebels was like a steamroller.

"Did you have any trouble adjustin' to the Rebel way of life, Leadfoot?"

"Not a bit, Axe. We enjoy it. It's pretty good over here."

"Beerbelly joined us," Wanda hollered. "The Rebels fixed up his teeth and he looks almost human."

"You don't say? All right, Leadfoot, I'll give her a whirl."

"There ain't no givin' nothin' a whirl, Axe. You either in, or you on your own, boy. Ben Raines don't cut nobody no slack."

Axehandle turned in the saddle at the sounds of half a dozen motorcycles coming up behind him. It was Danny and Corrigan and a few others. "You boys pullin' out?" he asked.

"You got that right, Axe," Corrigan said. "I'm tarred of bein' a loser. I wanna get on the right side for a change."

"Me, too," Axe told him. "That's Leadfoot and Wanda over yonder," he said, pointing across the Interstate.

"You don't say? How they likin' the Rebel way?"

"Said it's fine. The Rebels fixed up Beerbelly's teeth. Wanda said he looks sorta normal now."

"That'd be a sight to see. Beerbelly never did resemble nothin.' "

"Leadfoot?" Axe hollered.

"Right here, boy. With you in gunsights."

Axe swallowed hard. "Lower your guns, Beer. We's comin' acrost to join up!"


Ben Raines impressed the outlaw bikers.

There was nothing physically overpowering about the man. While he looked to be in middle-age he also looked in picture-perfect health. Which he was, except for a knee that bothered him from time to time and reading was a lot easier when he remembered to use his glasses.

There was just something about the man . . . the way he carried himself, maybe. Maybe it was some invisible aura lingering about him. For sure it was those cold gunfighter eyes.

"Why do you want to join us?" Ben finally spoke, his words soft. He was beginning to spook the bikers just sitting there staring at them.

" 'Cause we're all damned tired of gettin' kicked around," Corrigan said. "Outlawin' ain't much fun anymore. And us here"—he jerked his thumb at the other bikers—"is probably all that's comin' out."

"Why did you come out?" Ben never took his eyes from the man.

"I just told you . . . sir."

"No, you didn't. You told me you were tired of getting kicked around. If that was the only reason, you could have just kept on going. Now tell me why you came out."

Axehandle said, "To tell you the truth, General. Us here never felt like we really belonged with them others. Lamply there"—he jerked his thumb—"was always pickin' up stray cats and dogs and carin' for them and the like. Me and Corrigan and the rest of us here never would take no part in no gang-shaggin' of girls or women. I wasn't brought up like that. And, well, I guess we all got to thinkin' that the way we was livin' wasn't a very good one. I guess that about covers the waterfront, General."

Ben nodded his head. "You'll all undergo a battery of tests—some of them aren't very pleasant; I warn of that in advance. We won't throw them at you all at once, however. It might even come after this battle is over . . ." Ben paused. "Why are you smiling, Lamply?"

"That's another reason we come acrost, General. You don't even think of losin'. They got more troops than you have over yonder, but with you, it's just like, We'll win this one and then go on to the next one. They might be armies acrost the seas that can whip you. I don't know about that. But there ain't nothing left in the States that can do it; lessen all them Night Crawlers was to come together. But you done got them on the run."

"Ashley and Satan, are they looking for a hole to run out of and get gone from this fight?"

"Oh, yes, sir. They sure are. So is that Villar and Kenny Parr and Khamsin. They got 'em a place they want to get to, but they never did tell us where it was."

Ben stood up and shook hands with the bikers. "Welcome to the Rebels, men."

Grinning, Axehandle said, "We'll do you proud, General. We'll not let you down."

"I believe that. All right, Leadfoot. They're all yours, get them outfitted."

Lamar Chase had sat quietly throughout the brief interview, watching the bikers scratch. With a sigh, he picked up the phone that had recently been connected to the hospital and to other CP's throughout the area and requested some medics to take some strong soap and flea powder over to the bikers'

166

quarters.

He went out the door bitching. "Goddamnest army in the history of modern warfare!"

# Book Two

## Chapter 1

When the end is lawful, the means are also
lawful.

— Hermann Busenbaum

Ben had retired early and the camp sensed that
at dawn the next day, all hell was going to break
loose. For at the beginning of a new campaign, Ben
always went to sleep early and got up long before
anybody else, to sit with coffee at hand, brooding
over whether he had left anything out of his plans.

He awoke with a good feeling about the campaign. Not that it was going to be easy — it wasn't
going to be — but that he and the others had done
their best in the planning of it.

He showered quickly in cold water, shaved without cutting himself, and dressed in clean BDUs,
slipping into body armor and then pulling on his
battle harness. He checked his .45 and holstered it,
picking up his M-14 and slinging it. His personal
team was ready to go when he stepped out of his
quarters.

Jerre handed him a mug of coffee and stepped
out of his way. She knew his habits: until he had
mulled things over in his mind and was satisfied
with them, he wanted no conversation.

This morning, he surprised her. "Walk with me,
Jerre," he requested.

It did not surprise him to see the camp was up

and ready to go. The troops had their own grapevine and knew very accurately when a push was on.

"How do you read morale, Jerre?"

"Very high, Ben. As high as I've ever seen it."

Ben waved Thermopolis over to him. "Get your crew, Therm. I've got a surprise for you overage hippies."

"Might I ask what?"

"No."

Thermopolis walked away muttering and wondering what dangers Ben Raines had in store for them today.

"What are we going to do, Ben?" Jerre asked.

"Take in some sights. You ever seen Glacier National Park?"

"No. But I hear it's beautiful."

"It is. We're going to make it even more beautiful starting today."

"How?"

"Get rid of a lot of crap and scum that are littering up the place. What's the word on the units?"

"Everybody is in place."

Five and Six battalions were on the west side of the wilderness area, backed up by tanks and heavy artillery. Cecil's battalion and the bikers were at the south end of the area. Ike and West's people—with Emil and his fearless band of warriors with them—were taking the east side. Georgi and his people were at the north end. Dan, Buddy, Tina, Ben, and Thermopolis were curved around the northeastern sector.

Ben slipped his walkie-talkie from its pouch on his web belt. "Corrie, are the gunners ready?"

"Ready, sir."

"Soften up the edges."

"Yes, sir."

"Fire!" Corrie gave the orders.

"Get the team ready, Jerre," Ben said, just as the

170

sky was lanced with muzzle-blasts from eight-inch guns and from 105's. "Meet me at the trucks."

As the first rounds began dropping in, Malone's people started digging in deeper, which is exactly what Ben wanted them to do. It's difficult to see what's going on when one has their head down in a hole.

An hour later, Ben and his teams were linking up with Dan at the road that wound through the park—called Going To The Sun Road—angling west off of 89.

Ben stepped out into the darkness and walked to Dan's side. "Buddy and his Rat Team in?"

"Left half an hour ago, General. He reports no resistance. He's at the western tip of St. Mary's Lake. I told him to hold up and dig in there."

Ben waved his platoon leaders to him. "Make sure everyone is into body armor. Berets up and helmets on, people. Make sure everybody has rations, water, and plenty of ammo. We'll move in fifteen minutes."

"How big is this place?" Cooper asked.

"The park?" Ben turned to look at him.

"Yes, sir."

"Over a million acres. Even back when we had a working government in this country—laughable as it was—those dunderheads in Washington had the good sense to keep this area as primitively pristine as possible. It's wild country, people. Don't get separated or you'll get your butts lost in there."

Silver fingers of light were touching the east when Ben ordered his people into the park. The old rangers' visitor center had been turned into a fort by Malone and his people. But they had abandoned it when the Rebels moved into the area.

"General Striganov reporting that he has cleared the Prince of Wales Hotel and will be using that as his temporary CP," Corrie said. "He suffered one fatality, two wounded, and has taken ten prisoners. He has counted one hundred and two enemy dead. Rebet and Danjou have the area west of his CP under control and it is secure."

"Bump Dan for a progress report, please."

"He reports taking the Many Glacier Hotel, sir."

"That's just north of our position. Give me a status report."

"One wounded. No Rebel dead. No enemy prisoners taken. Seventy of Malone's people killed."

"Tell Buddy to move on and secure the Granite Park Chalet. Our pilots have detected people there. It used to be accessible only by foot or horseback, but fly-bys have shown that Malone cut a road to it. I'll use that for a temporary CP until the park is cleared."

"Yes, sir."

"And tell Buddy to warn his team to be on the lookout for grizzlies. They're all over this country, unless Malone and his people have killed them all. Which I doubt."

"Tina reports she's stalled at the south end of the park on Highway two. Meeting heavy resistance."

"Anything she can't handle?"

"No, sir."

Tina waved Ham to her, in a ditch alongside the highway. "Work around them, Ham. But stay this side of the Flathead River. See if you can't come up from the south. I think if we can get some sustained fire from that angle, they'll fall back."

"It's been raining pretty heavy in here, Tina. OK to use rockets?"

"Yeah. HE only. No Willie Peter and absolutely no napalm. HE's all that Dad's using in the big guns. He wants to keep fires down to a minimum." She grinned. "He's planning on reopening this park

172

. . . and charging fees."

Ham laughed. "Your dad, the economist. See you in a few minutes."

Ham's team of Scouts loaded up rocket launchers with antipersonnel warheads and moved out. Since Ben had no adequate way of fighting any forest fires, he wanted to keep that risk down to a minimum.

Malone's men had Tina's small contingent outnumbered, but the men behind the guns were getting more and more nervous. They knew the odds of their being taken prisoner was a toss-up, depending entirely upon whether the Rebels felt like taking the time to escort them back to a secure zone. Those manning the front position along the road didn't have to worry about being taken prisoner as two fragmentation grenades landed with a small plop inside their sandbagged bunker. Two seconds after landing, the grenades made a big mess inside the bunker and Ham's people moved up another one hundred yards, Tina's team right behind them.

Tina waved up a Duster and used the side-mounted phone to talk to the crew chief. "We've got to clear this roadblock and get to Essex. Main battle tanks will spearhead, you follow behind, and we'll bring up the rear."

"That's ten-four, Tina," the crew chief said, just as several main battle tanks arrived at the scene and rumbled by, all buttoned up and looking for trouble.

Tina lifted her walkie-talkie. "Hold what you got, Ham. The tanks have arrived."

The 52-ton monsters rumbled up the road, bullets bouncing off the heavily armored turret and chassis. One spun on a tread and clanked off the road, running over a sandbagged position, crushing those inside, then rejoined its companion on the two-lane highway, 105's lowered, looking for a target, the .50-

caliber machine guns spitting out death from the commander's cupola and the coaxial gun.

Malone's people had attempted to block the highway with trucks. The tanks shoved the trucks out of the way like knocking over a house of cards, and the Dusters, followed by Tina's command, poured through.

Malone's men gave it up and headed for the timber, looking for a way out.

"Essex is secure," Corrie reported.

"Tell Dan to drive south and secure Polebridge," Ben ordered. "We should have the park flushed clean by this time tomorrow."

By the time they got to the old Logan Pass Visitor Center, Buddy had cleared the chalet after only a brief battle and had radioed his father to come on it and make himself at home. He'd have coffee ready.

"Boy's full of himself today," Ben said with a grin. His smile broadened when he saw that while Malone's people had widened many hiking trails to accommodate vehicles, they had been unable to widen the trail between Dan's position at the Many Glacier Hotel, and Ben's CP at Granite Park Chalet. About five miles separated the two lodges. Dan could either hike it, or . . .

"We have many horses Malone's people left behind," the Englishman radioed. "But no proper saddles for the beasts."

Ben was laughing as he reached for the mic. "Use the western rigs, Dan. I know that isn't the way you were trained at Sandhurst, but bear with us."

Ben had to wait until Cooper climbed out of the pass and was on top of a mountain so he could repeat the transmission. Communications weren't the best in the mountains.

"Barbaric saddles!" was Dan's reply.

But at his CP just at the base of Vulture Peak, Villar didn't have to hear complete transmissions to know Malone's people were losing. The bits and pieces he could pick up were quite enough.

"The bastard is fighting an ecologically correct war and is still winning!" Villar said. He looked over at Ashley, Kenny, Khamsin, and Satan. "Ideas, gentlemen?"

"I do not like this place," Khamsin said. "Malone does not like me. I vote we leave our vehicles behind and walk out. We can always find vehicles once out of this wretched place."

"I ain't leavin' my Hog!" Satan said emphatically.

"Then go to hell!" Khamsin told him. "I don't like you either."

"Gentlemen!" Ashley said. "Please. We don't have to walk out. We can use horses to carry us and our supplies. I agree with Khamsin. We've got to get clear of Ben Raines and rebuild our forces."

"I'm with that," Kenny said. "But there ain't near-about enough horses for everybody. Somebody's gonna have to walk."

Khamsin waved details aside. "The question is *how* do we get out?"

"I'm ahead of you on that," Villar said. "Just north of us is a glacier. A hiking trail leads to a promontory overlooking the glacier. We take the trail east."

"East?" Kenny sat up and paid attention. "That's heading for Raines country."

"That's right. He won't expect us to cross territory that's been secured. Now we can't have over three thousand men all leaving at once and all of us using the same trails. None of us would make it." He looked at Satan. "Are you in or out?"

The big outlaw shrugged. "I'm in. Hell, Malone ain't gonna last long. Ain't none of us gonna last

175

long if we don't get shut of Ben Raines. I'm for gettin' on a boat and sailin' to Bullshit, Italy. I know the son of a bitch isn't goin' over there!"

"Don't bet on it," Khamsin said. "I will wager with any man that Ben Raines is going to conquer the world before it's all over."

"Odd you should say that," Ashley spoke softly. "I feel the same way about it."

Villar didn't say it, but he felt pretty much the same way.

A man came in and handed Villar a note. From the expression on the runner's face, Lan knew the message was not good news. He read it, balled it up and dropped it on the floor, then sighed heavily.

"Most of those units who headed south will not be joining us. The fools bunched up in Memphis and headed west from there. Pilots bringing supplies up here spotted them and radioed in. Ben Raines's damnable PUFFs from Base Camp One did the rest."

Villar sat down and rubbed his temples with his fingertips. "We had thousands of men, didn't we? We were going to conquer America and make quick work of it, weren't we? We were going to be kings, weren't we? Now look at us. We are certainly a pitiful bunch now, aren't we? Now we are reduced to tucking our tails between our legs and sneaking out . . . walking! Carrying a few possessions on our backs." He laughed, and much to the surprise of all, the laugh contained some genuine humor. "Pride goeth before a fall, gentlemen. And we all had much more than our share of that."

"So does Ben Raines," Satan said, a sour note to his voice. "He's shore kicked our asses all over half the United States."

"Ah, but no," Villar corrected. "The last part of your statement has merit. But not the first. Ben Raines has *confidence*. There is a difference. Ben

Raines has confidence plus patience. We had pride and impatience. We were cocky. Ben Raines was merely sure of himself and his people. We must be careful not to repeat our mistakes in the future."

Khamsin looked up. "Are you sure that any of us *has* a future, Lan?"

"As certain as anyone can be, Khamsin. That aside, the growing season is over in Alaska." He laughed once more. "Farmers, that's us. We're going to have to be farmers."

"I ain't farmin', " Satan bitched. "Not no, but hell no."

"Then how do you propose that three thousand mouths be fed three times a day?" Villar asked. "That's nine thousand meals a day, Satan. And we're running out of field rations."

"Steal it!" the biker said.

Villar laughed. "From whom? Think about it. No, we're going to have to go south where we can farm year round. Being very careful to stay clear of Raines's farms and ranches in Texas and New Mexico and Arizona. Malone was good enough to tell me about them. We're going to have to raise crops, vegetables and the like, and then learn how to can the food for preservation."

Ashley started laughing at the thought of these men hovering over pressure cookers and filling Mason jars. "Forgive me," he finally said, wiping his eyes. "But the mere thought is ludicrous. Lan, do you know how to operate a pressure cooker?"

"If I can construct a barometric bomb—and I have, many times—I can certainly learn to homecan foods." Villar's reply was not coldly given, for he, too, could see the humor in it all.

"Shhiiittt!" Satan said. "I shore am glad my original bunch ain't here to see this. Talkin' about farmin' and cookin' and cannin' foods. Good god amighty!"

Kenny stood up. "I'm taking my men and heading back to Florida, Lan. That's final. I got—or I had—a good operation going down there. You boys head on to Alaska. I'll take my chances down south. I'll head on out tonight and run interference for you guys. See you." The young man was gone from the room.

"Anybody else want' to split on his own?" Villar asked.

No one did.

"Get back to your sectors and start packing it up then."

"Our leaving is going to put a large hole in Malone's defenses," Ashley pointed out.

Villar smiled nastily. "Well, now . . . I guess that's his fucking problem, isn't it?"

# Chapter 2

It was summer in the rest of the battered nation, but in sections of Glacier National Park, it was plain damn cold.

Ben looked out the window of the lodge at the sunsprinkled and purple-shadowed remnants of a dying day and said, "The International Peace Park."

"What's that, sir?" Beth asked. She stood in front of the huge fireplace, warming her hands in the newly built fire. She had warmed her butt until Cooper, with a grin, pointed out that her BDU's were beginning to smoke.

"Back about the time you were being born, the Glacier National Park joined Canada's Waterton Lakes National Park, just north of us, to form the International Peace Park. It was a celebration of an open border between the two countries. It remained that way until the Great War."

Ben turned and smiled, holding up an old brochure. "I just read that, Beth. I'm no expert on the national park system . . . so it used to be called."

Ben had called for a cease-fire and had ordered Rebels with bullhorns to start calling for the surrender of all Malone's men. That move had at first startled the Rebels, for Ben was not known for magnanimous gestures toward the enemy.

Actually, the move was not as benevolent as it sounded. Under the cover of the cease-fire and the offer of surrender, Ben had ordered dozens of small teams to move into the enemy-held park at full dark, loaded down with plastic explosives and electronic detonators and the deadly Claymore antipersonnel mines.

"You're a sneaky, deceitful, son of a bitch, aren't you, Raines?" Chase spoke from across the room of the chalet.

"I certainly am, old friend. In matters of war, I am not to be trusted at all."

"General," Corrie called from the room where the communication equipment had been set up. "Patrols report a force of about two hundred and fifty men are attempting to walk out of the park. They're heading east; some of them are on horseback."

"Let them go and keep them under surveillance."

"You think they're trying an end-around, Ben?" Jerre asked.

He shook his head. "No. I think they're trying to escape. They've abandoned their vehicles and attempting a bug-out. Ask patrol if they can spot who is fronting the column. The leader will be on horseback, for sure."

It didn't take long, for Rebel patrols were now located in secret pockets all over the park.

"A young man, General," Corrie said. "They are just north of Mount Wilbur. Patrol leader says that will take them to a hiking trail just south of Chief Mountain and will eventually connect with Chief Mountain International Highway."

"That would be Kenny Parr. He's trying to make it back to Florida. Alert all units to get off the hiking trails and to allow any enemy troops who are hoofing it out to get clear of the park. Ike has moved up to take the area they will enter. Tell Ike to keep them under constant surveillance until they are out of the park and then ambush them. Wipe them out to the last person."

"Why wait until they're clear of the park, Ben?" Chase asked.

"So the sounds of the ambush won't be heard by any others attempting to escape and discourage them from trying it."

Lamar Chase sipped his cup of hot tea and studied Ben, as he had done a thousand times over the years. In all his years he had never known a man who was any harder than Ben Raines, but yet one who showed surprising compassion to those who were trying to live decently. Ben could be as brutal and vicious as an attacking grizzly, but yet halt an entire column to stop along the road to care for an injured animal. He could calmly order the deaths of hundreds of men, yet his top priority in setting up secure zone was education. He would shoot a criminal in a heartbeat and then pick up a broom to help in the cleaning out of a hospital to care for people.

The man was a damned walking contradiction.

Not a shot was fired within the over fifteen hundred square mile area of the park that night. But more than five hundred of Malone's people threw down their weapons and walked out of their bunkers to surrender to Rebels. Many of Malone's people were startled to find the Rebels not more than six feet behind them or to the side of them when they did make up their minds to surrender. The Rebels had slipped in on them as silently as a slithering snake, to lie waiting for the right moment to strike.

It was unnerving as hell.

By noon of the next day, Cecil had moved his people more than twenty miles north and Georgi had pushed twenty miles south, the Russian literally knocking on the back door of Malone's CP, forcing Malone to push deeper into the park.

"All units hold what you have," Ben ordered, after receiving the news that Kenny Parr's men had cleared the park confines and were moving toward

Highway Seventeen, and a slightly larger force was moving up the same trail Parr had used. "We don't want to spook any of the others who might be trying a bug-out."

"I have people in place just west of the highway, Ben," Ike radioed.

"Lan," Ashley said, "something's wrong."

"Yes," the terrorist agreed. "It's too quiet. Raines ordering a cease-fire caused warning bells to go off in my head. Kenny just radioed that he encountered nothing on his way out. He's now clear of the park."

"It's a setup, Lan. Ben Raines is setting the boy up for a killing."

"Yes. And Khamsin is only three or four hours behind Kenny."

"I believe this calls for an abrupt change in plans," Ashley said.

"Oh, quite." Villar smiled sourly. "Any ideas?"

"Get the hell out!"

"Not terribly original, but an idea whose time has come, I believe." Lan stuck out his hand and Ashley shook it. "Which direction would you prefer?"

"I'll take my men and head west. We'll find us a valley and pull the earth over us. No fires, no noise, no movement. It's the only chance we have of making it out of this mess alive."

"Yes. I'll push south and do the same. Raines won't use low-flying planes; he knows we still have Stingers. Maintain radio silence. Once Raines leaves the park, we'll link up. Good luck to you."

Kenny Parr's men walked right into an ambush. A mile from the highway, they walked into a Claymore-infested half mile of hell. What the Claymores didn't mangle, M-16's and M-60's and .50-caliber machine guns took care of.

Kenny had dropped back to the rear of the column to check for stragglers. At the first explosion, he left the saddle, grabbed his bedroll and took off into the timber, running hard for his life. He ran for over a thousand yards, then dropped into a moss-covered slope and lay still.

He had never been so frightened in all his life. Never. He was shaking all over. Even his eyelids were trembling. Ben Raines was a devil. He had to be a devil, straight out of the pits of hell.

Either that, he thought, and that thought frightened him even more . . . or a god, like some people believed.

A foul odor wafted to his nostrils and the young man grimaced in disgust.

Kenny Parr, outlaw, murderer, warlord, had shit his pants.


"Two hundred and forty-nine men dead," Corrie reported to Ben after speaking briefly with Ike. "Kenny Parr's body could not be positively ID'd."

"It's possible the Claymores mangled him so badly he couldn't be identified," Ben said. "But more than likely the little bastard got away. How about Khamsin's bunch?"

"Still moving up the trail. They were ten miles behind Parr's bunch and the terrain helped to muffle the sound of the ambush."

Ben didn't have to order the ambush site cleaned up. Ike's people were probably hard at work doing that right this moment. Either that or they had moved the ambush site farther west.

"No sign of anyone else coming up behind Khamsin?"

"Nothing. The trail is clear all the way back to Villar's old CP."

"And Villar and Ashley have been gone at least two hours."

"Yes, sir. That's when the rec team came up on the lodge."

Ben thought about that for a moment. "They're not taking the bait. The cease-fire spooked them off."

Dan had ridden over the mountain on a horse—trying to ride English-style, which some people, unfamiliar with equestrianship, have compared to the mating dance of certain large species of crane—in a western saddle.

"If they really want to hide from us," Dan said, "we'll never find them."

"True," Ben replied. "So I'm not going to look for them. It would take months to flush them out; that's providing they didn't slip out last night. We just don't have the time. Once Malone is finished, we're pulling out." Ben hand-rolled a cigarette and said, "Corrie, order all units to harvest what they can from the gardens they run across and then plow them up. Villar and Ashley can't stay here without food."

That hard smile once more crossed Doctor Chase's lips. Ben never missed a trick.


Khamsin had been a terrorist for years, considered one of the best. But as a commander of great armies, he had proved to be a bust. He had arrived in this country with thousands of men and the finest of equipment to be found anywhere in the world.

Then the Hot Wind ran smack into Ben Raines.

And over the years—they were only a few but seemed like a lifetime—Raines had steadily stomped him into the ground. Now he was walking out of a wilderness with little more than the clothes on his back.

Pitiful.

Khamsin's feet were wet and his boots were rubbing a blister on one side of his foot. He stopped to take off his boots and rub his feet. Then he slipped into dry socks and almost cried with relief. He laced up his boots and picked up his heavy pack, slipping his arms into the straps.

Abu, he spoke to his mentor in terrorism—now long dead—if you are watching me now, please turn away. I will recover from this humiliation. When or how, I cannot say, but I will recover.

Providing, he bitterly amended that, someone with more luck than I can kill Ben Raines.

Khamsin picked up his rifle just as the trail before him burst into a firestorm of death. Mangled bodies were blown a dozen yards in all directions as Claymores spread hellish death, rockets exploded against flesh, fired at almost point-blank range. The yammer of machine guns began putting the finishing touches on the scene of bloody destruction.

Khamsin flung himself off the hiking trail. He ran wildly through the thick brush and timber, ignoring the limbs that smacked and bruised and tore at his face and the thorns that ripped through his battle dress and lashed at the flesh of his legs. The Hot Wind ran until his chest was heaving, his vision blurred, and his legs rubbery and weak and he could run no more.

Khamsin dropped to the cool earth and buried his face against the vegetation. He wanted to weep and had to struggle to fight back the tears. Khamsin, self-proclaimed The Hot Wind, was now a commander of a nonexistent army. What was left of his army now lay broken and still, in cooling, bloody chunks along the narrow trail of this godforsaken wilderness. For a wild moment he thought of suicide as a way out of the deep humiliation he felt. He quickly rejected that. If by killing himself he could also kill Ben Raines, he would not hesitate to do so.

But that devil, Raines, was far away.

Khamsin regained his composure and took stock of his surroundings. All in all, he concluded, he was in a lousy position.

And all in all, he thought, I have been in a lousy position ever since I landed in America and discovered Ben Raines. He contented himself by silently cursing Ben Raines for a long moment.

He pulled himself to his boots and walked on, carefully measuring the terrain after each few slow steps. After walking about a mile, Khamsin found a blow-down: a wild jumble of trees that had been felled during some savage mountain storm. He slowly picked his way into the maze, being careful not to leave any sign of his entrance. One freshly broken off branch would have those devil Rebels on him like wild animals on a blood scent. And they were animals, Khamsin thought. They fought like animals, without the slightest shred of decency. The Rebels were savages led by the most savage of them all: Ben Raines.

Khamsin had food for several days, if he rationed himself. He could hear a spring bubbling, so water was nearby. If he kept his wits about him, he might survive to fight again.

Khamsin pulled himself into the darkness of the wild tangle and spread his ground sheet just as it began to rain, a cold falling of thick drops.

Raindrops began dripping down the back of Khamsin's jacket, running down his spine. Water collected on his nose and dripped off, puddling on the ground sheet.

He hadn't felt this miserable since those damnable Jews kicked his ass during a fight in Palestine, years back.

"Goddamn you, Ben Raines!" Khamsin whispered, as his ass got wet. *"IhateyouIhateyouIhateyou!"*

# Chapter 3

Meg Callahan had left Malone's side to strike out on her own. Malone was in an unreachable blue funk; so crazied thinking about his racist empire being pulled down around his nose, he was unbearable to be around. Meg had a strong suspicion that Malone, never all that stable, was having some sort of mental breakdown.

She had heard intercepted radio transmissions from the Rebels, deliberately broadcast uncoded, about the slaughter of Parr and Khamsin's troops, and about the hundreds of Malone's men surrendering; just throwing down their guns and giving up.

She knew, too, that the Rebels were now all over the vastness of the park. Malone might last a day, perhaps only a few more hours. Meg wisely wanted some distance between them.

What to do? was the question.

She entertained no thoughts of immediate revenge toward Ben Raines. That was so stupid it did not even enter her mind. What she had to do was hunt a hole and bury herself for several days. And she had that hole all picked out—if she could just make it.

It took her most of the morning, hiking through wilderness, but she made it, and crawled into the cave near the Continental Divide. She would be cold for a time, for she could not risk a fire, but she would survive.

Now she began entertaining thoughts of revenge—

at a much later date, of course.

Ben sat with his immediate staff and a few guests at the banquet table of the chalet, all of them enjoying fresh vegetables, just plucked from the gardens of Malone's people and cooked late that afternoon for the evening meal.

"The Hot Wind made it out," Ben said. "So did Kenny Parr. Villar and Ashley and their people have dug themselves a hole and pulled the earth in over them. We'll have to deal with them again, bet on that. But not during this go-around. What's the latest report on prisoners?"

"Just over eight hundred," Dan told him. "About half of them women and kids."

Ben had never taken eight hundred prisoners at one pop during all the long years of fighting. And he didn't have the foggiest idea what to do with that number.

Looking at the faces seated around the table, Ben knew that they didn't know what to do with those people, either.

"Malone?" he directed the question at Corrie who was busy buttering an ear of corn.

"Five Battalion moved across the line as General Striganov and his people pushed south, Buddy and Tina's teams on a parallel with them. Ike and West pushed in with West linking up with General Jefferys. Malone and what is left of his people are believed to have left the park and to be at that old lodge in the Lolo National Forest just west of the Indian reservation."

Ben nodded, thinking: It's almost over.

The body count of enemy dead had reached almost two thousand. Many of the prisoners were now being used to dig holes and bury their' dead comrades in hatred. The Rebels had been very lucky, suffering far less casualties than anyone could have predicted: ten dead and so far, just over forty wounded.

"We'll start interviewing the prisoners first thing in the morning," Ben said. "We'll see what we can salvage."

Not very damn much, was the general conclusion among the Rebels.

The prisoners, even though they had surrendered, were die-hard, hard-core racists and hate mongers.

Ben had shifted his CP over to the more easily accessible Many Glacier Hotel. The old lodge, built back in the 1920s by the Great Northern Railway, was huge, with rambling corridors and rough-hewn wood beams. It offered an impressive view of Swiftcurrent Lake.

The children of the surrendered, those kids still young enough to be taught — or reprogrammed as the Rebel doctors put it — were already being trucked out of the park, on their way to staging areas to be later flown to families in various secure zones and some back to Base Camp One.

A dozen of the leaders of Malone's pack of crud were standing at loose attention in front of Ben, who was seated in the lobby of the old hotel.

"I ought to shoot every damn one of you," Ben bluntly told the men.

Their faces paled and they sucked in their bellies and their assholes tightened at that.

"But I can't do it," Ben said.

The men visibly relaxed.

"But I don't really know what the hell to do with you."

"Turn us a-loose," one man spoke.

"And what would you do?" Ben challenged him. Ben gazed at the mountains across the lake, at the white lillies and the wildflowers growing impossibly next to the snow.

"Why . . . we'd leave!"

"And go where and do what?"

The question seemed to confuse the man. People of his ilk are easily confused.

"Let me put it another way," Ben said. "Perhaps I can somehow penetrate that murk that is called a brain. Believe it or not, you all have one, but in case you don't know where it is, it's located between your ears."

That got Ben some dirty looks but the men wisely kept their mouths shut.

"In case you men haven't heard the news, Malone is dead."

The men closed their eyes and silently cursed.

"He killed his wife, his son, and then stuck the gun in his mouth and blew half his head off. The bodies were found late last night. Now, as to what I'm going to do with you. I'm going to place you all on the old Flathead Indian Reservation. The few Indians that you have left alive will be in charge."

"I ain't takin' orders from no goddamn Injun!" one man blurted.

Ben looked at him. "Would you rather die?" he asked softly. "Because that is the only other option you have left."

"I don't believe you would just shoot me standin' here unarmed."

"Then you are a bigger fool than I first thought," Ben told him.

"What gives you the right to tell us what to do?" another challenged.

"Now that is a question I find worthy of a response. What gives me the right?"

Thermopolis was listening closely, leaning up against a wall in the corridor.

"Many things," Ben said. "Power is one reason I have the right. I have the biggest, finest, best-equipped, best-moraled army anywhere in America. That's one reason and I mention it only because

190

brute force is the only thing people like you really understand. But the most important reason of all is that the majority of the people we encounter like the Rebel type of law. *Majority* is the key word in that statement. And by majority, I mean those people who are trying to live decently, who respect the rights of those who are trying desperately to rebuild this nation; for all people of all races and creeds and religions. Not crud like you."

"So what happens to us?"

"You prove yourselves to me and the other Rebels. Prove that you can get along with people of all races and creeds . . . like the Indians you'll be living alongside of. And taking orders from."

"Not me," another said. "Oh, I ain't gonna try to walk away from you, Ben Raines. I got more sense than that. I'll go on the reservation. Then I'll leave."

Ben shrugged. "That's your business. Once we're gone, you all might try to run. And the Indians won't stop you. I've discussed this with them. But once you run, you better keep on running, and you'd better constantly keep looking over your shoulder. Because one of us might be gaining on you. And don't go into any Rebel-secured zone asking for help — any kind of help. Food, clothing, medical care. You won't receive it. Within a month, all Rebels and citizens living in Rebel zones will be issued ID cards. Complete with thumbprint and photo. And you asked this morning why we were taking your pictures and fingerprinting you? Here is your answer: we're starting our own criminal file."

Ben reached into his pocket and pulled out several crisp new greenbacks, holding them up for the men to see. "We're back on a limited monetary system. And without ID cards, you can't use money. You might steal it, but you can't use it. How's that grab you, asshole?"

The man glared hate at Ben Raines. But that was something that Ben was very accustomed to receiving. It didn't bother him a bit.

Malone and his jerks just thought they had killed or enslaved all the Indians. They were very wrong — as usual.

The weapons taken from Malone's people were given to the Indians and the zone declared secure. The Indians told Ben they had been praying for some Rebels to show up.

Ben reminded them they had been through the area south of the park just a few months back.

"You were also fighting a war then, General," a subchief reminded him. "And we were unarmed, except for bows and arrows, which most of us couldn't hit a barn with if we were standing inside it, and were afraid we'd get caught up in the middle of the war, with neither side knowing who we were."

"Good point," Ben said. "You're going to have trouble with the people we've saddled you with. Are you sure you want the responsibility?"

"They won't give us much trouble, General. You see, they're afraid of us. It is very a peculiar thing about white people. Most especially the ignorant among you. If they do not understand something, they are fearful of it. They do not understand the animals' way of life, such as the wolf and the coyote, and will make no effort to try and understand them, so they want to kill them. It is the same with people of another race. Very peculiar."

Ben smiled. "I think you and I will get along very well."

"I think so."

"Be careful. Villar and Ashley are still in the park, and they are dangerous men."

"Since the government disarmed us and slaughtered us right after the Great War, we have been virtually defenseless. Now with the weapons you have provided, we will be all right, I am thinking.

"There are secure zones just to the east of you. If you need help, don't hesitate to call. They're good people."

The men shook hands and yet another bond was sealed, and another secure zone set up.

The Rebels began making plans to pull out. Ben called for a meeting with his commanders to test their feelings on Alaska.

"It's pretty late in the season," Ike said. "We get caught up there, for whatever reason, and we could be in serious trouble."

"Yes," Striganov agreed, adding, "we are not adequately prepared for any type of arctic fighting. We could make it through the winter in the southern part, but without arctic gear, we would have to leave the rest of the state for another time."

"And we don't have any idea what we might be facing in the way of hostilities," Cecil said. "We do know there are people there — quite a few according to our monitoring of radio signals — but whether they are friendly or unfriendly is something we don't know. We have reason to believe they are hostile."

"We do know for certain there are no Night People there," West spoke. "Which brings me to this: let's make certain the lower forty-eight is as clean as we can make it before leaving it."

"I agree with that," Ben said. "Since we've learned that the massive nuking that the government told us about never took place, there are cities still standing that we've ignored for years. We can concentrate on the Northwest — including the coast — for the rest of the summer. Or for however long it takes. The Northwest takes in a lot of territory. During that time, our factories at Base can be working on gear for us to use in Alaska."

"Does that mean we will be taking our drive to rid the land of outlaws and warlords and creepies state by state?" Buddy asked.

"Yes. If that is what we decide our objective for

this summer to be. Let's take a vote on it. The Northwest, people?"

All hands were raised, including Ben's.

"That's settled, then. We'll cross the Bitterroot and take Idaho first. And that just might be easier said than done. We're looking at a lot of rugged country west of us." Ben spread out maps on a table and the men and women gathered around. "Now then, communications tells me they've been picking up a lot of very jittery signals from all over Idaho. We've got some very nervous people over there hoping that we just go away. That tells me the countryside is crawling with outlaws and the cities are filled with creepies. So we're not going to make them any more nervous than they are and send them into deep hiding. I want every commander to let a few uncoded transmissions through. Let those west of us think we're pulling out and heading back to Base Camp One. What we'll really be doing is gearing up to hit Idaho as hard as we've ever hit anything. But with the addition of Five and Six Battalions, we can pretty much effectively blanket the state."

"Utah, Dad?" Tina asked.

Ben grimaced. He had been waiting for someone to ask why that state had been left alone by the Rebels. "I wondered when one of you would bring that up."

Those in power in Utah had not been receptive to the Rebel overtures of partnership. All knew that Utah was, for the most part, clean of creepies and outlaws. It was also clean of anyone who did not subscribe to the way of thinking of the majority. And since it was known that Ben, Cecil, West, and Ike had all been employed, at one time or another, by a certain intelligence-gathering organization that had operated out of the Washington suburbs, the Rebels were not welcome in that state. That was a long-standing and little-known feud that went back decades.

Ben slowly met the eyes of those in the room. Cecil, Ike, and West were smiling. "They don't bother us, and they don't tolerate lawlessness in that state," Ben finally spoke. "They are and have been for some time completely self-sufficient. If they want to build a wall around themselves, that's fine with me. I can't and won't condemn someone for doing what we did in the Tri-States. Just as long as they stay inside that wall and don't interfere with us I'll leave them alone. But I will cross their borders, peacefully, whenever I feel like it. If they try to interfere with any peaceful crossing, they will be met with force."

Ben paused to pour a cup of coffee. Mug in hand, he returned to the table. "Georgi, take your people and head north. When I give the signal to jump off, drive south out of British Columbia and secure everything down to and including Coeur d'Alene and east along Interstate 90.

"Five and Six Battalions will position themselves north to south along Highway Ninety-three, from the Montana line to Shoshone.

"Cecil, you and West will drive straight across on Highway Twelve and secure everything over to and including Lewiston and Moscow.

"Ike, I want you to pull out today. Head north across British Columbia and then cut south, staying right on the Idaho line all the way down to just south of Hell's Canyon. Cut across there and start cleaning house southeast along the Interstate.

"I'll take I-Fifteen down to I-Eighty and then cut west. I'll link up with you somewhere along the line.

"Buddy, you'll split off from my columns at Pocatello and take your Rat Teams down I-Fifteen to the Utah line. Don't cross over. Take this road at Malad City and turn west over to I-Eighty then cut north and link up with me.

"Dan, your people will split off from me at Dubois and clean house down to Shoshone. Link up with me at Twin Falls. Everybody got it?"

There were no questions.

"Ike, you give me a bump when you're in position and ready to go. On Ike's signal, we go and we go in hard. That's it, people. Let's go get ready to kick some ass!"

# Chapter 4

It would be several days before Ike got into position, for nearly all of the roads he would be traveling were two lane, and it had been years since they had seen any maintenance. Georgi, on the other hand, was in position by that evening, massing his forces just south of Creston, waiting for the signal to drive south.

Five and Six Battalion began their move south, halting just north of the Continental Divide, at the approach to Lost Trail Pass.

Cecil and West stopped on the Montana side of Lolo Pass and waited.

Ben and his contingent were the last to pull out. They halted at Monida Pass and waited for word from Ike.

Each contingent that waited on the Montana side posted sentries on the high passes, but apparently the fake radio messages were taken in by the outlaws and the creepies, for the Rebels could spot no signs of trouble, and the radio chatter from the unfriendly side of the mountains was loose and easy.

Intelligence analyzed the transmissions and worked up an assessment of what lay on the other side of the Divide. Dan took the report to Ben.

"Starting from the west side of the state," Dan reported, "there is a very heavy concentration of Night People in the Caldwell/Nampa/Boise area."

"What does intelligence consider heavy?"

"Several thousand, at least. Possibly more, and they are heavily armed and confident. Heavily meaning .50's and rocket launchers and mortars. Between

197

Mountain Home and Rupert, there appears to be a constant struggle going on among several gangs of outlaws, jockeying for territory and leadership. The gangs are called—and only one of them appears to have more than a modicum of poet in his soul—the Bloody Bandits, the Hellraisers, and, get this, the Starlighters."

"The Starlighters!"

"Yes. Isn't that lovely." Dan waggled one eyebrow.

"They're not? . . ."

"Intelligence doesn't know and won't make a guess."

"Well, if they are gay, don't sell them short. One of the toughest men I ever knew was of that particular persuasion. That was one of the meanest men I ever knew in combat. He told me once there was only one thing he'd rather do than suck a dick, and that was kill communists."

"Good Lord, General!"

Ben shrugged. "Just telling you what he said. Go on."

"The Bloody Bandits control the area around Mountain Home—about a forty-mile stretch. The, ah . . . Starlighters control Twin Falls, about ten miles in either direction. The Hellraisers control the area around Burley and Rupert. Pocatello and Idaho Falls is hard creepie country."

"We have our work cut out for us. How about the interior?"

"Outlaws and a lot of them. Obviously they've been pretty much in control for years. This was one of the areas that President Logan left alone after the Tri-States fell and the outlaws simply enslaved or killed off the citizens and have had their way for years."

"They've got to live on something. I would say they have enslaved many of the people and are forcing them to work on farms. And the creepies probably have human farms of their own. That appears to be how they manage to survive."

A look of disgust passed Dan's face. "Yes. That is

their pattern."

"Up where Georgi is?"

"Outlaw country. Warlords have taken over some big ranching operations there and have some fairly substantial armies."

"Anything we can't handle?"

Dan smiled and then broke out in laughter.

"Right!" Ben said, joining him in the laughter.


Ike radioed that he was in position. Ben took note of the fact that Ike sounded very tired. And he should be; his Rebels had been pushing hard to get into position.

"Stay put for the rest of today and tonight and relax, Ike. You and your people have pushed awfully hard, day and night. Take a break. We'll shove off at 0700 hours in the morning." He turned to Buddy. "All right, son. Get your Rat Team and take off. Penetrate for twenty miles and don't mix it up with anybody unless it's forced on you. I want intelligence, not body counts."

"Yes, sir. On my way."

"Corrie, order the Scouts out from all units. The same orders apply to them as I just gave Buddy. I want intelligence, not heroics."

The Scouts began their incursion into what had been the state of Idaho . . . and would be again if Ben had his way; although Ben knew that the United States would never be restored to what it had been before the Great War—at least not in his lifetime. And, he often entertained this thought: perhaps it should not be as it was before. Ben felt it should be even better for those who tried to live good, decent lives. And worse for those who chose to break the law. That was his goal.

The Scouts reported roadblocks fortified with heavy machine guns about ten miles inside the area.

Ben took the mic. "Fall back. Let's see if they'll buy

a retreat. All Scouts and rec patrols fall back."

Those who now controlled Idaho and the rest of the Northwest were lawless thugs, but for the most part, their leaders were not stupid people. They knew that Malone had fallen to the forces of Ben Raines, and knew that Ben had sworn to rebuild the nation . . . under his rules. And outlaws could not exist under Rebel rules. Ben had thrown the Constitution away and written his own Bill of Rights and what laws would apply to whom.

The thugs and outlaws and warlords knew they were in a fight for their survival. And their leaders realized they could not fight the Rebels separately. They had to unite and they didn't have much time left to do it.

"Raines is knockin' on the door," Larry Rafford radioed from the Coeur d'Alene area. "We all knew this time would come, and now it's here. If we don't stand together, we're all gonna fall."

"I don't trust your ass, Larry," Ted Ashworth spoke from his headquarters in the Lewiston area. "And if you think I'm gonna hold hands with that bunch of fags down south, you're full of shit!"

"Screw you, you obscene redneck bitch!" Francis broke into the conversation from his listening post in the headquarters of the Starlighters located in the south of the state.

Ben listened as a cuss-fight broke out on the short-wave equipment.

Dan stood by Ben's side, his face expressionless, his arms folded across his chest.

"Aw, goddamn!" Red Manlovich cut in from his territory near the great primitive area of the state. "Both of you sound stupid! Larry's right . . . for once. We all got to get together in this fight if we gonna have any chance at all to whup Raines. Even if it means joinin' up with them swishes down south."

"Up yours, too!" Francis told him. "You ignorant savage!"

More cursing filled the airwaves.

A heavy, ominous voice silenced the wild cursing. "All our lives, our way of life, is threatened by Ben Raines and his army."

Ben knew that was probably a Judge from the Night People.

"And I damn shore ain't gonna tie up with no goddamn cannibal!" Ted screamed.

"Silence, you fool!" the Judge said. "We have existed side by side for years, have we not?"

"Except for the time you et my brother!"

"He violated our space. He knew the rules. And you have killed our people. Can you deny that?"

"Get to the point," Larry broke in.

"If we are to survive, we must cooperate. We must share information and anything else we have. And be advised that he is listening."

"How do you know that?" Red radioed.

"By applying simple logic, you lout," Francis told him.

"Go sit on a cucumber," Red replied.

"Whore!" Francis said.

"Turd!" Red shot back.

"Shut up! Both of you!" the Judge ordered. "We don't have much time. Hours, if we're lucky. We've got to break up in small bands and force Raines to do the same with his Rebels. That's the only way we stand a chance of surviving."

"I ain't breakin' my people up," Red said. "And I ain't gettin' nowheres near them weenie-chewers."

"Oh, go sit on your saddle horn, cowboy!" Francis told him. "I agree with the Judge. If we are to survive, we must unite and fight as one."

"You ain't gittin' your hands or nothin' else on my booty, Petunia."

"I wouldn't touch you wearing a suit of armor, horsefucker!"

"That does it," Red hollered. "I'm done talkin'. And I'm a-gonna kill you, Tulip-mouth!"

"Sticks and stones! Sticks and stones!"

"My word!" Dan said. "This is certainly shaping up to be a very interesting campaign."

"We are doomed," the Judge said.

"Kissy, kissy!" Red said.

"Go to scramble," Ben ordered. "You heard all that, Ike?"

"I wouldn't have missed it for the world."

"Georgi?"

"Every word, Ben."

"Cecil?"

"Oh, yes."

"Scouts and rec teams back in. We shove off in the morning with main battle tanks spearheading."

The 52-ton main battle tanks rumbled on the interstate as Ben walked back to the wagon and got in, cutting his eyes to Corrie.

"Move them out, Corrie."

The siege had begun.

# Chapter 5

At Dubois, where Dan was to split from the main column and head down Highway 22, Ben's command hit their first trouble spot.

The town itself was a burned-out shell. No more than a tiny village before the Great War, the town had been looted and destroyed over the years. The Night People had mined the area with Claymores, but it was too obvious for Ben's liking.

"They're getting smarter," Ben said, studying a map. "They want us to swing off the Interstate and take this secondary road that runs parallel to it. Check it out, Buddy."

"It's a death trap," his son reported back. "About ten miles down the road there is a bridge. It's wired to blow. It's you they're after, Father."

"Yeah. They don't like me very much for sure. Come on back. Our people are clearing the mined area now." He got out of the wagon and walked over to Dan. "OK, Dan. You and your people take off. We'll see you in Twin Falls. If you get into anything you can't handle, get the hell out, understood?"

"Understood, General."

Buddy and his team roared back in and once more took the point, main battle tanks rumbling and snorting right behind them. All the little towns they passed through were deserted and burned-out; relics of a dead society that blamed the war for its destruction, but in reality had legislated itself to death, the final blow coming with the disarming of the American citizens by a liberal President who was backed by an equally liberal House and Senate. The Great War only put the dying nation out of its misery.

And now, years later, Ben Raines was dragging the nation out of the ashes and dusting it off, propping it up, and telling its people to stand tall.

"John Wayne would have been proud of you, partner," Ike was fond of telling Ben. Then, in a more serious tone, he would say, "Tell you the truth, I wish Big John was here. We could use the help."

Buddy radioed back. "The creepies have barricaded themselves in the city, Father. They never learn, do they?"

"They have no other place to go, son," Ben replied. "For some reason unknown to us, they fear life outside the city. Tell the tank commanders to crank up their one-o-five's and start dropping them in. I'm splitting my people and I'll lead a contingent in from Highway Twenty. You take the airport."

"That's ten-four, Father."

Cooper meandered around back roads until reaching the new route and cutting southwest. Ben halted about two thousand meters outside the small city and told his gunners to set up and bring the city down. Damned if he was going to lose Rebels slugging it out with crud when he could use artillery and accomplish the objective faster and with practically no loss of life.

Ben stood with his team in the shade of what was left of a burned-out building on North Yellowstone Avenue when he thought he heard something that was totally out of sync with the bombardment. "Tell the gunners to cease firing, Corrie."

As the big guns fell silent, they could all hear it very clearly.

"What the hell?" Jerre said.

"They're on top of us, people!" Ben yelled. "Get down behind cover. The creepies are charging us."

The move had not been totally unexpected. Ben was intensely hated by the Judges—the ruling body of the earth's Night People—and he knew the creepies were so fanatical thousands would willingly die en masse if Ben Raines could be killed in the process.

Corrie was on the radio, urging Dusters and more troops to get the hell up to their position when the almost solid wall of stinking creepies came into view. The screaming, wild-eyed mob ran right toward and into the guns of the Rebels.

Corrie, Beth, Jersey, Cooper, and Jerre opened up with M-16s on full rock and roll. There was no need to aim; just point the muzzle in the general direction of the rampaging and screaming mob and hold the trigger back. Ben had bipodded his M-14 and was lying on his belly behind several hastily piled-up concrete blocks. The M-14 was pounding his shoulder as the big .308 slugs tore into flesh and knocked creepies spinning and wailing out their death songs.

Two Dusters came zipping around the corner and opened up with machine guns and 40mm cannon, the heavy fire tearing a great hole in the mob as the city smoked and burned and exploded behind the now bloody and body-littered street.

Rebels ran around the corner and stationed themselves behind whatever cover they could find and opened fire on the mob of cannibals. Others climbed up on rooftops and began firing into the still-chanting and screaming mob on the street below them.

But still they could not kill them all.

A Duster pulled in front of Ben's wagon to act as a shield just as creepies came charging from the burned-out building, breaching the Rebel security around Ben.

A stinking creepie hurled himself onto Ben, tearing the M-14 from his grasp and momentarily knocking the wind from him. Ben rolled from under the smelly cannibal and gave the man the toe of a jump boot to the balls. The creepie screaming and vomited, the puke just missing Ben's head. Ben kicked the man in the face just as another stinking creep jumped on his back. Ben flipped him off, regained his balance and jerked out his .45, carried cocked and locked, and shot the man in the head as he was getting to his knees. He turned the muzzle to the first creepie and blew a hole in the man's back.

Rebels surrounded him and forced Ben back, protecting him with their own bodies. They literally pushed him into the armor-plated and bulletproof-glassed wagon. His team was shoved in after Ben was inside.

"Get the hell gone from here, Cooper!"

Cooper spun the wheel and left the firefight area in a squeal of rubber. "What to, General?"

"Next block over," Ben said calmly. "Let's see if we can find some action there. That's where we left Emil and the bikers."

They found action. Emil and the bikers, joined by Thermopolis and his bunch were on one side of the street, a gang of creepies on the other side, both factions banging away at each other. It was a standoff.

A hard burst of gunfire struck the front of the wagon, the slugs blowing out both front tires. The wagon lurched to a stop in the street. To compound the problem, they were stalled much closer to the creepie side than to the friendly side.

"Let's go, people," Ben said. "We're ducks in a pond out here."

The team piled out of the wagon and ran for the cover of an office building, all of them carrying boxes of ammo as they ducked between abandoned and rusting vehicles littering the street.

Ben shoved Jerre inside the shattered front of the building and then jerked a grenade from his battle harness and chucked it into the building next to them. The Firefrag blew, clearing the front of the store of any creeps. Ben followed the blast with a clip from his M-14.

Ben ducked into the gloom of the ground floor. "Corrie! Bump those across the street and see if they've taken any casualties."

"Two wounded," she reported, after speaking briefly with the radio-person with Emil. "None of them serious. Emil had the heel shot off one of his cowboy boots. The force of it knocked him down and he got a splinter in his butt."

"Savages!" the voice of Emil Hite drifted to them during a momentary lull in the fighting. "Philistines! You'll pay for this, you . . ."

Whatever he called them was drowned out in a hard clatter of gunfire from the creepie side of the street.

"We're in a piss-poor position here," Ben said. "Cooper, check out the back and see what's going on."

"The alley's clear as far as I can see," Cooper called from the rear of the store.

"You can bet they've got people just above us, though," Ben said. "Waiting for us to try a run for it." Ben looked up at the ceiling. "This is an old section of town, with mostly two- and three-story buildings constructed fifty to seventy-five years ago." He handed his M-14 to Jerre and climbed up on a scarred countertop. Taking out his knife, he removed several pieces of ceiling tile and grinned down at his crew.

"What's so funny, Ben?" Jerre asked.

"The floor above us is wood."

Ben climbed down and retrieved his M-14. "Spread out," he told his team. "Let's give those above us a hotfoot before they figure out the floor is wooden and spray us with lead."

The team lifted their weapons and put two hundred rounds of .223 and .308 slugs into the room directly above them. Screaming bounced around the dusty room as blood began dripping down from the punctured floor above them, plopping amid the dirt and the torn paper and rat-shit-littered floor.

"Tanks," Beth said.

"Corrie, tell the tank commanders to spray the top floors while we get the hell out of here," Ben ordered. "As soon as the firing starts, head for the other side."

The .50-caliber slugs began knocking brick and

mortar from the top floors as Ben and his team ran for the other side of the street.

Ben plopped down beside Thermopolis. "I thought I told you to stay back with the artillery."

"It was far too noisy back there. Besides, I wanted to see what trouble you might be getting into."

"Did you satisfy your curiosity?"

"To the max."

"Tell the tanks to start using HE, Corrie. Bring that line of buildings down. And tell one of them to winch the wagon out of the street. Check out the back, Jersey. If it's clear, let's get gone from here."

"Them was my last pair of Tony Lama boots!" Emil wailed from the next building. "And they ain't nobody makin' no more of them. And I got a splinter in my ass. You creepie sons of bitches!" he wailed.


Those outlaws and terrorists Ben had left back in the park linked up and began their plans for moving on. Villar looked with disgust marking his face at the spot where they had concealed their vehicles.

"The bastard took them!" he griped. "Raines took every damn truck and Jeep we had. That son of a bitch doesn't miss a trick." He glanced over at Kenny Parr. The boy had the look of defeat on his face. They had all noticed the change in him since the ambush that wiped out what had been left of his command.

"He'd never known defeat before this," Ashley spoke in a low voice.

"It's more than that," Meg said. "He's scared. Ben Raines really frightened him."

"Leave him behind," Satan grumbled, contempt in his voice. "The punk's turned yellow. From now on out he ain't gonna be nothin' but a drag on us." The biker spoke loud enough for Kenny to hear.

"Screw you!" Kenny said, cutting his eyes to the outlaw biker.

Satan laughed at him. "You wanna be my punk,

boy? We ain't exactly overrun with wimmen around here and I'm sorta horny."

"That's enough!" Villar told him.

"You his sweetie now?" Satan faced the terrorist, an evil grin on his ugly face.

Villar stood nose to nose with the biker. "Don't push me, outlaw," he warned the man. "I'll chop you up in little pieces and feed you to the bears."

Satan wasn't afraid of the man, but he had enough sense to know his bunch would be no match for the men Villar had standing around him, weapons at the ready. And Satan wasn't really sure he could take Villar in a one-on-one fight.

The biker shrugged his shoulders. "No point in us fightin', Lan. But I still say the boy's lost it. What good is he to us?"

"Time will tell, Satan. Battle fatigue can strike any of us at any time. And don't think you're immune. Because you aren't."

Satan snorted, spat in Kenny's direction, and walked away.

"I think he is immune," Ashley said. "Because I'm not sure he's entirely sane. He rules by brute force and that's all he understands."

Villar nodded his head in agreement. "Perhaps you're right. Well, let's start walking out of this place. South," he added. "We'll pick up vehicles outside the park."

"We still goin' to Alaska, Lan?" Kenny asked, his voice trembly.

"After we stock up some food, yes. There must be government stockpiles of MREs that Raines's bunch missed. We'll start searching armories and military bases. That's our only shot. It's just too damn late in the season to grow anything." He struggled into his pack and glanced over his shoulder at Satan and his pack of bikers. A grin crossed Villar's face. The Rebels had not taken the motorcycles, but what they had done was even worse, and Satan had been livid with rage when he discovered it.

They had removed the handlebars and attached bridle and bit to the front hydraulic forks, looping the reins around the seat.

The look on Satan's face had been priceless.

"Well . . . mount up, Satan," Lan called cheerfully. "Time's a-wasting."

The look Satan gave him would have fried eggs. "I hate that goddamn Ben Raines!" the biker said.

# Chapter 6

With what was left of the small city being attacked by artillery from two sides, it did not take long for the town to become engulfed in flames. Rebels had spread out around the objective's perimeter and were shooting any creepies who tried to escape the inferno. The screaming of the godless cannibals could be heard over the crackling of flames and the bark of rifles.

By noon of the first day of the statewide assault to clean the area of thugs, punks, cannibals, outlaws, and warlords, the city and suburbs of Idaho Falls was burning, the flames pushing great clouds of smoke twisting into the skies.

In the northern part of the state, General Striganov and troops were meeting stiff resistance from a major gang of thugs, outlaws, and warlords. The crud had thrown up a defense line a few miles south of Sandpoint and were, because of the terrain, temporarily holding back the Russian's troops.

A huge lake, nearly forty miles long, made up the eastern line of the outlaw's defense perimeter, blocking Striganov's troops from that point. For the moment, Georgi's troops were stalled, slugging it out with machine guns and mortars, and being met by the same while Coeur d'Alene and Spokane were being beefed up by the outlaws' reserve forces.

Ike's people had yet to enter the Caldwell/Nampa/Boise area because of bridge defenders all along the line. Ike guessed that the bridges were wired to blow should his people bust through, and he did not want the bridges along the river destroyed.

"Leave it for the time being," Ben radioed. "Swing your people east until you can find a crossing and concentrate on cleaning out the crud along I-Eighty. That's supposed to be territory controlled by the Bloody Bandits. Ike, it's probably going to take you most of the day to get in position. Bivouac north of the area and hit them fresh in the morning. I'm going to hold what I've got and take on Pocatello at dawn."

"That's ten-four, Ben. Georgi is bogged down up north. It's about to get bloody up there."

"Only if we let it, and I'm not going to allow that. The hang-up is the crud have blown most of the bridges. I've told Georgi to pull back and wait. They'll probably do an end-around east or west in the morning and come up under them. Spokane is going to be a real bitch, I'm thinking."

"Five and Six Battalions?"

"They've had it pretty easy. Very little resistance along that route. Dan and his people haven't fired a shot. Buddy reports some light resistance and he was forced into two firefights. He and his Rat Team have since returned to this sector. They suffered no wounded or dead. Cecil and West are at a standstill at the intersection on the Middle Fork Selway. We're all going to stand down and dig in for the night. That's effective immediately."

"That's ten-four, Eagle. Shark out."

Ben and his people had moved several miles outside the city and were bivouacked between the Interstate and the Snake River, north of the Fort Hall Indian Reservation. The reservation, according to reports from Scouts, appeared to be deserted.

"Damn creepies probably ate them," Cooper said with a shudder.

Even after several months of close-in fighting with the Night People, just the mention of the cannibalistic clan still brought shudders of revulsion from the Rebels. Their way of life was so repulsive to any type of civilized behavior that none among the Rebels could come close to comprehending it.

Jersey looked at her just-opened packet of field rations and sighed. "Thanks, Cooper. I really needed that last remark."

Corrie took off her headset and said, "General, pilots are reporting in from their fly-bys east and west. They state that heat-seekers show several large human holding pens just south of Pocatello and just north of the Caldwell/Nampa/Boise area. Hundreds of people."

"Shit!" Ben said. He spread out a map on a table while Corrie was getting the coordinates from the pilots. After Ben had penciled in the locations, he said, "All right. We'll hold off any further attacks until we can get those people out of there. Tell Ike to take the western holding pens and we'll take this side. Buddy, you spearhead down this old county road—Dusters with you. The pens are just off Highway Thirty. About two miles north of this northernmost jut of the highway. You'll get into position and then give me a bump. We'll hit it just after dawn. Lamar, I want medics on hand to check for diseases and trucks to transport these people out."

"What are we going to do with them, Father?" Buddy asked.

It had been the Rebels' experience that once men and women were held for any length of time by the Night People, many of them were quickly reduced to near-mindless beings; that condition brought on by such intense fear and revulsion at what lie ahead for them, they were turned into babbling idiots. Most of the young could be salvaged, but the Rebels had to build or refurbish hospitals to care for the others; and it was a terrible drain on Rebel resources and personnel.

"Care for them as best we can, son. Allowing them as much dignity as possible, considering their condition." Ben again studied the map. "There is an airstrip a few miles east of the holding pens. Check it out, Buddy. It might be easier all the way around to fly the survivors out. Get some of your team moving on that right now."

"Yes, sir."

"Corrie, have the pilots found any holding areas of the creepies in the interior or up north?"

"No, sir. Only the two I gave you."

"That confirms that the Night People cannot exist outside urban areas," Jerre said. "For whatever the reason. Or," she added, "they want us to think they can't."

"I agree with the last part, Jerre."

Doctor Chase looked up from the map. "What time are we pulling out in the morning, Ben?"

Ben looked at him. *"We,* Lamar?"

"That's what I said, all right. Are you becoming hard of hearing, Ben?"

"Lamar, we don't know what in the hell we're going to find down there. I . . ."

"Dawn, then," he cut him off. "Fine. I'll be ready." He looked at Jerre. "How is his BP, Lieutenant?"

"Ah . . . just fine, sir."

"Good, good. Check it daily. You can't be too careful with that."

"Lamar!" Ben said, exasperated. "I've never had high blood pressure in my life!"

The doctor ignored him, turning to Jersey. "I hear your boss got you all in a jam earlier today."

"Nothin' we couldn't handle, sir," she said, sticking out her chin.

"You wouldn't dream of saying a bad thing about him, would you, girl?" Chase asked it with a slight smile on his lips.

"There isn't anything bad to say, sir."

"You know he walks a fine line, don't you, girl?"

"What do you mean, sir?"

"There isn't much separating loyalty from fanaticism. That's what I mean." The chief of doctors turned and walked away.

"Well, what got his back up!" Jersey demanded.

"What the hell's he talkin' about?"

"He's urging you all not to view me as anything other than a mortal man. The talk has sprung up again, Jersey."

"I heard it," she said.

Thermopolis was leaning up against a truck fender, Rosebud by his side. Both were silent, listening.

"But that don't mean I pay any attention to it," Jersey continued.

"You let me know if any Rebels start believing it," Ben said.

"Sure."

But Ben knew she was lying. He faced this same problem every two or three years, when the talk sprang up about him being more than a mortal man; somehow blessed by some higher deity. And Ben tried to squash the talk as soon as it surfaced.

"All right, Jersey." Ben smiled and walked off, over to where Thermopolis stood. "Have you heard the talk, Therm?"

"For years. You know, Ben, that Jersey would willingly die for you." It was a statement, not a question.

"Yes. I know."

"It doesn't bother you?"

"It bothers me. I try to fight it. If you ever hear the talk, try to get it through to them that I am not some sort of god, or blessed by some higher power."

Thermopolis laughed. "Oh, I've been doing that for years, Ben. The god business, that is. Blessed by some higher power? I don't know about that. God gave some damn strange characters a lot of power back when He was taking a more direct hand in earth matters."

Ben laughed. "Now, Therm, I really don't know how to take that. Are you saying I'm strange?"

"You were a writer, weren't you? I never knew a writer in my life — and I have known a few — who wasn't at least a little bit off the wall."

Ben couldn't argue that. "Therm, I am not blessed

215

by God. I am just a man who managed to put together an army—no, that's not even right. The army came to me. I avoided taking command for a long time and fought like hell when it was shoved on me. I am just a man."

Thermopolis smiled and patted him on the arm. "Sure, Ben. Right."


Buddy left in the wee hours of the morning and was a few miles from the holding pens several hours before dawn. The job that lay ahead of them was one of the most gut-wrenching of all the many missions a Rebel could be sent on and Buddy was not looking forward to it.

But one of the many reasons the Rebels idolized Ben was that he would be right in there with them, in any type of mission—including this one. And Buddy knew his father was much more deeply affected by the sight of these unfortunate people—chosen by the creepies to be eaten—than most Rebels realized.

Buddy and his team, backed by Dusters, waited for dawn to cut the sky.

As gray fingers touched the horizon and began streaking the land with lances of silver and gold, Buddy's radio popped.

"Lead the assault, Rat," his father's calm voice came out of the speaker. "And try not to get your ass shot off. Your sister worries about you."

With a laugh that broke the tension, Buddy waved his teams forward and within minutes the breeding farm and holding pens came into view.

Two Dusters, buttoned down as tightly as they could be, and rolling side by side, crashed through the gates and assumed a defensive posture, back to back, allowing Buddy and his Rat Teams to use them for protection against unfriendly fire.

Creepies came screaming out of the barracks, firing automatic weapons. The 40mm cannon fire turned them into quivering, bloody chunks as Buddy and his team raced toward the holding pens and the huge barnlike breeding area.

Ben and his people busted onto the scene moments after the Dusters had rammed through. Ben left the wagon before Cooper got it to a full stop and was running for what looked to be an office building of some sort, Jersey, Corrie, and Jerre right behind him. Ben threw himself at the closed door and crashed inside, rolling on the floor and coming up with his old Thunder Lizard banging and barking and biting.

He stitched three robed and stinking creepies in the belly, chest, and head as the M-14 rose up in his hands on full auto. The head of the last creepie exploded as the slugs impacted with flesh and bone and brain, splattering the wall behind him with gore.

Jersey, Jerre, and Corrie cleared the adjoining office of cannibals with automatic rifle fire and Beth tossed in a grenade for good luck.

They all came very close to losing their breakfast at what greeted them behind a closed door. Obviously the creepies had been having breakfast when Buddy's team hit the gates.

What was left of a young girl was lying on a table. The child had been carved on by the creepies.

They were all stunned into silence when the child opened her eyes and murmured, "Help me, please!" The plea was just audible.

Jersey crossed herself and muttered a prayer, joining in the astonishment silently written on everyone's face that anyone could be alive after losing so much blood and after having so much flesh carved from her. One of the creepies had just split her open, probably to get at her heart when the attack came.

Ben looked at Jerre. "Is there any chance at all she could make it?"

She shook her head. "No way, Ben. None at all."

Chase pushed through the crowd, took one look at the child, and turned to Ben. "Finish her, Ben. For the love of God, put her out of her misery."

Ben's hand dropped to the butt of his .45, carried cocked and locked. He hesitated.

"Ben," Chase said, "the medics are fifteen minutes behind. The damn truck broke down. I don't have anything with me to do the job."

The girl began screaming, the terrible pain ripping through her ravaged body.

"Goddamnit, Ben!" Chase yelled. "Shoot her!"

Ben jerked out his .45, placed the muzzle close to the child's head, and muttered, "May God have mercy on my soul."

He pulled the trigger, ending the child's agony. Ben holstered the weapon and walked outside.

Beth had gone outside to find a clean blanket to cover the ravaged body. She paused at the sight of Ben, kneeling between the buildings, his hands covering his face. He was alone, and crying.

# Chapter 7

The Rebels avoided Ben the rest of that morning, for they all knew that hell on earth was about to break loose. They got a small reminder of how enraged Ben was when he ordered a dozen creepie prisoners into a wooden shed.

"Douse it with gas and set it on fire," he ordered. "Any troop who shoots an escaping creepie to put him or her out of their misery will face a court-martial."

The building went up with a roar. The screaming of the burning creepies could be clearly heard over the howling flames. Several broke out of the inferno, running balls of fire. They fell on the ground and beat their hands and feet against the earth, howling out their misery.

The Rebels stood in silent lines, watching and listening. No one lifted a weapon to end the screaming. No one really wanted to.

The unmistakable and unforgettable smell of charred human flesh clung close to the earth. The day had turned out gloomy and overcast, the threat of rain evident.

When the last echoes of the wailing had died out, Ben turned to Corrie. His inner rage was still burning out of control. "Bump all commanders. I want prisoners from all sectors. I want to know if any outlaws or warlords or whatever those lousy motherfuckers call themselves have been dealing with the Night People."

"Yes, sir!" She got the hell gone from that area in a hurry.

The Rebels looked at one another, each man and

woman knowing that things were going to get very interesting, very quickly.

Leadfoot whispered to Axehandle. "The general is pissed."

"No kidding?" Axe returned the whisper. "I never would have guessed."

Wanda said, "I ain't never seen him this mad. Boy, he looks like the wrath of God, don't he?"

"That's plumb poetic, Wanda," Beerbelly said. "You ought to be the one to say something when we bury that poor little girl."

"The general's gonna bury her over yonder in the woods," Lamply said, pointing. "He asked me to pick out the spot and I found a real pretty place." He looked around the silent and stinking compound. "I hate these damn creepies, and anybody who does business with them. I figure the general is gonna go on a rampage now. We all think we seen action before. I got a hunch that we ain't seen nothin' yet."

That remark would soon prove to be a very great understatement.

Planes began landing at the secured airstrip and taking the survivors back to clean zones, most of them heading back to Base Camp One. Nearly all were in bad shape mentally. Some of the women had been held for years, used as breeders. Most of them were near total mental collapse.

Chase walked through a lightly falling mist, over to Ben, who was squatting under the low branches of a tree, sipping at a mug of coffee.

He waited until the sound of a plane taking off died away before speaking. "With this . . . shipment," the doctor said with a sigh, "our facilities at Base One will be strained to overflowing."

"We'll build more," Ben said, without looking up.

"We are desperately short of qualified doctors."

"That is your department. Mine is war."

"I don't need you to tell me what my job entails!" the doctor snapped. "I've been doing it for a good

220

many years."

Ben stood up, the weight of command heavy on him. "Lamar, I can't snap my fingers and produce psychologists and psychiatrists out of the air. On the other hand, I can't just turn these . . . survivors loose to fend for themselves. They wouldn't last twenty-four hours. All we can do is give them a secure place to live, with adequate food and clothing, and try to mend their minds as we get to them. If we have to jack down the more unruly ones with Thorazine to keep them stable, that's still better than what they had. Our success rate with these types is not good, but it's all we can do with what we have. Ol' buddy, I know how thin we are, and we're going to get thinner before it starts turning around." He paused as the last planeload of survivors took off. "Get your people rounded up, we're pulling out."

Ben walked away from the doctor and over to the bikers. "Leadfoot, you spearhead up I-Fifteen. Dusters will be behind you so don't try to break any speed records. I'll be coming up behind the tanks with the people here, while the rest of the battalion takes on Pocatello from the north. Shoot any creepie on sight. No pity, no mercy, no prisoners. Take off and stay in radio contact." Ben walked off, hollering for his team to gather around him.

"I told you it was gonna get busy around here," Lamply said.

Leadfoot checked his Uzi and the grenades hooked onto his battle harness. "Let's go, boys and girls. And keep in your mind the picture of that little girl we just buried. That'll make the job a whole lot easier."

The bikers hit a manned roadblock at what was left of a tiny hamlet just off I-15. The bikers smashed through and destroyed the creepies before the Dusters could even get to the scene. The bikers were piling up the bodies and pouring gasoline on their stinking carcasses just as Ben rolled up and got out.

He stood for a moment, surveying the scene. "Good

work," he complimented them. "Take any hits?"

"Sonny took a round through the leg," Leadfoot said. "He's over yonder gettin' patched up. Wanda got her Hog shot out from under her and busted her ass. Didn't hurt the Hog none. We killed forty creepies."

Ben nodded. "You feel like continuing the spear-heading?"

A wicked look sprang into the biker's eyes. "I wanna be the first one to ride into Pocatello and stick the muzzle of an Uzi up a creepie's ass, General."

Ben smiled at the Rebel-biker. "We'll follow you, Leadfoot."

The light mist was still falling as the bikers roared out, heading north up the Interstate. They hit no more roadblocks and pulled over two miles south of the silent city.

"Our people are in place north of the city," Corrie informed Ben. "Gunners have the coordinates and are ready for your orders."

"Have our troops spread out along the west side of the Portneuf River and the northwest side of the Snake," Ben said. "Heavy machine gun emplacements at all crossings. Let me know when that has been completed," he got out of the wagon and walked up the old Highway to where the bikers were sitting by their Hogs.

"We'll have our gunners soften up the city for us," he told them. "Then we'll personally go in and finish off any who survive the bombardment."

"Sounds good to me," Wanda said.

"What's the other battalions doin', General?" Beer-belly asked.

"Waiting for us. I told them all to hold what they've got. We'll overwhelm these bastards by sheer force."

Ben chatted with the bikers until Corrie got word to him that all troops were in position and machine gun emplacements set up.

"Commence firing," Ben ordered.

The area between the Portneuf River and I-15

erupted in flames as the tanks and self-propelled artillery began pounding it with HE, WP, and napalm. Scouts soon reported they had taken the airport, located just off I-86, and were busy clearing a runway for the resupply planes to use.

Three hours after the bombardment started, planes were landing at the field.

"He sure cuts it close, don't he?" Wanda remarked. "Damn city is under siege and he's orderin' planes in through the smoke. Them pilots must have ice water for blood."

"Cease fire," Ben ordered. "Let's go in, people."

What wasn't lying in ruins was burning and those creepies who survived the intense shelling were running for their lives. They ran straight into the guns of the advancing Rebels.

The advancing Rebels were savage in their seeking out and destroying of the cannibals. Tank commanders deliberately ran down many they could have much more easily shot, crushing the Night People under the treads. And all over the state, the outlaws and warlords listened to the reports coming out of the ravaged city with fear touching them with a cold hand. This was not like any battle they had ever fought. The Rebels were fighting with dark revenge in their hearts.

A small percentage of the men and women under the command of the thugs, outlaws, and warlords tried to leave. They soon found themselves looking into the cold eyes of Rebels who had gone in search of prisoners to interrogate.

And they found out the hard way that Ben Raines's Rebels got what they wanted from prisoners . . . easy or hard, it didn't make them the slightest bit of difference. One could be treated decently and speak into a mic while the PSE machines picked up on stress points in their voice, or if one was hostile and uncooperative, the other option was to be pumped full of truth serums and the information gotten that way.

Those who confessed to having direct dealings with the creepies over the years were promptly taken out and shot or hanged, depending on the mood of the Rebels who took them.

"The leader of the Starlighters is squalling on the horn," Corrie told Ben. "He wants to make a deal with us."

"What does the voice analysis show?"

"That he's lying through his teeth about never dealing with the creepies."

"Advise him that the only deal he's going to get from me is either a rope or a bullet. I don't make deals with crud."

Francis really started squalling when he heard that.

"We had to survive!" the leader of the Bloody Bandits hollered over the air. "We had to make deals with them. They outnumber us."

And on and on and so forth came the pleas from all around the state. Except for the outlaw leader in the interior of the state. And Ben was curious about that.

"Bump him," Ben ordered, just after the evening meal. The fires in the city still raged with only an occasional gunshot now. The Rebels were bivouacked in and around what was left of the small town of American Falls. "Let's find out who he is and what he represents."

It didn't take long for Ben to learn all he needed to know about Red Manlovich.

"I ain't no cannibal and I never dealt with them, Raines," Red radioed. "But I hate your ass as much as I do them cannibals down south."

"Why?" Ben asked.

"Bunches of reasons. You're a damn nigger-lover for one reason. And you got too goddamn many rules for me to live with."

"We have far less rules and regulations than the government had before us. And as far as my bending over backward for people of other races, you're wrong. There are plenty of blacks and Hispanics and people

224

of other races who despise me."

"Good for them. If I ever run up on one I'll shake his hand before I kill him."

Ben shook his head at Corrie. "He's hopeless. In his own way, he's as bad as the creepies." Ben lifted the mic. "Surrender now, Manlovich, and there is a good chance you'll live. Fight us, and you'll die."

"Then come and get me, Raines," was the shouted defiant reply.

"I certainly shall," Ben told him, then added, "Asshole." He handed the mic back to Corrie, who was laughing at the expression on Ben's face. "We take the next stretch of the Interstate in the morning. Get me a fix on Ike's position."

She got Ike's communication truck and handed the mic to Ben just as Ike was patched through.

"How's it goin', Ben?"

"Pocatello is gone and so are a lot of creepies. What's your position, Ike?"

"About thirty-five miles outside of Mountain Home. To the northeast."

"Take it in the morning, Ike. I'm pushing off at dawn, heading in your direction."

"That's ten-four, Ben. Consider it done. Where do you want to link up?"

"Twin Falls."

"See you there, ol' buddy. Shark out."

"Patch me through to Dan, Corrie."

"Good evening, General," Dan's voice came through the speaker.

Ben smiled at the ever-formal Englishman's greeting. "What is your position, Dan?"

"Shoshone. We hit a few pockets of resistance today, and neutralized them. Trash, mostly. All bluster with nothing to back it up. However, we do have some children with us that need to be flown out ASAP."

"That's ten-four, Dan. We'll try to keep the airport at Twin Falls intact. Right now, I want you to start throwing up a line between Shoshone west to the Interstate, Dan. Block all exit points north. I don't want these people to have any opportunity to link up with those outlaws in the north."

"How about south?"

"Negative. We don't have the people to plug all the holes. If they run into Nevada, we'll deal with them later. I've ordered all units north of us to hold what they've got. As soon as the southern part is clear, we'll turn and head north, clearing as we go."

"That's ten-four, General."

"Eagle out." He looked at Corrie. "Now bump Cecil, please."

Cec on the horn, Ben said, "Give me a position report, Cec."

"Twenty-five miles east of Lewiston, Ben. Rested and ready to go."

"Let them sweat awhile, Cec. Georgi has a plan to put them in a box."

"Affirmative, Ben."

Corrie got General Striganov on the horn. "Georgi, hold what you've got. Cec and West are doing the same. Put your plan into effect. If it works, I'm thinking this is not going to be much of a fight."

"Yes," the Russian agreed. "I think we can take them without losing a person."

"See you soon, Georgi." He turned to his immediate crew. "Get some rest, people. Tomorrow might get real busy."

# Chapter 8

With Leadfoot and his bikers again spearheading, Ben's column rolled out at dawn, heading west while Ike struck at the Bandits' position from the north. Ike hit Mountain Home on two fronts with main battle tanks punching the first hole through and crushed the resistance without losing a person or sustaining any wounded. The Bandits who survived ran east to link up with the Starlighters while the Hellraisers pulled out and headed west, to join them all at Twin Falls.

What'd you want to do with the town, Ben?" Ike radioed. "Or what's left of it I ought to say. Damn, but these people lived like hogs."

"Bring it down, Ike. I'm destroying as we go."

"That's ten-four, Ben. Putting the torch to it now."

"We're doomed!" Francis yelled. "If we stay, they'll wipe us out to a man."

"I hate to say it, but I agree with you," the leader of the Bloody Bandits said. "The first part anyways. You bein' a man is up for grabs. And we got nowhere to go but south."

"Look here," the leader of the Hellraisers said, pointing to the east. "Raines is burning Rupert and Burley."

Smoke was curving up into the skies, visible from fifty miles away.

"You know that savage Ike what's-his-name is doing the same west of us. So it's Nevada for us, people," Francis said. "We're packed up and ready to go."

But what they didn't know was that Ben had sent Buddy and his Rat Team out the night before, racing west over county roads to set up an ambush point on Highway 93, about twenty-five miles south of Twin Falls. And not telling any of the other commanders what he was doing. That was the only logical route for the bunched-up outlaws to take. Ben knew they wouldn't try for Utah, for they would not be welcome in that state.

The outlaws left the Twin Falls area very nearly in a blind panic. They had listened to radio reports and knew the rebels were closing in on them from three sides, burning everything in their path. And anybody who had dealt with the Night People could hang it up—the Rebels weren't taking any prisoners.

The outlaws pulled out in an assortment of cars, trucks, and motorcycles, leaving behind most of what they had stolen over the years. And rode right into death.

Buddy and his Rat Team had lined both sides of the highway with Claymores, set up machine gun emplacements, and then had taken turns resting for a few hours. With someone always on sentry duty.

Several miles north of the ambush site, Buddy had ordered an observation post set up, well off the road and concealed. The observation post radioed in as the outlaws roared past their position, fleeing Ben Raines and his Rebels.

Several hundred died during the first five seconds of the ambush, as Claymores unleashed their deadly barrage, literally blowing bikers out of the saddle, shredding flesh and breaking bones and slamming bits and pieces of outlaws all over the road.

The car Francis was riding in was riddled with machine gun fire and the gas tank exploded, cooking any left alive after the machine gun fire. They screamed in agony for only a few seconds.

The leader of the Bloody Bandits lived long enough to see his little empire literally blow up before his eyes as his driver's head exploded from .50-caliber machine gun bullets, splattering him with brains. He rolled out of the car and stood for a second, wiping the gore from him. He turned his head and looked straight at a Claymore placed by the side of the road.

"No!" he managed to say, holding out his hands. "Gimmie a break. I'll join up with you boys." Then the Claymore blew and splattered him all over the other side of the highway.

The Rebels continued spraying the bloody and burning ambush site for another full minute, all their weapons set on full rock and roll.

Buddy called for a cease-fire.

The Rebels surfaced from both sides of the road, to stand or squat, leaning against their rifles, as they looked down at the body-littered highway.

"So much for that shit," a Rat Team member summed it all up.

"They're some alive," a medic called. "What do you want to do with them?"

"Nothing," Buddy said, his eyes as cold as the eyes of his father. "They had a choice. They just chose the wrong one. Let's go."


Ben, Ike, and Dan joined forces on the western edge of Twin Falls. Behind them, the city was burning.

"Buddy reports the ambush was a success," Corrie said. "His ETA is one hour."

"We'll wait until he joins us before pulling out," Ben said. "We've got to wait for the birds to fly these kids out, anyway." He lifted a map. "Dan, the breeding farm of the creepies is located just north of the Snake River. Right here." He laid a finger on the spot and grimaced. "You cut off of the Interstate here and neutralize that obscenity."

"Right, sir. With pleasure."

"Beth, have trucks and medics waiting to go in at

229

Dan's signal."

"Yes, sir."

"We'll secure the airport at Boise first and fly out any survivors from the farm from there. Now then, this Ted Ashworth and his bunch are putting up a fairly stiff fight against Cecil and West; but Cec says the area should be secured by late afternoon. We'll hit the Boise/Nampa/Caldwell area at dawn. Start moving the artillery out now."

Villar, Khamsin, Ashley, Kenny Parr, and the bikers had found transportation and headed east out of Montana. At an old military base in North Dakota, they found a huge underground warehouse filled with field rations, cold weather clothing, and ammunition.

The terrorists were back in business.

After studying a map, Villar called the men together. "We're going to take the southern route. I don't see where we have any choice in the matter. We can't cut across Canada to get to Alaska. The Russian, Striganov, has people who would report us immediately. If we try to cut straight west from here, we're going to run right into Ben Raines. So we'll cut south and work our way west, avoiding the Rebel outposts. Just north of the panhandle of Texas, we'll cut west. We've got to stay north of those secure zones in New Mexico and avoid the outposts in Arizona. After that, we're home free. L.A. is hot with radiation; one of the few places that really did get hit, I think, so we damn sure have to avoid that. Once we hit California, we cut north and keep going."

"Lan," Kenny Parr said. "What in the hell are we going to *do* in Alaska?"

"Rebuild our armies. Don't worry, we'll find people up there who will be willing to join us. The place is teeming with outlaws. The trick is to pull them all together. And that's very easily done. I know; I did it all over Europe."

"And it will give us a couple of years of freedom from that goddamned Ben Raines," Ashley said.

"Exactly," Lan agreed. "We can also use the time to build up artillery and tanks. There were several military posts up there that Raines's people didn't get to. We'll get to them and get that equipment in shape."

"And then?" Khamsin asked.

"We return to the lower forty-eight and kick the snot out of Ben Raines and his Rebels."

"It's time for us to haul our asses outta here," Red Manlovich told his people. "We've had a good thing goin' for a good many years. Now it's over. Thanks to that goddamned Ben Raines."

"Pull out to where?" Red was asked. "There ain't no place safe no more."

"Yeah," another said. "Utah sure ain't safe. Them goddamn Mormons is worser than Ben Raines."

*Nobody* is as bad as Raines," Red said. "That ain't possible. We'll just slide on over into Oregon and work our way up to Alaska. Ever'body I've talked to says Raines ain't interested in Alaska. So I reckon that's where we'll head. Pack it up, boys. We're gettin' gone from this place."

"How?" he was asked. "Them damn Rebels done sealed off ever' damn road all around us."

"All the main roads, Jackie. The main roads. But we know roads them bastards don't even know exist. It'll take us awhile, but we'll get out. We just got to be careful and take our time. Let's do it."

"Go," Ben gave the orders.

The airport had been cleared and the big guns began roaring, sending their lethal loads crashing and roaring into Boise. A light rain was falling as the artillery opened up.

Trapped inside the city, the Night People cursed

Ben Raines; they were unable to do much else, for Ben did not commit troops when he could use artillery to destroy an enemy.

The savage bombardment ripped the morning as Ben gave the creepies all the fury he could muster from every gun at his disposal. Stretched out along the Interstate, the guns of Ben Raines soon had the downtown area flaming as Willie Peter and Napalm turned the buildings into infernos, driving the creepies into the street, where antipersonnel shells exploded and ripped their flesh with shrapnel.

The Rebels had the battle plan worked out to perfection; none of them had to be told their jobs. All around the besieged city the Rebels had set up ambush and sniper points and machine gun emplacements. The creepies had no place to run except straight into the outstretched arms of death.

Ben ordered his people in closer, working the shattered, smoking, and oftentimes still burning streets like a grid, flushing out those creepies who thought they could hide and be safe from the guns of the Rebels. Most were wrong in that thinking.

The Rebels hunted them down ruthlessly and killed them without pity or remorse. The Godless cannibals did not cry out for help as they lay wounded. They knew better. For the Rebels would not show them one morsel of compassion. The only soothing balm the creepies could expect from Ben Raines's Rebels was a bullet to the head. And any wounded creepie the Rebels came up on got just that.

The creepies' last act of desperation came when they tried to make a deal with Ben.

"Let us go and we'll tell you the locations of all our breeding farms and holding pens around the nation," a Judge radioed from the burning city.

Ben's eyes were killing cold as he listened to the message being repeated. He smiled at Corrie. "Tell the gunners to cease firing."

Boise fell eerily silent as Ben consulted a map.

232

"Are you accepting our offer?" a Judge radioed.

"Tell him I'm thinking about it," Ben said. "And to shut up until he hears from me."

The message was related.

"Get voice-stress equipment up here," Ben ordered. "And a qualified operator with it."

When the equipment was in place, Ben said, "Get the bastard on the horn."

"Yes, General Raines?" the Judge spoke.

"Go to CB equipment," Ben told him. "I would imagine you don't want your fellow Night People around the country to know what you're doing, right?"

"That is correct, sir."

Low power CB's were hooked up.

"If I think your information is valid," Ben radioed, "I'll let you walk. You and your . . . people will use Capitol and Americana to cross the river and get out. Those will be your only exits. Is that clear?"

"Yes, General."

Ben turned to Buddy. "Set up machine gun emplacements at the intersections along Crescent Rim Drive. Go!" Ben looked at Corrie. "Tell the bastard to start talking and record all this."

After a moment, the PSE operator nodded his head. "He's telling the truth, General."

"That's nice. Very cooperative fellow. It's refreshing to meet someone who keeps his word."

Jersey and the others laughed. They knew Ben wasn't about to let the creepies go free.

"Every city in Washington seems to be full of the bastards," Ben said. "Goddamnit, we were led to believe that the Seattle area took a nuke. Now we're learning that it's clean. Did *any* area take a hot strike in the Great War?"

"Kansas City and the Washington/Baltimore area are the only ones that have been confirmed," Jerre said. "Now I'm curious about Europe."

"So am I. Even the areas we've avoided because the government threw up Hot Zone warnings are beginning to intrigue me. To declare L.A. hot would be one way to keep any people out, wouldn't it? Oh, shit, if what I'm thinking is true . . ." But he would not say his thoughts aloud.

"What do you mean, General?" Cooper asked.

Ben was silent for a moment before sharing part of his thoughts. "I think that goddamned general at Shaw AFB lied to me years back. He told me . . . no, he didn't," Ben muttered. "He just implied that many cities had been hit. The government lied to the people. Deliberately lied." He laughed bitterly. "Hell, what else is new? Kansas City is hot; that's a fact. We know that. And we know that Washington is hot. But everything else is *clean!*"

Ben turned and put his hands on Jerre's shoulders, gripping them hard. It was the first time he had physically touched her in a long time, other than tossing her to one side during an ambush. "Do you know what this news means?"

"Ben, you're hurting my shoulders! Ease up, please."

He laughed and let up on the pressure. "Sorry, kid."

"What does it mean, Ben?"

"It means . . . there was a massive cover-up, but one within a cover-up. President Hilton Logan was fed misinformation, and he took the bait."

"Fed it by whom, and why?" she questioned. "Who would do it. It would have to be someone very close to the man, right?"

"Probably. And certainly someone who shared the beliefs of the Night People. We've learned that the creepie movement is about fifty years old. That's a fact. So that means that probably people in congress were actually closet-cannibals; practicing this . . . bizarre religion while they were supposed to be representing the people. Not only here, in America, but all around the world."

"General," Jersey said. "That means . . ." She trailed it off.

"Yes. It was a hoax. A massive, sick, and very ugly hoax on the part of our leaders; leaders from all around the world. Corrie, radio Buddy and tell him to abort the ambush. Tell him that I want these people alive. I want every shred of information they've got stored in their heads."

"Ten-four, sir."

Dan had returned from the rescuing of the men and women and children at the breeding farm. He had heard Ben talking and hypostatizing. And the news had shaken even his usually calm demeanor.

"They were neutron bombs, General. Not hot, but clean. Destroy the people, but not the cities. Maybe a half dozen very limited nukes were detonated around the world. Only two here in the States."

"Yes, Dan. That's what I'm thinking. L.A., Seattle, Miami, those cities were hit by clean bombs; very low level strikes. Then the creepies surfaced and moved in. What an ugly, profane joke to play on the decent peoples of the world."

"London, Paris, Berlin, Madrid, Dublin, Geneva, Moscow," Doctor Chase muttered. "All the great old cities of the world and the huge cities in America. They're still standing."

"Yes," Ben said. "Havens for Night People. That was the plan all along. And we bought it. All of us. We were so accustomed to Big Brother's slop from the mouth, we all bought it. Hell, we didn't even question it! That was why the relocation plan went into effect. To hide the truth from the people. And I'll bet you all every damn country around the globe did the same thing. It was an international hoax."

"Ben," Jerre said softly. "If that is true, and I suspect it is, that means there are, at the most, eight or ten thousand of us, and *millions* of Night People around the globe."

"Yes. Hundreds of thousands of them right here in good ol' America. That's why we don't see many survivors. That's why those still alive are afraid to approach us. They don't know what side we're on."

"What do you mean, Ben?" Chase asked.

"The creepies are constantly working the country-side, rounding up people."

"At night," Dan added. "Probably always working at night."

"General," Beth said. "Those uniforms we found in New York City. The creepies are wearing uniforms just like ours."

"Yes. Telling the people they're Rebels and then when they've won their trust, they grab them."

"To eat," Dan finished it.

# Chapter 9

"You tricked me," the Judge said, staring balefully at Ben. "I was told you were not a man of your word."

"I'm fighting a war, whatever-your-name-is. Not running the Boy Scouts. But I'm curious as to who told you that."

The Judge did not miss the very obvious fact that Ben was pulling on thick leather gloves although the day was warm and it didn't appear very likely that General Raines was preparing to go work in a garden or change a flat tire on a vehicle. The Judge had a pretty good idea that what was going to happen was Ben beating the shit out of him if he didn't tell the truth.

"We don't have to resort to violence, General. I'll tell you."

"I'm waiting."

"It's doubtful you will remember him. He was a man who tried to live in your old Tri-States but simply could not abide by the rules."

"Name?"

"I . . . think his name was Peter something. He is dead."

"By your hand."

"Yes."

"And then you had him for dinner."

"Lunch, actually."

Ben suppressed a shudder at the man's cold reply. He was not trying to make a joke. He was deadly serious. "Where did this . . . movement, this religion of yours have its beginning?"

"I was told it began in the forties. Before I was born. I suspect it began long before that. But its roots are in California."

A light sprang into Ben's.

"Yes," the Judge said, seeing the glimmer of understanding in Ben's eyes. "Los Angeles."

"Pieces of the puzzle are beginning to fall into place. I had guessed L.A. Go on."

"By the mid to late 1960s, many were groping for something to believe in. They came to us. Already the group was big and growing larger very rapidly. It was inevitable that people of power would join."

Ben nodded his head. Everything was falling into place. And he had guessed very accurately. "Give me some names and positions of people in power."

"Names are unimportant now, are they not?" the Judge asked. "Most are dead. We had United States senators and representatives among us. Police chiefs and sheriffs. Military people. Mayors and city council members. State senators and representatives. Millionaires and paupers. Housewives and CEO's. Young and old."

"How did you get them in? Nobody in their right mind would willingly accept such a life as yours."

The Judge smiled at the slur. "General, we are now in our third generation of Believers."

"Believers?"

"You call us the Night People. A misnomer. We are the Believers."

"Go on."

"Drugs, General. It's easy to find recruits among those hooked on drugs. And easier still to keep them."

"You bastards! You people controlled the flow of drugs into America."

"Oh, not just America, General. The world. Certainly, we did. And still do, to a large degree."

Ben recalled back in the Midwest; the woman telling him about drugs, and something dark stirred in his mind.

238

"You people are not just in the cities, are you?"

"No. That is something you people dreamed up, General, and we let the myth continue. We are in cities and hamlets. Urban and rural."

"Everywhere."

The Judge nodded his head.

"Miami?"

"Alive and doing very well."

"I've sent fly-bys over that city! The pilots reported a dead city. Destroyed."

"It appears that way only during the day, General. Not at night. Parts of that city, and others thought to be hot, have been destroyed. But only small parts of them. You yourself concluded years back that few nuclear bombs were used in the Great War; that most were germ and neutron. You were right."

"And how I wish I wasn't."

"You won't win, General. You have made small gains, yes. But you can't win in the long run. We are too many and growing."

"Yeah," Ben said, disgust thick in his voice. "By feeding off the population."

The Judge shrugged. "It is our way of life and we are entitled to it."

"Are you saying you have a *right* to eat other people!"

"Of course. We don't subscribe to your silly concept of God and Jesus and life after death and all the rest of that absurd bullshit. This is all there is, General. When one is dead, one is dead. Period. The only rules one must follow are the ones he or she believe in."

"The Believers."

"Precisely."

"Obviously you and your followers don't believe in it too strongly, or you wouldn't have offered me the deal you did."

"Let's just say I'm flexible."

Ben stared at the cannibal and the man stared back, no fear in him. He pointed to the equipment and to the mic in front of the Judge. "You know we can tell if you are lying or telling the truth."

"I am aware of that."

"Your answer to the next question I ask will determine if you live or die. Be aware of that."

For the first time, Ben saw a flicker of fear dance across the man's eyes. "All right, General. I fully understand."

"You'd damn well better understand," Ben warned. "If I cut you loose, will you return to the ways of the Believers? Yes or no."

"I cannot answer that question."

"Why?"

"I must have time to think on it. You're asking me to change a life-style that I have practiced virtually all my life."

"A life-style that is wrong, damnit!"

"I was taught that it was right."

"You cannot believe that the eating of human flesh is in any way right."

"But I do."

"Is that your answer."

"I will not change, General."

"That's firm?"

"That is firm."

Ben looked at the man and shook his head. "You just signed your own death warrant."


Ben and the Rebels waited until the area had burned down to the point where it presented no danger of spreading before pulling out. He then ordered all troops in the southern part of the state to begin working their way north. Search and destroy.

Some of the buoyancy had gone from the Rebels after hearing of the massive numbers of Believers still alive, not just in America, but around the world. But the missing buoyancy was quickly replaced by a feeling of determination and resolve. All right, so the battle isn't very nearly over, as we thought. We'll just keep on fighting until we win, was the single thought in Rebel minds. The thugs and outlaws and punks and creepies are wrong, we're right, and with the help of God, we'll win.

So let's go!

The Rebels never missed a bet on their move up north. They checked out every road, paved, gravel, dirt, or grass — if it looked as though it had been recently traveled — all the way to trail's end. And in doing so, they made some thugs and outlaws who thought they were safe very unhappy for a moment, and very dead for a long time.

Ben had taken his contingent north by Route 95, while Ike had taken Highway 55 which connected with 95 at New Meadows. Ben would send troops checking out county roads to the east while Ike sent troops to the west. Five and Six Battalions had already cleared everything in their sector along Highway 93. They had backtracked into Montana and picked up Highway 473, which ran west for a few miles before turning into an unimproved road, which eventually and very slowly, would take them to Highway 14 at Elk City.

Ted Ashworth had seen the writing on the wall and had packed up and pulled out of Lewiston, slipping across the border into Washington and taking his outlaws with him. Ted wanted no part of Ben Raines and his Rebels.

North of him, Larry Rafford had different thoughts, those thoughts brought on with a slick and quiet maneuver from General Striganov.

"Goddamn Russian bastard!" Rafford cursed, after his patrols west out of the city came staggering back in, all shot to hell and gone.

Georgi, with time on his hands and nothing to do except wait for Ben to push north, had sent the troops under the command of Rebet and Danjou first west into Washington, and then south down to between Spokane and Coeur d'Alene, seal⋅ off any escape by

241

Rafford.

Danjou's men had blocked all exits west from the Washington state side, while Rebet had placed his troops in a defensive line against possible attack from the creepies in Spokane.

Larry Rafford's arrogance had sealed his fate.

Ben cut off Highway 95 and took a rutted old county road west, which finally changed to blacktop, and came up under Lewiston from the south. Ike took his troops on up 95, crossed the river, and pulled up on the east side of Lewiston.

On their way in, they had been met by several hundred men and women, who had been forced by the outlaws to work on farms, producing food for the punks and various other crud. With the advance of Ben's Rebels, the outlaws had fled the countryside, heading for Lewiston, leaving the now freed prisoners to fend for themselves.

Most of them bore both old and new scars on their backs from the frequent use of whips, their captors trying to get more work out of them than was humanly possible.

"Nice folks that we'll be facing in the city," Ben observed. "Real salt-of-the-earth types."

"How big was this place, General?" Cooper asked. "Back when."

"About thirty thousand. It won't take long to bring it down. Corrie, is everybody in place?"

"That's ten-four, sir."

"We'll strike at dawn. I want those sorry bastards in there to sweat some."


They were doing more than sweating inside the small city.

"Well, I ain't never dealt with none of them cannibals!" an outlaw who had just come in from the interior yelled at the leader of the outlaws who had taken refuge in the town. "And by God, I'll surrender if I

242

want to, and I *want* to!"

"You're part of my bunch now, Dick," Jenkins told him. "When I took you and your boys in, you swore loyalty to me, and by God, you'll damn well keep your word."

"Screw you, Jenkins! I'm callin' it quits. Man, it's a damn death trap in here."

"It's a death trap out there, you fool!" The outlaw waved his hand. "Raines will never believe you didn't deal with the creepies. Besides, you've heard them talkin' on the radios. They're deliberately talking on an open frequency so we can hear. Anyone who kept forced labor is to be dealt with the same as those who helped the creepies. And that's you, Dick. You! Think about that. I'm not going to be put up against a wall and shot. I'm going to die on my feet fighting that son of a bitch Ben Raines. And if you got any balls, you'll do the same."

"Yeah, yeah, Jenkins. I know how tough you are and all that happy crap. But if you think Raines is going to send troops in here to fight us, you' re crazy as a road lizard. All he's going to do is sit out yonder and blow us all to hell and gone with artillery; just like he's done all over the damn state. What's so glorious about dyin' like that, huh?"

"It beats bein' put up against a wall, Dick. Not by much, I'll admit. But some." He shook his head. "There just ain't no stoppin' the man."

Dick turned to leave the room.

"Where the hell are you goin'?" Jenkins shouted.

Dick slowly turned around. "To make my peace with God, pal; if He'll listen to me. 'Cause this time tomorrow, we all gonna be dead."

# Chapter 10

The Rebels waited for the signal to destroy the town. They had rolled out of their bedrolls long before dawn, eaten breakfast, and cleaned their weapons. Now they waited.

The gunners manning the artillery drank coffee, relaxed, gossiped, and waited for the general's signal.

Ben turned to Corrie, standing beside him, wearing a headset. "Everybody in place?"

"Yes, sir. All exits blocked."

"Let's get it over with then. Bring the city down, Corrie."

The earth trembled as the big guns unleashed their destructive fury against the outlaws and thugs trapped inside the town.

Fifty shells, most of the warheads containing HE charges, struck the town. The second barrage from the guns with that capability was napalm, and the third was Willie Peter. Ben kept up a steady barrage for one hour then ordered the gunners to stand down.

"Take the point, Buddy," Ben said, after pulling the plugs from his ears. "Find out if there are still any snakes wriggling in the pit."

"Prisoners, Father?" the young man questioned.

Ben cut his eyes to his son. "No," he said flatly.

What was left of the town was put to the torch while Georgi and his men moved against those troops still massed around Coeur d'Alene. Many had

244

fled Rafford's command, running off in small groups. Some made a successful escape. Most did not. The Russian was just as ruthless as Ben and by mid-afternoon, the small city was rapidly becoming no more than a fading memory as the afternoon skies filled with greasy smoke.

Ben and Ike had pulled their columns up 95, clearing towns as they advanced north. They stopped at the junction of 95 and 5 and waited for word from Georgi.

"The town is finished," Striganov radioed. "I just hanged Larry Rafford."

"That's ten-four, Georgi," Ben told him. "Hold what you've got until I get there. Spokane is not going to be an easy ride." He turned to Buddy. "Take the bikers and work your way around to come up on the city from the west. Check out this old Air Force base. Secure anything we might be able to use and wait there. Work your way in close to Spokane but do not enter the city unless you get orders from me. Draw supplies and take off."

At the time of the Great War, Spokane was a nice-size city, with a population of nearly two hundred thousand. It had colleges, a university, museum, and an international airport.

"We can expect a lot of creepies in this city," Ben spoke to Ike. "And they're very heavily armed. The Judge told me that they keep their breeding pens and food factories inside the city, so standing back and destroying it is out. We're going to have to take it nose to nose with the uglies."

"Be like old times," Ike said with a smile. "Back when we knocked heads daily."

"Yeah. And you keep your big ass out of the line of fire. No heroics, Ike."

"Look who's tellin' someone to be careful," the Mississippi born and reared Ike said. "Talk about the pot callin' the kettle black!"

Ben ignored that. "Cross over the line and take your people up 195. Pull up about ten miles south of the city and bump me when you're in position."

"I'm gone," Ike said, tossing him a grin and a very sloppy salute.

Ben got Georgi on the horn. "Georgi, swing your people around and come down Highway Two, approaching the city from the north. Cec, you're going up Highway Twenty-seven. West, go in on Highway Fifty-three. Five and Six Battalions stay in reserve. I'll go straight in on the Interstate. Take off and get in place."

Ben got a mug of fresh coffee and wandered around, looking for Doctor Chase. He found him sitting under a shade tree. "Alert your people to expect a lot of wounded, Lamar."

"We going in nose to nose?"

"Yes. They're holding captives in there. We're going to have to take it block by block."

"Can you delay for a day?"

"Yes. Why?"

"That will give me time to get whole blood flown in here."

"Tell me when you're ready, Lamar."

"No, you tell me when you've got a toehold so I can set up a field hospital close in."

Ben laughed at him. "You're a hard-to-please and cantankerous old bastard, you know that?"

"Stick it up your kazoo, Raines!"


Ben walked through the busy camp, chatting with Rebels as he went, Jersey and Corrie shadows beside him.

"I better not find anyone without their body armor when we go in," he warned platoon leaders. "Or they'll be back in the mess tents washing dishes."

To Thermopolis: "You ever been to Spokane,

Therm?"

"No."

"You're about to get the scenic tour."

"Don't tell me if you've planned a welcoming party. I like surprises."

"We'll see in a day or two."

To Emil: "Ready to go, Emil?"

"Forward to victory, Great General Raines! We shall rid the land of the hordes of barbarians and restore America to its former greatness!"

"Right, Emil."

"We'll strike them down with a mighty sword and trample them under our boots."

"Don't get too carried away, Emil. Save your strength for the creepies."

"When I'm fighting on the side of righteousness, I feel I have the strength of ten men, the courage of an eagle, and the heart of a lion."

"One thing about it, Emil," Ben cut him off before he could really get wound up, "we have to pass right by Michelle's position."

Emil froze rock-still for a moment, his eyes glazing over at just the mention of her name. Back in New York, he had fallen ass over elbows in love with a French-Canadian lady named Michelle Jarnot, part of Danjou's troops. Sadly, his affection was not returned, and Emil had moped around for days.

"Oh, my Michelle!" he wailed. "How do I love thee? Let me count the ways."

While Emil was counting, Ben quick-stepped the hell away from that area.


Chase informed Ben that the whole blood had arrived and to get this goddamn campaign in high gear. Whole blood doesn't keep forever.

Ben had his people moving within the hour.

Dan's Scouts took the point. Ben bitched about it,

247

but he agreed to be stuck back with the tanks. Chase was bringing up the rear, with his mobile field hospital and doctors and nurses.

Buddy had radioed in that the old AF base was a mess, but he had uncovered some underground tunnels that looked very promising and had proved to be more than that. Thousands and thousands of cases of MREs and winter clothing encased in heavy plastic bags; just like new. M-16s and M-60s and ammo.

"Looks like we're set for a winter campaign," Ben had told the others. "And finding those MREs was a godsend. They might not be the tastiest meals around, but they damn sure beat the goop that Lamar dreamed up."

"Screw you, Raines!" the doctor had told him.

"Dan is reporting that none of the little towns approaching Spokane are inhabited," Corrie told Ben. "And no sign of creepies."

"Believers," Ben corrected her with a smile.

"They're creeps to me, General."

"Me, too," Ben admitted. "How far have the Scouts advanced?"

"To what is left of a town called Opportunity."

"Tell him to hold up there. Cooper, pass these tanks and put the pedal to the metal."

"Do what, sir?"

Ben smiled. "Sorry, Coop. You're a little young to remember that phrase. Just get us there."

"Yes, please do that," Jersey said. "How come the worst driver in the entire Rebel Army gets to be your driver, General?"

"Just lucky, I guess, Jersey."

"You're just jealous because I get to sit up front with the general," Cooper said with a grin, a wriggle and a bad lisp.

"You wanna trade places with me, Jersey?" Ben said quickly, looking over his shoulder.

"Hell, no!"

Cooper got them to Opportunity in one piece and slid to a halt by Dan's Jeep. There was nothing left of the town; every building had been gutted by fire. The only thing left standing was the road sign, and it had several bullet holes in it.

Every town they had passed since moving across the state line had looked the same. And all other units were reporting the same thing.

"Let's see if that Judge leveled with us," Ben said. "Beth, get a map with population figures and find every town that had a population of say, oh, seventeen thousand or more back before the war. We'll see if the creeps destroyed or ignored anything less than that when they settled in."

Ben studied maps while Beth got to work. It did not take her long.

"Twenty-nine, sir. Some of them with populations somewhat less than seventeen thousand—before the war. I've circled them on this map."

Ben looked at the map. "And ten to one that out-laws are working the interior of the state."

"No bet from me," Dan said, looking over Ben's shoulder. "Big state."

"Almost sixty-seven thousand square miles. And before the Great War it had a population of four and a half million." Ben shrugged. "Well, we've got about six hours of daylight left and we all know we have it to do, so let's get to it. Corrie, radio all units to begin the attack."


General Striganov's troops knocked open a hole coming down from the north and set up his CP at the old Whitworth College complex. He did not want to penetrate in too far and get trapped, so he pulled up there and waited.

Ike punched a hole big enough to get a toehold

and a route over to the Spokane International Airport and get it secured. He left it in the hands of Buddy and the Bikers and told them to start clearing a runway for the planes to land.

Cecil took his column and cut off of Highway 27 between Mica and Freeman onto a county road, coming up just south of Glenrose, about five miles east of Ike's position.

West had come in on Highway 290 and was just north of Ben's position, almost within shouting distance.

All units pushed off at Ben's signal and immediately ran into heavy fire from the creepies. The Judge had told Ben that after their defeat in New York City, the Believers had better armed themselves, knowing they were in a fight to the death with Ben and his Rebels.

And the Judge had not been wrong. The Rebels found themselves slugging it out with an enemy that was just as well-armed as they were, including heavy mortars and rocket launchers.

There was no doubt in Ben's mind that he was going to eventually take the city, but after several hours' fighting, he knew it was going to be a slow process. The creepies were not giving up an inch of ground without it being turned bloody before they backed up.

And by the approach of dusk, the creepies had backed up damn little.

The forces of West and Ben had advanced only to Argonne Road before they were stalled. Georgi held onto the Whitworth College complex, but only with an all-out effort from his people. Cecil had made it to the city limits and ran into a solid wall of resistance. Ike had punched through to High Drive Parkway and then was forced to back up because of a tried end-around from the creepies that threatened to cut him off.

Jerre found Ben on the floor of an old service station-turned CP, studying a map of the state. His personal team was scattered around the building, in defensive postures. She squatted down beside him.

"Grim, Ben."

"Yeah. Slick move on their part, pulling the prisoners inside the cities. Limits us and pulls us down to fighting their way."

"What's with the map?"

"If I was in the creepies' position, with help all around me, I'll pull something sneaky."

"Such as?"

"Just a guess. But we know that the Pullman area is filled with Believers. As is Walla Walla and the Kennewick/Pasco/Richland area. I'd pull reenforcements up from Pullman to attack Ike's position and people up from the tri-city area to come in from the west, on the Interstate, to attack Buddy and the bikers."

"Buddy wouldn't stand a chance."

"Yeah. And Ike would be put in one hell of a situation."

Ben waved Corrie over to him. "Get Five and Six Battalions on the move. Five will set up along Highway One-ninety-five at this little town of Spangle, while Six will move on over to the Interstate and set up ten miles from Buddy's position at the airport. Get them moving now. When that is done, get all commanders on the horn."

"Double the guards," Ben told his people, scattered all around the fringes of the city. "No fires, no smoking, and maintain noise discipline. They might decide to hit us tonight. Be ready for anything. Eagle out."

Ben and his team bedded down on the floor of the old service station, with Rebels on guard all around the outside of the building.

Ben suspected that the creepies would try a night

251

raid, and he was on the mark with that suspicion.

He sensed someone was about to touch him and came wide awake, looking up into the eyes of Jerre.

"They're coming, Ben," she whispered. "All sectors reporting creepies moving up."

"Get our people outside the garage inside," Ben said, pulling on and speed-lacing his boots. "Everybody up?"

"Just Corrie and me."

"Get them up, kid."

"Coffee's hot in the back room, Ben."

"Thanks." Ben picked up his M-14 and slipped into body armor and battle harness, then went into the back room and poured a cup of coffee that was as black as sin is purported to be and hot as hell.

But after several sips he was wide awake.

Jerre came into the room, the only light the dim illumination from the moon through a very dirty window. She poured a cup and leaned against the counter. "Sarah slipped into this sector last night. Doctor Chase said he was getting tired of her moping around and sighing and making goo-goo eyes in the direction of Colonel Gray."

Ben chuckled softly. "They're both smitten, that's for sure. In a way I'm glad for them."

"In a way?"

"The battlefield is a hell of a place for romance, Jerre. Dan is a professional; he's not going to let thoughts of a loved one interfere with the business at hand. Sarah, though, is another story."

"They're getting into position, General," Corrie called softly. "Two blocks in front of us. All field commanders are urging you to fall back and get into a safer CP."

"Tell all field commanders their concern touches me deeply. I'm staying right where I am."

"I'll get that message right out, General," Corrie said, laughing softly.

252

Both knew she would not send it.

"Gray coming in!" the call came from the darkness just as Ben got into position. "With company."

"Come on, Colonel," Cooper called.

Dan slipped in, pushing Sarah Bradford in front of him. "Sorry for the interruption, General," Dan said. "But I wanted to get Sarah to a more secure location before the creepies struck us."

"Perfectly understandable," Ben replied.

"Did I screw up?" Sarah asked, looking at Ben.

"Not really. People who are fond of each other like to be with each other. Human nature. But from here on in, I would suggest you stay with the hospital unit while we're in a combat situation. And Sarah," he smiled at her, "that isn't an order."

She returned the smile just as Ben's eyes caught silent and furtive movement across the street. "Down!" he yelled, and hurled himself against Jerre, putting both of them on the floor just as a light machine gun opened up from across the street.

Dan had done with Sarah the same as Ben with Jerre and the other Rebels had automatically hit the floor before Ben's yell had stopped echoing around the big room.

"Corrie!" Ben shouted, above the yammer of weapons, both Rebel and creepie. "Alert all commanders that we've been infiltrated and watch out for the same."

Sarah cut her questioning blue eyes from Ben and Jerre back to Dan.

"Later," Dan said, and rolled away from her. He jerked his walkie-talkie from a side pouch and keyed it. "Scout leader here. Are you infiltrated?"

"That's ten-four, Colonel," the Scout XO spoke calmly. "They're all around us."

"I shan't be rejoining you. I'll stay here with the general. Take command."

"Yes, sir."

253

Ben had bipodded his M-14 between piled-up bags of sand and dirt dug that afternoon and laid out a line of full clips to his right. "Berets off and helmets on," he ordered. "Pass it up and down the line, Corrie. Leave chin straps loosened to prevent concussion injury."

"Yes, sir."

"Dan, get a rocket launcher and neutralize that son of a bitch across the street, please."

"Right, sir." Dan scrambled across the concrete floor on hands and knees and grabbed a tube and rockets. He slipped out the back.

"All units have been infiltrated, sir," Corrie told him. "Five and Six Battalions reporting coming under heavy mortar fire."

"They're throwing it all at us tonight," Ben said. "It's going to be a long and noisy night."

The Rebels in the old service station stacked the creepies up in dead stinking piles on the street in front of them. The creepies tried an end-around and found that Ben had planned for that by setting up Claymores at the rear of the building. They tried twice from the rear and then gave that up as a very bad idea.

"Five and Six Battalions getting bloodied, but holding," Corrie reported. She listened to her headset for a moment and said, "Doctor Chase is cut off. Creepies coming out of Balfour Park have blocked the street and our people can't bust through."

"That isn't worth a shit," Ben said. "Main battle tanks rolling, Corrie. Break through and secure the field hospital zone."

"Ten-four, sir."

"Tell artillery back of the lines to ready flare-shots and to stand by for my orders. I want the sky lit up until I say darken it."

Ben went to another frequency and alerted all commanders that flares were going up.

"Major Halloran is dead, sir," Corrie reported. "Sniper got him through the head."

"Who's the XO of Five Battalion?"

"Steinberg, sir."

"Tell Steinberg he just got promoted and to take command."

"Right, sir."

Jerre looked at Ben during a momentary lull in the gunfire. "Jerry Halloran?"

"That's him."

"He's my age. I met him at the gathering of the young people, just after I left you in Virginia. He got married after that and he and his wife had some kids. I met her and liked her. She's really nice."

"Yes. He was very much in love with his wife. She and the kids were killed in an ambush by a pack of white trash two years ago."

"I'm sorry. He must have taken that terribly hard."

"He got over it a few minutes ago." Ben's reply was given much more coldly than he intended, and he knew she would take it the wrong way, and she did. Jerre's look was strange for a moment before turning away from his eyes.

"Gunners reporting flare-shots ready to pop, sir," Corrie said.

"Fire."

The darkness over the besieged battlelines was lit up as the flares popped open high in the sky. "Creepie-killing time, people!" Ben yelled. "Pick your targets and put them down."

For the creepies nearest the old service station, caught in the harsh artificial light, there were but two options left open to them: either die where they stood, or charge the CP and try to kill the leader of the Rebels, Ben Raines.

They ran screaming toward the CP.

# Chapter 11

A half-dozen creepies made the service station area, literally climbing over the bodies of their fallen kind and hurling themselves through the glassless front of the building.

Ben swung his M-14 like a club, the stock catching one Believer on the jaw and breaking it, sending bloody and broken teeth flying out of his mouth. Beth jammed the muzzle of her CAR into a creepie's mouth and pulled the trigger, blowing away the back of the cannibal's head. Jersey was rolling on the dirty and brass-littered floor, battling a creep with a knife in his hand. Jerre stepped over, stuck a .45 to the creepie's head, and pulled the trigger, ending the struggle.

"Yukk!" Jersey said, crawling to her knees and shoving the stinking body from her.

"Here comes more!" Cooper yelled, jerking the butt of his M-16 to his shoulder.

Dan reached down with his knife and cut the throat of the jaw-broken creepie, then turned to the outside action, Sarah by his side.

Over the din of battle, and the sound was enormous in the concrete block building, Ben sensed more than heard movement on the flat roof of the building. He could see the plywood decking of the roof where the tile had rotted away over the years. Motioning to Jerre and Corrie, they nodded understanding and lifted their M-16s, waiting for Ben to give the signal.

Ben opened fire with his old Thunder Lizard, .223 rounds from the women following the .308s from the M-14 a half second after Ben opened the dance. The slugs tore through the decking, knocking great holes, mangling the bodies of those on the roof, and exposing the harsh light of the flares. Already overloaded from the weight, a portion of the decking collapsed, sending howling creepies tumbling inside the service station and another hand-to-hand battle was on.

A creepie jumped onto the back of Dan and the Englishman expertly flipped him off and smashed his face with his boots, kicking the man unconscious.

Grenades exploded outside the service station, killing several Rebels and knocking to the floor those closest to the front. Jersey was slammed to the floor as a piece of shrapnel struck her helmet, denting the metal and giving her a hell of a headache.

Cooper took a piece of hot flying shrapnel on the arm that knocked him down, addled but not seriously hurt. Ben got to his knees and again bipodded his M-14 at the front of the building and let the lead fly.

"All units under heavy attack!" Corrie yelled over the roar of battle. "Holding."

"Fuck this," Ben said, and turned to Corrie. "Order all units to charge! Charge, goddamnit, charge!"

Roaring like an enraged tiger, Ben left the building and led his contingent in a charge through the brilliantly lit night.

The creepies had expected a fierce fight from the Rebels; what they had not anticipated was a charge of screaming Rebels coming dead-bang at them. The move momentarily confused them and that was all that the Rebels needed.

The charge broke the attack from the Believers and forced them back. From all points around the city, the Rebels advanced two blocks before Ben called a halt to it.

General Striganov's forces had pushed to Francis Avenue and now controlled — at least for the moment — everything from Nine Mile Road to Morgan Acres to the east.

Ben had pushed his people all the way up to the old

fairgrounds and now held everything from the Interstate north to the river.

West and his people controlled the area from Highway 290 up to the Russian's perimeter.

Ike and Cecil had bulled their way up to the Interstate and were holding.

Five and Six Battalions had held tough and beaten back the creepie attacks west and south of the city.

"Good night's work, people," Ben radioed. "Damn good work."

The commanders met at Ben's new CP the next morning.

"Goddamnit, Ben!" Ike got all up in Ben's face. "You could have ended up like Custer last night, you . . . you . . ." He sputtered to a red-faced halt.

"I concur," Cecil said. "It was a very foolhardy thing to do. You could have been killed."

"But I wasn't," Ben pointed out. "And it broke the back of the creepie attack."

"Can't you do something with this hardhead!" Georgi yelled at Jerre.

Jerre only smiled and shook her head.

Ben didn't let the argument gather any more steam. He slapped a map that had been thumbtacked on a wall. "We can't let the creeps regain any of the momentum they once had—or thought they had. Order all units to attack at once. Push the creeps toward the center of the city. That's it!" Ben's voice was sharp and all gathered around knew the meeting was over. "Attack!"

The Believers had no chance to recoup from the battering they'd taken only hours before. Slowly, a building at a time, the Rebels began taking the city, pushing the creepies into a corner from which there was no escape.

The Night People were well-armed, but they had put themselves into a box and they could but fight and die; they knew that for them, there was no surrendering to Ben Raines and his Rebels. A few had tried. The Rebels promptly put them up against a wall and shot them.

At the end of the third day of bitter fighting, most of it close-in, eyeball to eyeball, using grenades and rifles — and sometimes pistols, camp axes, knives, and entrenching tools — Ben called for a halt to the advance and stood his people down for a rest.

The Rebels had forced the remaining creepies into a small downtown area.

Ben called for a face to face with his commanders. "How many more prisoners do the creepies hold in the city?"

"Only a handful," West told him, leaning on a cane to give his aching ankle some relief. "In my sector, the creeps are shooting the prisoners as we advance, rather than have us rescue them."

Ben received the same grim report from the rest of his people.

"Damned if we do and damned if we don't," he muttered. "All right." He made up his mind, and it was not a decision he liked. "The artillery has had a good long rest. Time for them to go to work. Corrie, order all artillery into place. Ring the city. Tell them to use WP, napalm, and HE, in that order. Gentlemen, pull your people back and give the city to the big guns. Let's bring it down."

The Night People were barbaric and godless, but they were not fools. They knew as soon as the Rebels began withdrawing there was no hope left for them. Ben Raines had made up his mind and death stood just around the corner, waiting patiently.

The Reaper did not have a long wait.

The center of Spokane erupted as the shells began dropping in, spewing fire and shrapnel and exploding destruction.

Interstate 90 had been cleared all the way through the city and Ben had ordered his command post be set up at the airport. Chase had moved his facilities to an old hospital not far from the airport.

The Rebels had taken casualities during this fight; more casualities than they had suffered in a long time, and it was not to Ben's liking.

While the monotonous shelling of the city boomed and the earth trembled, with the center of the city now engulfed in flames, black smoke drifting into the skies, Ben drove over to the hospital.

He found a very unhappy Lamar Chase.

"All right, Lamar," Ben said. "You look like a thundercloud. What's on your mind?"

"Is it worth it, Ben?"

Ben stared at him, knowing what the doctor meant, but wanting him to say the words.

"We've got a hundred dead, Ben. Three times that many wounded. We've rescued four hundred-odd people from the creeps. Perhaps, and this is a very optimistic guess, seventy-five out of that number will recover enough to lead normal, useful lives. One Rebel dies and approximately two are wounded for every four freed prisoners. Are the numbers worth it?"

"It's a hard thing you're asking me, Lamar."

"Yes. And as a doctor, it's a dreadful thought to have in my own mind."

With a sigh, Ben sat down and took the offer of coffee from Chase. "Lamar, you know as well or better than anyone how the Rebels operate. Those men and women would charge the gates of hell if I asked them to. But something like this? I've got to put it to them. You've often said that this army will go down in history as the damned army ever to roam the earth. I think perhaps you're right in that. But no one's come along to whip us yet."

"That's certainly true. Your personal feelings on the loss of life, Ben?"

"I don't like it, Lamar. And now I'm going to tell you something that you're not going to like. Out of all those men and women we rescue, nine tenths of them were losers to begin with."

"What do you mean by that, Ben. Goddamnit, they're human beings that were captured to be *eaten*, for Christ's sake!"

"Why were they captured? Why didn't they stand and fight or join a larger group." He shrugged. "Losers, Lamar. They'd be losers in any environment."

"You don't believe that, Ben! You've heard their stories. Many of them did fight, and fight hard. I can't believe this is coming out of your mouth."

"What's the big uproar, Lamar? You're the one who brought up concerns about the losses we're taking rescuing these losers."

"They're not losers!" the doctor roared. "What the hell do you want to do, Raines: kill them along with the creeps?"

"That was your original idea, wasn't it?" Ben asked innocently.

"Hell, no, it wasn't! It certainly was not. I was just . . . talking, that's all. The idea is barbaric, Raines. Hideous."

"Well, I'm glad that's settled them. Personally, I'd just as soon lay back and blow hell out of the cities and not lose one Rebel. Damn, I thought I'd found someone who agreed with me."

"Well, you haven't!"

"Well, I'm very sorry to hear that." He drained his cup and placed the mug on the desk. "Anything else on your mind, Lamar?"

"Not at the moment, no."

Ben hid his smile as he stood up. "Well, then, I'll just be going. I want to see the wounded and talk to them. If that's all right with you?"

"Sure, it is. Just stay out of the ICU wards. We've got some seriously wounded."

"I'll be sure and do that. See you around, Lamar. Oh, by the way: how are the rescued?"

"They're doing just fine! We're making real progress with them. And I'd appreciate it if you'd leave them alone."

"I'll do that. See you, Lamar." He looked at Jerre. "You coming with me?"

"I think I'll stay and chat with Doctor Chase. I'll catch up with you later."

Ben nodded and stepped out into the hall. No longer able to contain his laughter, he leaned against the wall and laughed out loud.

Jerre sat down and watched as Chase stormed around his office, cussing and bitching and in general low-rating Ben Raines. The chief medical officer stopped and listened to Ben's laughter in the hallway, a frown on his face.

"What the hell does he find so goddamn funny about all this?"

Jerre shrugged. "You know Ben, Doctor. He has a strange sense of humor."

"Damn sure does." Lamar sat down behind his desk and fiddled with a pencil. He suddenly broke the pencil in half and glared at Jerre. She could not contain her laughter, laughing at the expression on the man's face.

"That son of a bitch!" Lamar said.

"What's the matter, Doctor?" she managed to ask.

"He conned me again! The bastard did it to me again! He shifted the idea from my shoulders to his and I didn't even realize he was doing it."

They could hear Ben' s laughter fading as he walked up the hall.

# Chapter 12

The Rebels stood on the outskirts of the city and watched it burn. When the fires had died down and there was no danger of them spreading, Ben ordered the columns out. Five and Six were to head north, checking for survivors in the northeast corner of the state. Ike was to take his battalion and clean out Pullman. Cecil was to take Walla Walla while West took care of the tri-cities along the Columbia River. Ben was going to travel the Interstate over to Ellensburg, then cut down to Yakima. Five and Six would eventually wind their way west and south to Wenatchee and all would link up outside Yakima to plan out the western campaign.

The Rebels began fanning out all over the eastern half of the state, searching for survivors who might like to join them in setting up outposts — small pockets of civilization in the midst of a world gone mad — and seeking out and destroying those who wished to continue their anti-social and outlaw ways.

As the Rebels fanned out, they began finding small groups of survivors who had banded together for strength in combatting not only the many outlaw gangs who roamed the state, killing and robbing and raping and enslaving, but also the hideous Night People, or Believers.

Ben found one group of survivors concentrated around the Moses Lake area, led by Tom Loomis.

"Two hundred and fifty adults and seventy children," Tom told him, after introducing himself.

Ben was taking a walking tour of the town with Tom and a few of the survivors. His practiced and experienced eyes had picked up on the well-bunkered machine gun emplacements that dotted the town, and also how the survivors had strung together the buildings on the outskirts of the town, creating a walled fortress.

Tom smiled as he noticed the direction Ben's eyes were taking. "Kind of sad, isn't it, General? Here we are in the twenty-first century and we've reverted back to a fortress existence."

Ben shook his head. "We do what we have to do in order to maintain some degree of civilization, Tom. In a way it is sad, but you and your people have done a fine job here. You've carved a pocket of order and reason while being surrounded by human crud."

"I was born in the sixties, General," Tom said. "I remember the pampering and coddling of criminals and the stripping away of the rights of the law-abiding." His eyes were hard as they met the eyes of Ben Raines. "And the taking away of the citizens' right to own and bear firearms. I'll not see that happen again."

"It won't as long as we're alive, Tom," Ben assured him. "But we've got to make sure those who come after us always remember what led up to the downfall of civilization—and never forget it."

Tom nodded. "It's being taught in our schools, General. We've based our philosophy on what we've been able to intercept—by radio—from your Base Camp One and outposts."

Ben nodded. "I'll leave two squads of Rebels here. See that your clinic is completely restocked and brought up to date. We'll clean up the old airport and outfit you with radio equipment. We've got to set up other outposts; we can't leave you stuck out here alone. Any suggestions on that?"

Tom paused and pulled a map from his pocket, spreading it out on the hood of a truck. "Seventy miles north of here," he pointed it out, "is Grand Coulee. There is another group of survivors there. We stay in radio contact. Man by the name of Mike Mitchell is in charge. He's a good man."

Ben nodded. "Corrie, bump Five Battalion and tell Steinberg to check that out and set them up. What about this area here?" Ben outlined it with a finger.

"A gang of thugs took over Ephrata years ago. Probably four hundred strong. They pretty much leave us alone now; but that came only after we showed them that we'll fight to protect our way of life."

"That's usually all it takes. We'll clean out Ephrata and that'll take some of the strain off you people. How about south of here?"

Tom shook his head. "There's a few pockets of survivors along the Snake. But other than that, it's mostly the Believers and outlaws. It's been grim in this state, General. Really grim."

"Conditions will improve, Tom. I promise you that. It's going to take us some time, but we'll clean up this country. Town by town and city by city."

Tom grinned. "You people sure played hell over in Idaho, General."

"That we did. But you can bet that as soon as we pulled out, the outlaws who ran into the wilderness areas resurfaced. But the main thing is that we got rid of the creepies."

Tom could not hold back a shudder. "If you're wondering what happened to many of the people in this area, General, you just spoke the word."

"I know. We'll deal with thugs and outlaws as we come to them. Getting rid of the creepies is our first order of business."

"Did you really destroy New York City, General?" *

"Yes. And with it perhaps the largest concentration of Believers in America. We'll win the fight, Tom. But it's going to take a long, long time."

*Valor in the Ashes & Trapped in the Ashes—Zebra Books

"Voleta and her Ninth Order?"

"I think she's dead. My son says she is still alive. I hope I'm right and he's wrong."

"That bunch is almost as bad as the Believers."

"Almost."


Voleta had been moved to a secure zone in Michigan, and with the passing of each day, her chances for a complete recovery improved. If love cures all things, for Voleta it was her burning hatred of Ben Raines that aided her recovery.

Villar, Khamsim, Parr, Ashley, and the bikers made their way furtively across the country, being very careful to avoid Rebel outposts and raping and killing in only the most out-of-the-way locales. They maintained radio silence and when communication was necessary, they used low-range CBs. None of them liked this tippy-toeing around, but they knew their survival depended upon stealth.

They all silently cursed Ben Raines as they made their way across country, with Alaska to be their final destination.


Ephrata was a piece of cake for the Rebels.

Ben told the outlaws to lay down their arms and surrender, or die. Those were the only two choices he gave them. The thugs and punks and crud elected to fight. They died.

Ben stood over a wounded man while the town smoked and burned around them. The outlaw glared hate at him.

"I'll never live under your rules, Raines!" the thug gasped.

"Your choice," Ben told him, then turned away to leave the man to die in the littered street.

"Ain't you gonna patch me up?" the wounded thug

hollered at Ben's back.

"No," Ben told him. "I won't waste medicine on the likes of you."

"I got rights!" the outlaw squalled, his hands bloody as they gripped his bullet-punctured belly.

"Not with me, you don't," was Ben's reply. The man was still screaming and thrashing on the street as Ben found Buddy.

"See that all the outlaws' guns and ammo are collected," Ben said. "Arrange for the weapons to be transported to the new outposts. When you've seen to that, get your Rat Team and take off for Ellensburg. Give me a report on conditions there just as soon as you can."

Dan walked up. "We have prisoners, sir. Among them some of the trashiest women I believe I have ever had the misfortune to encounter."

Ben sighed. He knew the answer to his question before he even asked it. "Children?"

"A goodly number of them. All of them malnourished and most of them showing the signs of abuse — of one kind or another."

"Let's get the kids over to Doctor Chase and then we'll deal with the women."

Chase was muttering curses under his breath as he watched his medical teams examine the kids. He stood up and walked over to Ben.

"Nearly all the girls over the age of eight or nine have been sexually molested, both vaginally and anally," he reported, disgust on his face. "Some of them much younger than that. Many of the boys show initial signs of having been sexually abused . . . anally. We'll know for sure once tests are done. In addition, both the girls and the boys have been severely beaten. Most of the physical scars will fade. The mental scars are quite another matter."

"What are they saying about it, Lamar?"

"They were abused with their mothers' permission.

Several of the women traded their childrens' sexual favors for protection or whatever."

"All right," Ben said. "We'll bivouac here and sort this thing out. I want the kids to positively ID the women who willingly sold them out, then we'll PSE the women for further confirmation."

"And after that?" Sarah Bradford asked.

"I'll have them shot," Ben said flatly. "I will not tolerate sexual abuse of children."

"I will be more than willing to be a part of that firing squad, General. Anyone who would force their children into prostitution doesn't deserve to live."

Ben looked at her grim face. "Find some other men and women who share that, Sarah. And then meet me at the west end of town tomorrow morning."

Jersey, Corrie, and Beth stepped forward, as did Tina, who had just joined her father's contingent.

Ben nodded his head. "That's a starter," he said softly. "Dan, convene a panel. We'll meet at dawn tomorrow for the hearing."


The vote of the twelve-member tribunal was unanimous: death by firing squad. Ben read the sentence aloud and then the sobbing men and nearly hysterical women were taken from the old gymnasium onto the old football field, placed against the side of a field house, and shot.

"Bury them in a common grave," Ben ordered, after the gunfire had died away, his eyes on the crumpled bodies on the ground. "We'll mount up as soon as the kids are airborne out of here."

Some of the outlaws in the town had escaped the attack from the Rebels, and they had watched and listened as Rebel justice was served. They wasted no time in fleeing the area and getting on the air and telling other outlaws what had happened. Most outlaws, thugs, punks, and trash wisely decided that Washington state had become very unhealthy for them. They began scattering in all directions, getting the hell away from Ben Raines and his Rebels. Many of them left with just the clothes on their backs, not even taking the time to pack. The older ones remembered the good times, when liberals ran the country and they could plea-bargain and holler about discrimination and every "i" not being dotted and every "t" not being crossed and they could walk free on the slightest of trial technicalities.

That was before Ben Raines.

Ben Raines didn't give a tinker's damn about constitutional rights; he'd strap your ass to a table and pump you full of truth serum to get at the truth. The truth was what Raines was all about: whether or not you did the crime.

"Things are goin' to hell around here," one outlaw observed. "I think I'm gonna clean up my act and join up with some survivors. Take to farmin'."

"You're not serious!" a friend in crime remarked. "You mean actually *work* for a livin'?"

"It's either that or have Ben Raines prop you up agin a wall and shoot you! We just ain't got that many choices left us."

"Wait a minute," his partner said. "I'm goin' with you."

Wherever Ben Raines and the Rebels went, those who chose to live outside the rules of society had but two choices: straighten up or die.

Ben did not believe in many options.

# Chapter 13

Ellensburg, Pullman, Walla Walla, Wenatchee, and the tri-cities fell to the Rebels' relentless and ruthless advance. Those creepies who had felt themselves safe in Yakima took stock of their situation and deserted the city, fleeing westward toward the bigger cities, taking their prisoners with them.

Ben had found another group of survivors and set up an outpost near the Canadian border. Now the entire eastern half of the state was, for the most part, a secure zone. There were still bands of outlaws in that section of the state, but they were keeping their heads down and looking for a way out.

For the moment, outlawing was the last thing on their minds.

Ben stood his people down and called for a meeting with his field commanders.

The men and women gathered at the old Yakima airport, where Ben had made his CP. He pointed to a map taped to a wall. "Ike, whenever you feel like your people have had enough rest, shove off for the northwestern corner of the state and start working your way down to just north of Seattle. Five and Six battalions will take that sector—Everett and the towns just south of it—and clean it out. Cecil, you and West take the Tacoma/Olympia area and secure it. Buddy, you and your Rat Teams are with Ike. Tina, you're with Cec and West. Dan will come with me. We'll take Vancouver and Portland. La-

270

mar, how about supplies?"

"We need to be resupplied, Ben. I'd say another two or three days."

"That's fine. That'll give us all time to clean weapons, rest, and get the birds up here. We need to start an inventory of all that gear we seized from the Air Force base. Wherever we go, scrounge around for maps of Alaska; we're going to need them. Now then, Seattle is going to be a screaming bastard, people. It was one big metropolitan area when the Great War hit, and the creepies have had years to fortify. Same with Portland and all the rest of the cities out here. And we know they've got hundreds, maybe thousands of prisoners in those cities. These cities are going to have to be taken block by bloody block. We'll grab prisoners when we can and get the locations where the prisoners are being held out of them; try rescue raids. These aren't nice people, so I don't particularly care how you get the information we need. We all know that the more the rumors say how brutal we are, the more outlaws decide to stop outlawing and try to turn straight. All right, people. That's it. Good hunting."

Ben waved Dan to his side as the others filed out. "If we try to stay on the north side of the Columbia River, the creepies will blow the bridges and cut us off from Portland. Start moving our people out now, crossing the river and coming up on Interstate Eighty-four and south of the city on Highway Twenty-six."

"I'll get them moving now, sir. Do we destroy the cities after we've taken them?"

Ben hesitated. "I don't know, Dan. We need ports on both coasts and on the Gulf. We'll just have to play that tune when we come to it."

The Englishman smiled. "Still thinking about going to England, sir?"

"Oh, yes. We'll get there, Dan. One of these

days. I promise you that."

Ben began moving all units out, stretching them south to north. Ike began his pullout immediately, traveling north until junctioning with Highway 20, cutting west across the Cascades. He would turn north on Interstate 5, spreading his people along a line from Mount Vernon in the south to the Canadian line.

Five and Six Battalions crossed the mountain range on Highway 2 out of Wenatchee. They moved to within fifteen miles of their objective and halted, waiting until everyone got into position.

Cecil and West pulled out from Yakima on Highway 410, crossing the lower end of the mountains and bivouacking just north of the Clearwater Wilderness area, about thirty miles east of Tacoma.

Ben and his columns rolled south out of Yakima. They crossed the Columbia River into Oregon and connected with Interstate 84, turning westward toward Portland. At Hood River, Dan cut off from the main columns and took his people south on 35. About fifty miles later he would connect with Highway 26 and move toward Portland, approaching the city a few miles south of Ben.

Far south of the Rebels, Villar halted his people in California and stood them down, to wait out the battles soon to take place north of them. He would monitor the events by radio and move toward the north only after the Rebels had either won or lost; but Villar knew that thoughts of the Rebels losing was only wistful thinking on his part. Ben Raines and his Rebels did not lose — ever! Over the past few days he had been entertaining the idea of somehow getting ships and sailing back to Europe, and to hell with Ben Raines and America.

But his ships were three thousand miles and a continent away, and now in Rebel hands, according to radio transmissions he'd picked up. Ben Raines commandeered everything that wasn't nailed down.

Good*damn* Ben Raines to hell!

Villar stood his people down in the Marble Mountain Wilderness area and dared them to even breathe hard, warning them, "This is a little too close to the Rebels for comfort, people. But we'll stay undetected if we're very, very careful. Maintain strict radio silence. Don't even use CBs—the signals might skip and the Rebels pick them up. If that happens, we're fucked. Build your cook fires under low-hanging branches to break up the smoke and douse them as soon as you' re done. It'll take Raines two to three weeks to settle the Believers' hash, and then he'll move on. That's his pattern and I doubt he'll change it this late in the game. As soon as he moves out, we move up toward Alaska and safety. Don't screw up, people. Ben Raines doesn't give an enemy a second chance."


"General Jefferys on the horn, sir," Corrie said.

Ben moved to a mic and picked it up. "Go, Cec."

"Bad news, Ben," Cecil spoke from outside Tacoma. "The Believers have looted McCord AFB and Fort Lewis. This West Coast bunch now have long-range artillery capabilities and battle tanks."

"Have you any news about Portland? Dan's Scouts haven't been able to grab a prisoner for interrogation."

"That's ten-four, Ben. The creepies there raided numerous Army and Marine Corps depots. They are very heavily armed with enormous firepower at their disposal. This is going to be a slugfest."

"That's ten-four, Cec. We all expected it to be a tough one. I'm in position. We strike at dawn. Good luck." Ben glanced at Corrie. "Get me Colonel Gray, please."

"Standing by," she told him a few seconds later.

273

Ben lifted his mic. "Dan, you monitored that transmission from Cec?"

"Yes, sir."

"What's your situation?"

"Looking down the barrels of long guns."

"Do the approximate locations of the holding pens for the prisoners still tally up, Dan?"

"That's ten-fifty, General. I ordered a fly-by and heat-seekers showed no large concentration of human beings at the locations the Judge told us about."

"Damn!" Ben muttered. He lifted the mic. "Then they've moved them, Dan."

"Or eaten them," came the Englishman's reply.

Jersey looked at Ben and swallowed hard. The disgust all felt was very evident on the faces of those in the command post.

"We launch attack at dawn, Dan. We'll just have to take the city street by street and try to somehow rescue the prisoners. If that is at all possible," he added.

"That's ten-four, sir. We strike at dawn."

Ben clipped the mic and turned to his personal team. "This is going to be a son of a bitch, people. A bloody son of a bitch."


All Rebel units struck at dawn and were thrown back by heavy fire from the creepies' well-fortified positions up and down the west coast of what had once been the state of Washington and the extreme northwestern part of the state of Oregon. The Rebels did not gain one inch of ground, but neither did they lose any.

It was an impasse. At least for the time being.

Ben stood alone, outside his CP on the edge of Portland, making some hard and difficult decisions in his mind. His team knew he did not want to be

274

bothered, and they left him alone.

Ben walked back into his CP and told Corrie, "Order all units to hit it again. If we can't gain a better toehold, and keep it, fall back to original lines."

"Yes, sir."

From Bellingham in the north to Portland in the south, the Rebels attacked, and were once more thrown back, suffering heavy casualties.

After hearing the field reports, Ben made up his mind. But it was not a decision he liked or an order he enjoyed giving.

"Corrie, tell all commanders to fall back. Order the artillery up. I won't kill any more of our people. I just can't justify it. Tell the FO's to get in place and artillery to commence firing as soon as coordinates are charted."

"Yes, sir."

Chase stood in the CP, sipping coffee and watching Ben. Although the doctor knew the emotion was there, Ben's face did not mirror his inner feelings. Chase sat his coffee mug on a scarred table and walked to Ben's side. "It was the only logical order to give, Ben," the doctor said. "You tried to save the prisoners; you did your best. What would have been the point in losing more people?"

Ben shook his head. "Logical, yes. But I just signed the death sentence for a lot of prisoners in the cities, Lamar."

"If they are even in the cities, Ben. If. I don't like it either, old friend. My business is saving lives, remember? But you don't kill an entire ward of patients to save one. That isn't logical. If you hadn't tried a frontal assault, I'd have been in here jumping up and down and screaming at you. You tried it—twice. It didn't work. Now we've got field hospitals filled with wounded Rebels and with no gain against the Believers. You did the right thing. Keep that in mind and put the other thoughts out of your mind."

The artillery began booming, the shells whistling and howling as they roared overhead. Downtown Portland exploded as the HE rounds impacted. High explosive was followed by white phosphorus and that was followed by napalm. The downtown area, from the waterfront over to 14th Street was soon blazing. From Hoyt Street to Lincoln, fires were soon burning out of control as Ben ordered done what the Believers had bet their lives he would not do.

Ben walked outside, to stand watching as the skies above the city and the suburbs around it soon turned dark with smoke. He cut his eyes as Thermopolis walked around the corner of the building and up to his side, to stand quietly.

"There was a lot of history in that city that I wanted to save," Ben said. "A lot of history is now going up in smoke, never to be seen by the generations that follow us."

"Yes," Therm agreed. "That is true. But we'll be able to save some of it. Just like we did in New York City and all the other cities. It won't all be destroyed. Ben, you had no choice in the matter. The ratio of lives lost against possible lives saved was just too high."

They stood in silence for a time, watching and listening as the historic district along the waterfront burst into flames as shells impacted and the gunners raised the elevation and began working toward the center of the city.

Ben lifted his walkie-talkie. "Corrie, order Dan's Scouts in, tanks spearheading, and our people to follow. Tell the artillery to take a break just as soon as the troops are in unfriendly territory."

Ben waited a moment. Corrie's voice popped out of the walkie-talkie. "Tanks up and spearheading, sir."

"That's ten-four, Corrie." He turned to Thermopolis. "Would you care to come along and visit the suburbs of this city, my friend?"

"Gee," Therm feigned great surprise. "I thought you'd never ask."

# Chapter 14

"See if you can get us to Burnside Street, Coop," Ben said. "Get off the Interstate here. This old high school should do nicely for a CP." He glanced over his shoulder. "Where's Jerre?"

"Coming across with the medical team," Beth said. "They're shorthanded due to all the wounded."

Ben knew the figures and just the thought made his face tighten up. They were far too high for the little ground the Rebels had gained.

"Look out, Coop!" Jersey yelled, just as a wildly driven car filled with creepies shot out in front of them. The big wagon slewed around as Cooper fought the wheel, the tires grabbing for traction on the rain-slick street. Ben lowered his window and gave the creep car a full clip from his old Thunder Lizard. The drivers' side window blew apart, taking most of the driver's head with it. The car crashed into a building and exploded into flames.

"That building used to be part of the Bensen Tech High School," Beth said, after consulting a map.

"Thank you, Beth," Ben said, one eye on Cooper's antics as he tried to straighten out the still-fishtailing wagon, fighting the wheel. "I believe it would help if you would take your foot off the accelerator, Coop."

"Creepies," Cooper said, jerking his head forward.

Several carloads of creeps were gaining on them as the wagon slid backward around a corner.

"Pure luck," Jersey muttered. "Cooper, if you keep this up, we'll crash into that big building that is rap-

278

idly coming upon us—from the rear. And going backward like this is making me sick at my stomach."

Muttering under his breath about women in general and Jersey in particular, Cooper got the wagon under control and roared toward the huge building Jersey had mentioned. He spun the wheel, did a sickening, sliding turnaround in the middle of the wet street, and drove the wagon up onto the sidewalk, with Ben's side facing the building.

"Your new CP, General," Cooper said with a grin on his face.

"Thanks, Coop," Ben said drily. "The ride was certainly . . . unforgettable, to say the least."

"That ain't exactly the word I'd use," Jersey spoke from the second seat. "Shitty, would be my choice."

Slugs began yowling off the armor-plate of the big wagon. "Out, people!" Ben yelled, bailing out onto the sidewalk. "Grab everything you can and follow me."

"And away we go," Jersey said, scrambling out of the vehicle.

Inside the littered building, Corrie began radioing their position to prevent any artillery or mortar fire from hitting them, and to let other Rebel units know their position.

Ben pointed toward the rear. "That's your baby, Beth. Don't let any buggers surprise us."

Beth nodded and dropped into a protected position to cover the rear, laying out several grenades and clips for her CAR-15.

"Dan's people have a firm hold in their sector," Corrie announced. "Six blocks have been effectively neutralized."

"Where the hell are we?" Ben said, looking at a map just as Jersey and Cooper opened fire on the creeps who had made the mistake of charging the building. The creeps were chopped down by automatic rifle fire. "I don't like this position," Ben muttered. "Coop! Is it clear out there?"

"For the moment."

"Let's get the hell gone from here and get to the airport. We need a landing strip in case we get stuck in here and have to be resupplied by air."

They left the building and immediately ran into another group of creeps. But this time they caught the creeps in a cross fire between themselves and a Rebel patrol and reduced the cannibals to bloody rags in the rain-slick street. Ben waved the patrol to him and knelt down on the sidewalk, while the sounds of combat boomed all around them. Using a flashlight, Ben traced the route to the airport while Corrie radioed for tanks to come to their location.

Only a few moments passed before several main battle tanks clanked and rumbled up to their location. Using the outside phone so the commander would not have to unbutton, Ben said, "We'll stay off the Interstates. The creeps probably have them mined. Spearhead us over to Ninety-nine and then gradually work toward Airport Way. We'll pick up other units as we go and take the airport. Move out."

The tanks clanked out in front and Ben waved his people in behind him and then told Cooper to follow the huge machines of war. Little pockets of war were raging all around them as they made their way toward the airport: grenades slashed the wet day, followed by automatic weapons fire as the Rebels hammered out their advance. Ben's team slammed through the suburbs then cut under the Interstate and roared toward the airport, the tanks leading the way.

"Picking up a lot of creepie traffic from the airport," Corrie said. "They're waiting for us."

Ben nodded and twisted in the seat, his eyes picking up Thermopolis's bunch right behind them. Emil and his followers were close behind Therm. "Should be an interesting fight," Ben muttered.

The tanks shifted on their treads and cut off the main road to the airport, taking a blacktop road that ran alongside a chain-link fence that paralleled a runway.

"Tell them to bust through and let's take it," Ben told Corrie.

The tanks slammed through the fence and the column raced onto a runway, heading for the terminals.

Ben looked at the jets parked at the terminal gates. "Those jets will still have aviation fuel in them," Ben said. "Tell the tanks to lower their guns and let's see some fireworks."

Corrie relayed the orders, the tanks fired, and the jets blew, spreading flames all over the outside of the terminal. The flames soon ignited the interior of the long buildings as dusty carpets and tile caught fire and thick, choking smoke forced the creepies out of the terminals and into the rain and the guns of the Rebels.

The Rebels needed no orders; they opened fire. Within minutes, the burning southeast corridor of the airport was in Rebel hands.

The rain became a downpour as the leaden skies opened up. The rain slowed the fiery march of flames, and then extinguished most of the fires outside the terminals.

From his position on the river side of the airport, Ben lifted his mic. "Mortar teams set up and tank commanders lower elevation. Take the terminal down," he ordered.

The Rebels began to systematically destroy the main buildings of the airport. Ben pointed out a smaller building off to the side. "Check it out and clean it out. That's my new CP for this campaign." To Corrie: "Tell Chase he can set up a field hospital here. And we can fly the wounded out. We've got a firm toehold."

By late afternoon of the second day, most of the suburbs were solidly under Rebel control. That is to say the ashes of the suburbs were free of creepies. The Rebels had burned everything that could be torched and now stood poised to cross the Willamette River at eight points.

Ben glanced at Corrie. "Take the city, Corrie," he ordered.

She gave the orders and the Rebels poured across, tanks spearheading the drive.

Ike's people had cleared out their sector from the Canadian line down to Bellingham and were now driving south along Interstate 5, burning as they went.

Five and Six Battalions had completed their sweep and Everett was no more than a smoking memory. Five and Six Battalions had shifted over to Highway 9 and were waiting to link up with Ike.

Cecil and West had fired Tacoma, driving the creeps out and west onto the peninsular and over into the Olympic National Park area. West bivouacked his people north of the smoking ruins and Cecil put his troops south, waiting for Ben to finish up in the Portland/Vancouver area.

Dan had taken his people across the river into Vancouver and had pushed the creeps out of the city, driving them north with fire.

At the end of the fifth day, Ben ordered his people out of the smoking ruins of Portland and across the river. He linked up with Dan and the long columns began their northward push.

Several hundred miles south, Villar monitored radio reports and shook his head in grudging admiration for Ben Raines. "He'll never be stopped," Villar said. "There is no force on earth that is large

282

enough or determined enough to stop the man. He is the most ruthless person I have ever encountered. He is going to pull this nation out of the ashes of ruin and if he has to burn the son of a bitch down to accomplish that task, he'll do it."

"Where does that leave us?" Satan asked. The big outlaw biker was beginning to get it through his head that Ben Raines was really as awesome as legend stated.

Villar looked at the man. Satan was the ugliest human being he had ever seen. "Screwed, if we get in his way," he said flatly.

"Send it in code to all unit commanders," Ben said, after handing Corrie a note. "Take the word Alaska out of all vocabularies. I don't ever want to hear it on the air. We're facing too many unknowns to give our destination away. Code name it Northstar."

Ben was resting his people just north of Kelso. They had encountered no creeps on the push north along the Interstate. The Believers had fled across the river into Oregon and were, Ben guessed, making their way north, to cross back into Washington at Astoria, to spread out along the coast. He would deal with them later; for now, the taking of Seattle was paramount in his mind.

Ben walked through the sprawling camp, filled with men and women and their particular instruments of war.

"When does Seattle fall, General?" a woman called out, looking up from cleaning her M-16.

"Tomorrow," Ben told her. "So get your beauty rest, Rosie."

"Why?" she called to him. "I sure as hell don't plan on kissing any of those creepie bastards!"

Ben laughed and waved, walking on. He spent

283

more than an hour prowling the encampment, stopping to exchange a few words whenever he could, with Corrie and her headset and Jersey with her M-16 constantly at his side. He joked and kidded with his Rebels as he walked the camp. He noticed a group of Scouts running for their Jeeps and turned to Corrie.

"What's going on, Corrie?"

"A little trouble over by the river, General," she said blandly. "Nothing much."

"What kind of trouble?"

"A small ambush by some outlaws, General. The Scouts put it down almost as quickly as it happened."

"Anybody hurt?"

"Two Rebels wounded. They're being taken to the field hospital now."

"Tell Coop to bring the wagon around. Let's go see what happened."

"Yes, sir," she said glumly.

"What's the matter with you, Corrie? Aren't you feeling well?"

She sighed and Ben caught the glance that passed between the two women.

Before he could ask what the hell was going on, Dan ran up to him and faced Ben.

"Dan. What's the problem?"

"There is no way to say this except straight out, sir. You better get over to the field hospital. It's Jerre. She caught two bad ones and Lamar says she's just hanging on."

# Chapter 15

Lamar Chase blocked Ben at the door to the field hospital. "She isn't conscious and she is never going to regain consciousness, Ben. She caught a bullet in the head and one in the back. The bullet went right through her head. The second bullet severed her spinal cord. They were both hollow-nosed slugs and did terrible damage to her brain, her right lung, and one kidney after it impacted and began spinning. I'm not sparing you, old friend. Because there is no hope."

"I'll sit with her," Ben said, his voice dull.

"I fixed up a private place for her, Ben. And put a chair in there for you."

"Is she in pain?"

"No." Lamar shook his head. "I ordered her heavily sedated. I wanted to make it as easy as I could for her."

"Leave us alone, Lamar."

"I understand, Ben."

Her head was wrapped in bandages and her skin was very dry to the touch. Ben looked at the chart hooked to the foot of her bed. He couldn't make any sense out of it and rehooked it. He sat down in the chair by her bed and took off his beret. He looked at the bottles hanging above her and the tubes from them running into her arms. He called for a nurse.

"Unhook them," he ordered.

"Sir! . . ."

"I said unhook them. You didn't know her. I did.

She would not want to live like this. Now either you unhook them, or I will."

Chase stepped into the room. "Remove them, Sergeant. I'll take full responsibility for it and sign the order myself."

When the tubes and bottles and needles were gone, and the room empty except for the two of them, Ben sat down and put his big hand over hers. He gently squeezed. No response.

He touched her hair and gently touched one cheek. He leaned back in the chair and waited. One hour and fifteen minutes later, Ben stepped out of the canvass-walled room in the field hospital.

"She's dead," he told a nurse.

Dan was waiting outside the field hospital. "I have the men who ambushed the pair of them, General."

"I didn't even think to ask, Dan. How is the person who was with her?"

"It was Thermopolis's wife, General. She received a wound in the shoulder. She's going to be fine. They were over by the river with a group of people, picking flowers."

"The outlaws?"

"Six of them surrendered."

"Dispose of them."

"Yes, sir."

"Jerre wasn't especially religious. So we'll not have any elaborate service." He looked north, toward the Mount Saint Helens monument about ten miles away. The foothills were green with fresh growth, gentle appearing. "She liked the mountains and the sighing winds. We'll bury her in those foothills. They look very peaceful. The service will be at dawn in the morning. Tell unit commanders we'll delay the push until noon."

"Yes, sir."

Ben pointed toward a copse of trees several thousand yards away.

"I'll see to that personally, sir."

Ben walked away. He had not shown any visible signs of emotion. But Dan knew that men like Ben Raines, and yes, Dan Gray, too, did not go in for much public display of emotion.

But Dan knew only too well that inside, Ben was torn apart and hurting.


Ike, Cecil, and West, along with Buddy and Tina flew in that evening for the service, landing at a strip just south of Kelso. Buddy and Tina went directly to their father's quarters.

They found him sitting on the front porch, holding a little Husky puppy in his lap. Ben smiled at his kids. "She found me this afternoon. I guess I've got a new pal."

Tina kissed him on the cheek and opened her small duffle bag, hauling out an unopened bottle of Glenlivet Scotch. "I found this about a week ago. How about a belt, Dad?"

"You know that was Jerre's favorite, don't you?"

"I know."

Ben sighed. "Sure, why not? Hell, let's have a snort or two."

"What's the pup's name, Father?" Buddy asked while Tina was digging around for clean cups.

Ben laughed. "When she found me, she started making little funny noises. Sounded like she was trying to say smoot. So that's what I called her. Smoot."

The Scotch poured and their bellies warmed from the first sip, Tina said, "How are you doing, Dad?"

"I'm all right. I said good-bye this afternoon, sitting in a little grove of trees behind the field hospital. Really, Tina, I said good-bye a long time ago."

"Are you going to get drunk, Father?" Buddy asked. "I've never been drunk, I don't think, so if you want company, I'll join you."

Ben smiled. "No, son. I'm going to go easy on the hooch. I don't know what my feelings are right now. All jumbled up, for sure. But neither of you has to worry. I'm not going off the deep end and do something stupid. Probably go to bed early. The funeral is at dawn tomorrow. I'm escorting the body out about an hour before then. I drove over this afternoon and found a peaceful place in the foothills. The grave won't be marked."

Both his kids looked at him at that.

"That isn't Jerre wrapped in that blanket at the hospital. Her soul is free now. And I hope she's happy."

When Tina looked at her father, he was crying soundlessly, tears running down his tanned face.

The wind sighed gently in the foothills around the Mount Saint Helens monument as one of the Rebel chaplains conducted the brief ceremony and Jerre was laid to rest. The final prayer was an echo in the wind and still no one made a move. Ben was conscious of eyes on him. The Rebels were not going to start covering the body until Ben made a move.

"It's all right," Ben said, then reached down and sprinkled a handful of dirt on the bodybag.

The grave was quickly filled in.

Ben looked at Dan. "We'll pull out at noon, Dan. Have the people ready to go."

"Yes, sir."

"Now leave me for a time."

Dan shooed the Rebels away, leaving Ben alone on the crest of the hill. He began gathering good-size rocks and placing them on the damp mound of dirt, working for more than an hour, covering the grave, insuring that no animal could dig through. Smoot played around his feet as he worked.

Satisfied that he had done all that could be

288

done—with the materials at hand—Ben sat down close to the grave and memories; mental pictures that spanned a decade.

He recalled when he had first met her, back in Virginia just after the Great War. And he knew and accepted, finally, that he had fallen in love with her on that first day, many years back.

There had been many other women over the years, but always in the back of his mind, there was Jerre. Untouchable, unreachable except for mental images that he would always carry with him.

Ben picked up Smoot and walked down the hill, away from eternal rest. The wind seemed to cry as he walked toward the column of Rebels waiting for him on the road. Ben did not look back at the solitary, unmarked grave.

Ben had changed, and everyone around him picked up on that fact immediately. How he had changed quickly surfaced as the columns headed north.

"Corrie, when we stop for a break this afternoon, go to communications and give Base Camp One a bump. Tell them to start printing flyers. The wording will be this: The forty-eight contigious states comprising the United States of America are now under the rule of the Rebels. All citizens must come forward to be photographed and fingerprinted for identification. Noncompliance to this order will not be construed as a criminal act. Refusal to comply with this order will mean a complete denial of medical care and protection from the Rebel army and it will carry the implication that those refusing to do so wish to live outside the law. It will also mean that the children of those refusing to comply, when found, will be taken and placed in Rebel homes. The people have one year from this date to comply."

"The shit's gonna hit the fan now," Jersey said.

"It's communistic, Ben," Thermopolis said.

"That's crap and you know it, Therm," Ben told him. "I'm not a dictator and you know that too."

They had bivouacked for the evening and the news had spread like unchecked fires throughout the camp. Ben had expected Thermopolis to confront him and the aging hippie had not disappointed him.

"Big government brought this nation down, Ben. Now you want to bring big government back."

"Horseshit, Therm! It's your nature to challenge rules and regulations; but you know damn well civilization cannot flourish without rules. There is only two directions we can go: forward or backward. And I don't intend to go backward. I want a census count, and this is one way to do it."

"It's also a way to know where people are and to keep an eye on them."

"True. But I don't mean to do anything sinister with that knowledge."

"There are a lot of individuals out there, Ben." He waved a hand.

"Sure. That's fine. I don't care if people want to go off and live a hermit's life. People can live as they damn well please. Just as long as they obey the few laws we have on the books. Therm, we can't get anything done pulling in single harness, all going in different directions. We're either going to pull together to rebuild something good and lasting, or this country—the world—is doomed."

Thermopolis glared at him. "You've got a lot of politician in you, Ben."

"Yes. I'll agree with that. And being a politician can be either good or bad. I like to think of myself as somewhere in the middle." He noticed the surprised look on Thermopolis's face. "Hell, I've got faults, Therm. I'm no saint. I tilt at windmills too. And so do you. But haven't things been so much more interesting since we started tilting at them together?"

Thermopolis gave him a disgusted look and walked off, muttering about totalitarianism, imperialism, socialism, communism, big-brotherism, and Ben Raines . . . all in the same breath.

# Chapter 16

Ben and his Rebels slammed northward, clearing out the towns as they went. They crushed any resistance with sheer brute force and a total lack of compassion or mercy. By the time the columns reached Olympia, the city had been abandoned by the creepies.

"Strip it of anything we might be able to use and then burn it," Ben ordered.

He ordered Ike, Cecil, and West to reclaim Seattle and put Five and Six Battalions stretched out between what was left of Olympia over to Aberdeen. Ben took his columns and began working the two hundred and seventy-five-mile circle formed by Highway 101, which would end back at the smoking ruins of Olympia.

Ben found a strange assortment of creepies and outlaws within his perimeter, each one oddly dependent upon the other for survival. Ben cut their survival factor down to zero during the sweep.

And at night he dreamed of Jerre.

The Rebels roared through the towns on the southernmost stretch of their perimeter before reaching Aberdeen. There, the creepies had massed for a last-ditch defense against Ben Raines.

But the Rebels were on a victorious roll and by now had the procedure worked out to perfection. They stood back a mile outside of town and blew it off the map without taking a single casualty. They rolled through the still-burning and body-littered town, main battle tanks spearheading, and smashed into a mixed bag of outlaws and creeps who had holed up in the next town, about five miles up the road.

The battle was brief, with the Rebels taking no prisoners and leaving nothing that could be salvaged behind them. They went up the coastline as far as they could, rolling through all the tiny towns. The Rebels found where outlaws and thugs had taken over, killing off any survivors and occupying the beachfront homes. But the outlaws and thugs had left when Ben Raines entered the state. They wanted no part of the Rebels.

"I wonder where they went?" Buddy asked, eating the evening meal with his father and sister, both of whom had joined Ben on this campaign.

"Probably inside the Olympic National Park," Ben said. "Stinking up and screwing up the beauty of the park. Or they might be one jump ahead of us. If that's the case, they're in for a surprise. Whatever way they try to get off this jut of land, they'll run into Rebels."

Corrie stuck her head into the room. "Fly-bys report a large concentration of outlaws and creeps in Port Angeles, General. Or rather they're gathered all along that stretch of road. They're going to make a fight of it."

"They're finally wising up, Dad," Tina said. "They know now that holing up in the cities is a death trap."

"It's about time the dumbasses learned. What's the word from Seattle, Corrie?"

"The creepies are trapped, sir. General Jefferys is at the south end and General Ike to the north. West is on Mercer Island and they're all pounding the city with heavy artillery. Seattle is burning. Five and Six Battalions are bitching because they don't have anything to do."

"Tell them to hang tight. I'll see if we can't drive

the crud out of Port Angeles and head them their way. Get me all available data on the location of the enemy, Corrie. Tell the people we'll pull out in the morning."

"This should just about wind this campaign down, Dad," Tina said.

"It won't take long. Then we have to see about getting the people counted and ID'd."

"We'll do that this fall and winter?" Buddy asked.

"Yes. That and try to reclaim Southern California."

"Do you feel that will be as big a job as New York City?"

"At least that much and probably more. The island of Manhattan was a compressed area. L.A. is huge, sprawling all over the place. And I don't know yet what we'll be facing there; probably gangs of every size and description and belief, in addition to the creepies."

Smoot came over and puppy-attacked Ben's boot until Ben gave her a scrap of food from his plate. She wandered off to a corner, ate the scrap, and promptly came back for more. When she didn't get it she again declared war on Ben's boots.

The three ate in silence for a moment, with Tina and Buddy sneaking little glances at their father, both of them wondering how he was really coping with Jerre's death. Outwardly, he seemed fine; but with Ben, outward appearances could be very deceiving.

Dan entered the building and Ben pointed toward the coffeepot.

"The mixture of creeps and outlaws are stretched out along a line that extends approximately ten miles east and west from Port Angeles," Dan said.

Ben glanced at an old map. "Along One-twelve or One-o-one?"

"Both."

Ben nodded his head. "All right. Dan, you and

294

Tina cut off at Sappho, using this secondary road north, and link up with One-twelve. I'll take my bunch and push east on One-o-one. We'll hook up at this airport about five miles outside of the objective."

Dan looked at the map and smiled; a grim soldier's curving of the lips. "We've got them in a box. Any escape route they try will put them up against Rebels."

"Yes. And surely they must know that. They'll put up a pretty good fight, I'm thinking."

"Prisoners, General?"

"Not unless you're feeling unusually charitable."


The outlaws, thugs, punks, and creepies were trapped and knew it. They could not go north to Vancouver Island; that would mean crossing the Strait of Juan De Fuca and they did not have the boats to manage it. West lay Ben Raines and his people. East lay the Rebels. Their only hope was south into the Olympic National Park. That might buy them a little time, but all knew the Rebels would eventually hunt them down and kill them.

Besides, there were no roads that led all the way through the huge park; only hiking trails. The outlaws and creepies made an uneasy pact with each other and made ready to die under the guns of the Rebels.

Seattle was gone, virtually destroyed by the round-the-clock shelling from Rebel guns. There were crud still alive in the city, huddled amid the burning rubble, but their numbers were now so few as to be inconsequential.

Some had tried to surrender to the Rebels. They were either shot or hanged. Ben Raines's get-tough policy left no options open for those who chose the path of lawlessness. Before making this sweep, he had offered surrender terms to the outlaws — only the outlaws, not the creepies — and a few had accepted those terms. The majority of thugs, punks, and crud, being arrogant from the start, or they wouldn't have chosen the life-style they did, had jeered at the offer of surrender.

Now they had only death before them.

And word was being radioed all over the nation, from one outlaw gang to another: Ben Raines is offering a one-time deal — surrender now or die later. Past sins will be forgiven, but you'd better get your asses to a secure zone, 'fess up, and do it now. There is no tomorrow. Tomorrow, all bets are off.


Ben and his Rebels pushed north at first light, traveling through the now-deserted and barren coastline and inland towns. There had been Indians living on reservations on this jut of land. The outlaws enslaved them and the creepies ate them.

Buddy's Rat Team found, to their amazement, a pocket of survivors in the town of Forks. Nearly four hundred men, women, and children had turned the town into a fort and had survived for a decade.

"You're kidding!" Ben radioed back.

"No, sir. These survivors control everything up to Sappho and have for years. They got tough right after the Great War and stayed tough. But they sure are happy to see us. They request to be made a secure Rebel zone."

"Tell them request is granted. I'll be there in about an hour."

The survivors were a mixture of Indians and Whites, living proof that people of different cultures could live and work together in harmony . . . all they had to do was expend a little effort and understanding to make it work.

Ben met with the leaders and another outpost was in place.

"After you leave Sappho," one of the leaders, a Quinault Indian told Ben, "you'll be in hostile territory. We just weren't strong enough to extend our area of control any further."

"Why did you choose to settle here?" Ben questioned, although he felt he knew the answer.

"It's so isolated we felt we'd be safe. Obviously, others felt the same way. When the outlaws and Believers came, then it was a matter of pride and stubbornness for us. We just weren't going to be chased away from our homes. So we got tough and fought them. When the government ordered all weapons to be turned in — before the Great War — we ignored the order; as did thousands of others around the nation. So we had something in place to fight with. Those who meekly turned over their weapons to the government were slaughtered after the country, the world, went belly-up."

The citizens had kept the small airfield in good shape, anticipating the day when the Rebels would arrive. Ben ordered supplies and a platoon of Rebels willing to resettle flown in to beef up the small outpost. Then it was on to reclaim the northernmost part of coastline.

Dan and Tina exited 101 at Sappho, traveling the old county road north to 112, while Ben and his contingent stayed on 101.

Smoot spent most of her time riding in the back with Beth and Corrie and Jersey — usually sound asleep. She had grown accustomed to the sound of gunfire and cannons booming, and after a jumpy first time, she paid no attention to the sounds of war.

Dan hit the first resistance at what was left of a tiny town named Joyce and Ben's people locked horns with the outlaws and creeps at Elwha. There was nothing left of the towns but rubble and smoke and fire after the Rebel gunners took their morning exercise.

The Rebels drove slowly through the still burning rubble, looking at the sprawled and broken bodies of those who chose lawlessness over civility. No medical team stopped to help any wounded, for the survivors back at Forks had briefed the Rebels well, telling them that all decent people had long since left, been killed fighting the thugs and creeps, or had been captured and eaten.

No doubt history would write that Ben Raines and the Rebels were hard men and women, and no doubt some would write that they were too hard, too lacking in compassion toward the enemy. To a person, the Rebels' reply to that would be that the enemy had a chance to surrender, to change their ways. They didn't take it, so tough shit!

By the middle of the afternoon, Dan and Ben had linked up at the junction of 112 and 101 and were now five miles from the town of Port Angeles.

"Seventeen miles between Port Angeles and the town of Sequim." Buddy traced the line on the map with a blunt finger. "And fly-bys show the outlaws and creeps are stretched out between the town."

"Order Six Battalion up, Corrie. Start them moving immediately. They're going to hit some resistance at a couple of places, but it should be light. Tell them to get in position at Blyn and wait for my orders."

Tina looked at her dad. "And what'll we be doing until then?"

"First having dinner and then getting a good night's sleep," her father replied with a grin.

Ben was working on his second cup of coffee the next morning, alone with his thoughts, when a man with a white flag appeared, walking up the center of the highway from the direction of Port Angeles. He shouted that he wanted to see Ben Raines.

Ben was notified. Using a bullhorn, he asked, "What the hell do you want?"

"A chance to surrender!" the man shouted.

"You had a chance to surrender. You didn't take it."

"Well, goddamn! Can't nobody change their minds with you people?"

Ben lifted the horn. "Come on in closer. I want to talk with you face to face."

The man hesitated.

"Don't be a fool!" Ben told him. "You've a hundred guns trained on you. If I was going to kill you you'd already be dead."

The man walked up to the truck where Ben was leaning against a fender. "We done broke with the creepies. They know you ain't gonna let them surrender. But we ain't no cannibals."

"You're just as bad," Ben told him.

"Huh? What'd you mean by that?"

"If you play with shit you're going to get some on you."

"Maybe we didn't have a chance to begin with. You ever thought of that?"

"What am I going to hear now, some crap about your misspent childhood? Or maybe the coach wouldn't let you play or you had pimples or some other equally terrible traumatic youthful experience that caused you to turn bad? Which is it, and it better be something original, because I've heard all the rest and I wasn't impressed."

The man's eyes met those of Ben and lingered only briefly. He dropped his gaze with a low curse. "You're a hard bastard, aren't you, Ben Raines?"

"Yes, I am. And I'll admit that I've had some few successes in rehabilitating the criminal element. But I had something there to work with. You're a total loss, partner."

"How do you know that by just looking at me?"

"I don't. It's a guess."

"I don't get a another chance?"

Ben studied the man for a moment. "Tell you what. I'll let you come on through if you'll agree to take some tests."

The man grew wary. "What kind of tests?"

"PSE tests. Polygraph tests. Drug-induced hypnosis. We'll be asking you questions about your past and of your thoughts for the future. Questions about decency and criminal history and, oh, just all sorts of interesting and fascinating topics. If you pass, you're in. How about it, partner?"

The man cussed him, loud and long, until he was breathless. He knew he was going to die, now or in a few hours, so that short a span of living really didn't mean all that much.

When he paused for breath, Ben said, "That will be all. You may return to your sector and prepare to die."

"You ain't human, Raines! There ain't no human man can be that hard to another."

Ben's smile was thin. "Have you ever raped?"

"Yeah. I've took pussy by force. So what? The whole goddamn world is turned upside down. There ain't no damn laws!" he screamed the last.

"Have you enslaved people and sexually abused young children?"

"Yeah. Yeah, I have. Again, so what? It's the law of the jungle out here."

"You really believe you were justified in doing that? You believe it's the law of the jungle out here?"

"Yes, to both questions. The biggest and toughest animal wins."

Ben pulled out his .45 and shot the man between the eyes. Holstering his pistol, he looked at the cooling body and said, "In that case, the big Eagle just won."

# Chapter 17

The Rebels struck the town at dawn, throwing everything they had at the town and its defenders from the east. To the west, Six Battalion had worked feverishly throughout the night setting up Claymores and other devilish devices of surprise and pain and destruction. When the creeps and the thugs ran from the burning town, they ran right into ambush points set up along the highway, then the troops of Six Battalion moved in to mop up anything that might be left alive . . . but not for long.

Ben stood in the trashed library building of what had once been a small college in the town. He looked at the hundreds of ruined and rat-chewed books. He knelt down and picked up one rat-chewed volume of Durant's eleven-volume *Story of Civilization* and carefully brushed away years of dust and neglect. "Anybody who would allow this to happen to a book deserves to be shot," he muttered sourly.

"I concur," Dan said, looking around.

Thermopolis walked in with some of his group. He looked around and shook his head in disgust. "They had the whole world at their fingertips . . . and refused to turn a page."

The hippie and his group began searching the library for volumes they could salvage.

Ben pulled a map out of a pocket and studied it for a moment. "Corrie, order Five Battalion up and Six Battalion down; have them start cleaning out the Bremerton area. We'll bivouac outside of town tonight and finish up Port Townsend in the morning."

"And that will just about do it for this state," Tina remarked. "One more cleaned out."

By listening to radio transmissions, Lan Villar made certain that all Rebels were in the western section of the state and then he made his move. He ordered his people up and moved them quickly to the eastern side of California. He then moved them into Southern Oregon and began working his way north, keeping an entire state between his forces and the Rebels.

Villar put scouts far out in front of his proposed route north. The short and very infrequent communications between the scouts and the main body were done in code and with jacked-up CBs.

As Ben and his forces were beginning their move south, Villar and his bunch moved north. The two columns paralleled each other, a state apart.

Ben headed his battalion down the extreme western edge of the state, working the towns that dotted the coastline while Cecil, West, Ike, Georgi, and Five and Six drove south out of the still-smoking Seattle area.

"We're clear," Villar said with a sigh, removing a headset. "We've finally got them behind us, and, thank the gods of war, heading in the opposite direction."

"It'll suit me just fine if I don't never see Ben Raines again," Satan said. "Just thinkin' about that bastard gives me a headache."

Ashley glanced at the man, having serious doubts that the outlaw biker was even capable of thinking. But he kept that to himself. "We'll be in Alaska in time to prepare for the winter. I would suggest we start stocking up on fuel oil and the like."

Villar shook his head. "From reports I've heard I

302

don't think there is much need for that. Supplies are more than adequate. What we have to do is go in looking like professionals; show the outlaws there a strong force . . . whether we are or not. We've got to go in with the upper hand and keep it. Our objective is still a thousand miles away, so we've got plenty of time to clean up our act." And Villar also knew that the confidence of the men would grow with each mile they gained putting Ben Raines behind them. He stood up from the camp stool and adjusted his battle harness. "Let's go take Alaska."


Ben's forces crossed over into Oregon at Astoria. He would stay on 101 all the way down the state. Cecil and Ike entered through the rubble of Portland and would stay on the Interstate all the way down. Georgi and West moved east and picked up Highway 395 down, while Five and Six Battalions were ordered to wander the state.

All units began reporting pockets of survivors as soon as they entered the state and Cecil and Ike found a huge concentration of Believers in Salem. All other units stopped where they were while Salem was being neutralized and destroyed.

Five and Six Battalions set up an outpost at Madras and swept the zone, soon declaring it secure and requesting supplies be flown in.

Ben had found a pocket of survivors on the coastline, in a small town named Garibaldi and was working to establish yet another secure zone. A few miles down the road, however, a band of thugs had set up shop and showed no signs of being intimidated by Ben Raines or anybody else.

"He's called Bull," the leader of the survivors in Garibaldi told Ben. "And he's a bad one. You'd be hardpressed to name a crime that he hasn't committed and he's proud of every vile thing he's ever done.

There are pockets of survivors all over Oregon, General Raines. But only the older, and by that I mean the more established groups, manage to survive."

Ben smiled. "What you're saying is that you folks finally and totally rejected the liberal beliefs concerning the poor put-upon criminals that were jammed down our throats years back."

Ben's smile was returned. "That is certainly one way of stating it, sir."

"We'll deal with Mister Bullshit in the morning," Ben told him. "Do you want to save the town he and his bunch have occupied?"

"If at all possible. He's massed a lot of materials that we could use."

"Materials such as?"

"Medical supplies he found at an army base. Thousands of cases of MREs, clothing, weapons, and ammunition."

Ben held up a hand. "I get the point. We'll take the town intact."


"Fair-size little town," Ben said after looking the town over through binoculars. "And they've done a bang-up job of setting up defensive position."

"They have a lot of military hardware," Dan observed, casing his field glasses. "So we can bet they've also got Claymores planted around, as well."

"Let's take it," Ben said, glancing at his watch. Seven o'clock. "Corrie, send in the tanks and we'll fall in behind them."

The main battle tanks began rumbling forward, Rebels on foot using them for cover. Heavy machine gun fire sprang up from the edges of the town, but the slugs could not penetrate the armor of the tanks. No mortar rounds fell from the town, and that brought a sigh of relief from all the Rebels, including Ben.

The Rebels overran the outermost positions of the outlaws and dug into the just-vacated bunkers, establishing a well-defended front for themselves and forcing the outlaws to go on the offensive.

Bull reviewed the situation and came to the conclusion he was in a piss-poor position. He'd been hearing about Ben Raines for more than a decade, but up until now had felt the man was more myth than reality.

Until myth rolled up with fifty-five-ton battle tanks and practically stuck the snouts of the cannon up the asses of his men.

And this was just one contingent of the Rebels, for Christ sake!

"Get Raines on the radio," he told a woman seated behind the equipment. "Him and me got to talk."

"What do you want, Bullshit?" Ben's voice came out of the speaker.

Bull ground his teeth together and fought to hold on to his temper. "A deal, Raines."

"I don't make deals with crud."

"Well, what the hell do you intend to do with me and my people?"

"I intend to kill you," Ben said flatly, and a chill ran up and down Bull's spine with the words.

Bull knew then that everything he'd ever heard about Ben Raines was solid truth. Even before the Great War, Bull had been notorious up and down the West Coast, staying in trouble with the law. But he never had to spend more than a few weeks in jail for his infractions. A month at the most. The cops never could pin any of the rapes and assaults on him and Bull would walk out of the jail laughing.

He always had money in his pocket to buy some shyster lawyer to get him off, and the judicial system was so screwed up back then that half the time he could plea-bargain out of a case with only a slap on the wrist.

With a cold glob of fear in his belly, Bull knew those days were long gone and would never be back . . . not as long as Ben Raines ran the show.

Bull lifted the mic. "No trial, no nothin'?"

"You got it, Bull," Ben told him. "You've been tried, convicted, and sentenced *in absentia.*"

"I know what that means and that ain't legal!" Bull hollered.

"Sue me."

"Well, come and get me then!" Bull screamed. "You cocky bastard!"

"Oh, I plan on doing that, Bull. After lunch."

*"Lunch!* What kinda shitty war are you runnin', anyways?"

"Enjoy your last meal, Bull. Eagle out."

"Let's get the hell outta here!" Bull said.

"We cain't," one of his men told him, a mournful sound to the words. "Raines has done called for some more people to come in behind us. He's got us in a box."

"How, for Christ sake?" Bull yelled. "We got all the streets blocked off."

"It's another unit, I guess. They come up from the south early this morning, I reckon."

"What the hell are they doin'? They ain't fired a round."

"They're eatin'."

"Eatin'!"

"Yeah. They're sittin' around their trucks and tanks and Jeeps eatin' lunch. They don't seen to be worried about nothin'."

"Bull," another man asked. "How are we gonna get out of this mess? Ben Raines don't fool with folks like us. He just puts 'em up agin a wall and that's the end of it."

The radio operator started crying. "You said you'd take care of us, Bull."

Bull slapped her out of the chair. "Shut your

damn mouth, bitch! We ain't dead yet."

"No," a man said. "I figure we got until lunch is over."

The look he received from Bull would fry eggs.

The woman Bull had slapped to the floor jumped up and ran from the room, screaming curses at him. Bull stepped to the door, cocked a pistol, and shot her in the back. She fell to the ground, twitched once, and died.

"Shit on you," Bull muttered to the lifeless form. He walked back into the room and sat down while his men stared at him.

Long bursts of heavy machine gun fire from both sides of the Rebel perimeters ripped the temporary quiet and somewhere in the town, a man screamed in pain.

"Lunch must be over," an outlaw said, absolutely no humor in his voice.

# Chapter 18

The Rebels simply overwhelmed the outlaws by sheer numbers. Attacked from all sides, the outlaws died behind their guns, died screaming for mercy— their pleas falling on deaf ears—or were shot down as they tried to run away from the relentlessly charging Rebels.

Bull sat on the ground, his hands tied behind his back, while Ben and a man from the now secure zone north of the outlaw town stood to one side.

Another man from the secure zone was forming a noose out of heavy rope.

"I ain't believin' this," Bull said. "No trial, no jury, no chance to tell my story. You just gonna hang me!"

"You can tell your story, Bull," Ben told him. "But you'd better make it a condensed version; you don't have much time."

Bull spat at Ben's boots and cursed him until he was breathless.

Ben glanced down at the clipboard in his hand and shook his head in disgust. "Says here you tortured animals to death as a kid, Bull."

"Yeah? So what?"

"Did you?"

"Yeah. What's the big deal about that?"

"Did your parents see that you got professional counseling after that?"

Bull laughed. "Yeah. She was a good-lookin' bitch, too. I raped her. Right there in her own office. You should have heard her squall when I bent her over the desk and shoved it up her butt."

"And because you were a juvenile you didn't get any prison time for that."

"That's right, Raines."

Ben looked at the man beside him. "We will never, ever, return to that form of judiciary nonsense. Anytime you start feeling sorry for scum like this"—he jerked a thumb toward Bull—"recall my words. Now hang him!"


The Rebel push continued south, flushing out gangs of thugs and finding pockets of survivors all over the state. Almost always the survivors were in small groups, living far off the beaten path and maintaining a very low profile. And not all of them were thrilled to see the Rebels.

There were those who had set up little cults, and the cult leaders were not happy when the Rebels came around. Others were filled with religious zealots, worshipping everything from a kumquat to a blank computer screen. Still others had reverted back to the caves, fleeing when the Rebels came around.

"What are you going to do with these people, General?" Emil asked.

"Leave them alone," Ben told him. "I left you and your bunch alone, didn't I?"

"Yeah, but we never turned down any help you offered. I had more sense than that. What's gonna happen when these people get really sick and need attention?"

"I don't know, Emil. All I can say is that they've chosen their life-style and they're welcome to it. We've offered them help, they've turned it down, and that's the end of the story as far as I'm concerned. As long as they pose no threat to us, they're free to do as they damn well please."

"I tried to talk to some of them," Emil said. "Tried to tell them I been where they are. Tried to tell them that sooner or later they're gonna need our help, and they're gonna be told to go sit on a candlestick. They said they didn't care and to leave them alone." He shrugged his shoulders. "What can you do?"

"Nothing," Ben said, knowing that Thermopolis was listening and a pretty good debate was sure to come out of this. "You all know that the government — back when there was a government — tried to take care of all the people; even the people who refused to step into the mainstream of society. I thought it was a mistake then, I think so now. I have no patience with people who chose totally different alternate life-styles and then when something goes wrong, expect the central government to help them. Piss on them!"

The push southward was slow going, for the Rebels checked out every town and every building. They cut off the main highways and traveled the backroads to roads' end. They missed nothing in their searches and they collected everything that might be of use. They offered help to anyone who would take it, but the help was not free, not without strings attached. You want help? You join us. You don't want to join us, you're on your own, pal.

"You're setting up a form of government," Thermopolis finally geared up for debate, "that doesn't leave the people any choice."

Ben poured them both coffee and waited.

"You're setting up a goddamned monarchy!"

"I most certainly am not"

"You're the absolute ruler. What the hell else do you call it?"

"The people rule, Therm. You're trying to split hairs. I'm asking for a little cooperation in return for help and protection, that's all. You're a fifty-year-old man with a ponytail, for Christ sake. Have I asked you to cut your hair? No, I have not and never will. You're just as much an individual now as the day we first met."

"King Raines," Thermopolis said with a smile.

"You're a fraud, Therm."

"Oh?"

"You just don't like—or profess not to like—any form of authority. But you can't have organization without it. And you know it."

"If I'm a fraud, you're a walking contradiction, Raines."

"Sure. I admit it."

"Hardheaded, obstinate, stubborn, die-for-the-flag, and all that crap."

"To a degree. But then, so are you. If you weren't, you wouldn't be here with me."

"I'll certainly argue that!"

"You would argue anything, Therm. Anytime, anywhere, and with anybody."

"I'd certainly argue that!"

Both men looked at each other for a moment and then burst out laughing.


The Rebels had entered the center of the state—Ben in Florence along the coast, Ike and Cecil approaching Eugene, Georgi and West cleaning out Prairie City, and Five and Six Battalions roaming along Highway 26—when communications received a frantic call and patched it through to Corrie.

"A group of survivors in Roseburg, sir," Corrie said. "They're under heavy attack by the outlaws and crud we've been pushing ahead of us."

Ben quickly opened a map case and found Roseburg. "It's about a hundred miles from here. Ask them how many they are and how many they esti-

311

mate they're facing."

"Two hundred and fifty of them and probably fifteen hundred to two thousand outlaws. They have creepies mixed in with them."

"Ike's going to have his hands full in Eugene. Hell, we're just about as close as he is. Tanks out now, Corrie. Main battle tanks and Dusters. We'll catch up with them along the way. You get cracking on that. I'll find Dan. I would send the bikers to spearhead but the citizens would probably think they were with the outlaws."

Dan had heard the frantic call for help and anticipated what Ben would do. He was forming his Scouts when Ben found him.

The tanks were already gassing up for the run, huge tanker trucks pulled alongside. Over the rumble of tanks and the shouted commands of crew chiefs, Ben said, "Spearhead, Dan. Take Buddy and his Rat Team with you. I'll pull out in about an hour with Tina and her bunch."

"That's ten-four, General. See you in Roseburg."

Tina had jogged up. "Get your teams together. We'll be pulling out in about an hour."

She nodded and ran off, shouting for Ham, her second-in-command.

Ben spotted Thermopolis and waved him over. "You're in command of the bikers and Emil's bunch. Push on to Coos Bay and stay north of the city. It's occupied by creepies."

"Command! To hell with you, Raines!"

"Shut up and listen. The North Bay/Coos Bay/Charleston area is crawling with creepies. Set up your defenses anyway you like; just be alive when I get back."

"Command, my ass! I'm not taking . . ."

Ben waved Leadfoot over while Thermopolis was still sputtering. Emil joined them while Ben was explaining to the biker who was in command.

312

Emil promptly drew himself to attention and saluted Thermopolis.

"Will you stop that!" Therm shouted.

"At your service, my captain," Emil said.

"I'm not your damn captain!"

"Suits me, General," Leadfoot said. "All my bunch likes and respects Therm. We'll take his orders. Whatever he says, goes with us."

"I'll get you for this, Ben Raines," Thermopolis said. "I promise you that. I'll put a chipmunk in your PortaPotty."


"Reports are really getting frantic, General," Corrie said from the second seat in the wagon. "The crud is knocking on the town door pretty hard."

Ben checked his watch. "Dan should be just about there. He'll take off some of the pressure. Get him on the horn, please, Corrie." He picked up his mic and waited.

"Go, Eagle," came Dan's voice.

"Dan, I'm going to cut off One-thirty-eight just up ahead and take this secondary road. That'll put you coming straight down from the north and me coming in from the west."

"That's ten-four, General. I have the town in visual now. Attacking."

Cooper anticipated Ben's next question. "Thirty minutes away from the town, General."

"And kindly get us there in one piece, Cooper," Jersey requested.

"Never fear, my dear, Cooper is here," Coop told her.

Even Ben had to join in the groans after that.

Beth was reading an old tourist's guidebook to Southern Oregon. "I wonder what happened to all the animals at this Wildlife Safari thing outside of the town? It was one of those places where the animals wandered around free."

"Hopefully they made it out and are alive and breeding," Ben said. "There have been unconfirmed reports of cheetahs in this area."

"Then some of them made it out," Beth said. "This place was where they bred the cheetah. Gee, wouldn't it be nice to see one?"

Jersey looked at her. "Only from a distance," she muttered.

"Jerre was really into saving the animals and all of that type of. . . ." Beth trailed that off into an uncomfortable silence.

"Yes, she was, Beth," Ben said. "And you don't have to be uncomfortable speaking about her in my presence. That's one way of insuring that she will never be forgotten. As long as one person remembers her, she'll never be forgotten."

"That's beautiful," Jersey said.

"Unfortunately, it's not terribly original. I don't remember who said it."

"Colonel Gray reporting the outlaws have been strengthened, sir. Much larger force than originally thought."

"How much larger?"

"Colonel Gray reports facing several thousand outlaws and creepies."

"Kick it in the ass and get us there pronto, Coop," Ben said.

"Oh, Lord!" Jersey moaned as Cooper put the pedal to the metal and grinned as the big wagon surged forward.

Ben and his command roared through the burned-out remains of Umpqua and a few miles later could see the smoke rising from the besieged town of Roseburg.

"Order the column to pull over and wait for the tanks to arrive," Ben ordered. "Order one weapons' platoon up to join us. We're going in."

Ben led the platoon into the outskirts of town and surprised a knot of crud who were huddled around and manning a machine gun. A round from a rocket launcher took out the machine gun nest and the Rebels had a toehold.

"Get whoever is in charge on the horn, Corrie. Tell them where we are and that we're friendly."

"Tom Martin says to tell you God bless, General," Corrie said. "They're just about out of ammo."

"Tell them to hang tough. We've got a toehold."

"Would you look at that watermelon patch over there," Coop said. "Don't they look good?"

A rocket from the enemy side exploded the building next to them before Jersey could wisecrack about Cooper's love for watermelon.

"Tanks are here," Corrie said.

Main battle tank up to our location, please," Ben said. "Spread the Dusters out in a line and tell them the enemy has rocket launcher capabilities."

"Martin says all his people are grouped in the downtown area, General. Everyone outside that area is the enemy."

"That makes it easier," Ben said as the big tank clanked up. "House to house, people. Let's go."

The Rebels worked their way up the block, darting from house to house.

Cooper tossed a grenade through a window of a frame house then sprayed the interior with .223 rounds. A man staggered out onto the front porch, bleeding from a dozen shrapnel wounds and several bullet wounds. He expelled his last breath cursing Ben Raines then toppled off the porch, dead.

"Dan reporting they've taken some prisoners," Corrie yelled over the bang and confusion of combat. "Every thug and creepie that we've shoved off their turf have gathered here for a last-ditch stand."

"I can believe it," Ben said, after ducking a long burst of automatic weapons' fire from a house across the street. He leveled his Thunder Lizard and made life miserable for those behind the guns in the house. Popping out the empty clip and fitting a full one in place, he turned to Corrie. "Tell our tank to put a round into that house."

The main battle tank swiveled and lowered its 105. The house went up in a roar as a round of HEP (high explosive plastic) exploded.

Ben led the charge across the street and the taking of another block began as Rebels on all sides of the town started working toward the center of town, block by block, house to house.

Ben stepped over the body of an outlaw, sprawled in death on the sidewalk and ran around the corner of a brick home. He came face to face with a trio of creepies; the Rebels could distinguish creepies from others because of their pale faces and horrible body odor.

Ben reacted first and pulled the trigger of his M-14, holding it back. The weapon yammered and bucked in his hands and the lead sent creepies screaming and jerking and hunching obscenely backward as the slugs tore into flesh and shattered bone.

Ben stepped over their bodies and ran for the back yard, his team keeping pace with him. "There!" Ben yelled, pointing toward a well-kept home constructed out of some type of native stone.

Two of Dan's Scouts joined them and took the point, checking out the house and waving Ben forward.

"We're just a few blocks from the downtown area, General," a Scout informed him. "This would make a great CP for you. Tanks have busted through to the survivors and have set up a wall around them. All Rebel teams have worked their way in and are steadily advancing."

Ben smiled. The Senior Scout had told him, very politely, that the battle was going well and would the general please keep his ass out of the fray and let someone else do it?

Ben turned to Corrie. "We'll set up shop here, Corrie. Inform the other units where we are — as soon as I figure out where we are."

The Scout told him the street name.

"Thank you. You may return to your unit."

"Colonel Gray ordered us here, sir. With you."

"Very well. See if you can find the coffeepot. I seem to be momentarily out of a job."

# Chapter 19

Ben met with Tom Martin and the others as the Rebels were disposing of those thugs and creeps who were not killed during the battle for the town. Ben was watching the people for signs of displeasure over the disposition of the captured. He could see none. The townspeople apparently had had a gutful of criminals and creepies and anyway the general wanted to get rid of them was just fine.

Beth was holding Smoot to keep the puppy out of mischief. The way she was growing, now that she was getting a proper diet, the Husky pup would soon be big enough to leash.

"You understand the way we operate, Tom?" Ben asked. "And you and your people are willing to abide by those rules?"

"One hundred percent, General," came the very quick response.

"We have us another secure zone," Ben said, smiling as he shook hands with Tom Martin.

The thugs and creeps were buried in a mass grave outside of town, in a huge hole scraped out by a bulldozer. The citizens of the town were fingerprinted, photographed, numbered, and put on record.

The securing and stabilizing of America was under way.

Ben waited in Roseburg until he received word that Eugene had been neutralized by the forces of Ike and Cecil. Georgi and the mercenary, West, had set up another secure zone in the town of Burns and were now paralleling Five and Six Battalions on the way south to the California line, following Highway 395. Five and

Six would enter Nevada and work their way over to the rendezvous point on Interstate 5 at Yreka, a town reportedly held by outlaws.

On a rainy and cool morning, after much deliberating by radio with all his commanders, Ben made his decision on the next campaign.

"Alaska can wait," he said. "Let's secure the lower forty-eight and then move toward Northstar when that's done. Saddle up, people. We're pulling out."

From the coast to the border of Idaho, Rebels cranked up and began the pullout toward the rendezvous point in California.

Buddy and his Rat Team was spearheading the drive. Ben knew he would have to secure Medford and Klamath Falls, the last two remaining strongholds for creeps and thugs in the state. The Rebels had worked this out to a fine art, and scouting reports showed no innocents being held in either town. The two cities would go down in flames.

That morning, as his people began gearing up for the pullout, Ben took a Jeep and drove north out of the town, alone, except for a patrol of Dan's Scouts that stayed well back but always keeping the general in sight.

Ben drove up high ground and parked, getting up and squatting down on the shoulder of the road. He looked to the north. Hundreds of miles away, Jerre rested on a lonely, lovely, windswept hill.

Memories came rushing to him, enveloping him in a mist of emotions. He recalled the first time he'd seen her, and the last time. He recalled the laughter, the quarrels, and the tears. There had been many women in his life, and would be many more, but none would touch the part of him that Jerre had sought and found. None would know the man as she had known him.

The mist turned into a rain, but Ben didn't notice it. The Scouts had fanned out, covering both sides of the road, staying in the timber around Ben, securing

319

him.

Ben knew it was time to let go. To put the memories of Jerre away. To get on with life. To find a woman to share the years with.

He didn't know if he could. He didn't know if he wanted to do that.

But he knew he had to. Too many people depended on him. He could not allow himself to wallow in self-pity, to remain shrouded in memories, to only love a person who was now with the angels.

Ben sighed and stood up. He remembered the note she'd left for him back in Virginia, so many years ago. He had committed it to memory.

*I don't know what my feelings are toward you, Ben. I like you a whole lot and I think I probably love you a little bit. That's a joke—I think I probably love you a whole lot. That's one of the reasons I've got to split. There are other reasons, of course, but my feelings toward you are right up there at the top.*

*You've got places to go and things to do before you find your-self—your goal, preset, I believe—and start to do great things. And you will, Ben. You will.*

*I hope I see you again, General.*

Ben still had the note, carefully tucked away with other precious memories.

He looked toward the north one more time. One more time before he finally accepted her dying and went on with his living.

"I loved you, Jerre. More than I ever loved anything in my life. Good-bye."

Ben Raines walked back to his Jeep and headed south. He had a war to fight; a country to put back together. A world to explore.

Smoot jumped into his lap and licked his face. .

"OK, Smoot," Ben said. "Let's go see what's left of Los Angeles."